Grievous

Also by Robert T Price
Nickers (1998)

GRIEVOUS

Robert T Price

Constable · London

First published in Great Britain 1999
by Constable & Company Ltd
3 The Lanchesters, 162 Fulham Palace Road
London W6 9ER
Copyright © 1999 Robert T Price
The right of Robert T Price to be identified as the author
of this work has been asserted by him in accordance with
the Copyright, Designs and Patents Act 1988
ISBN 0 094 79660 2

Typeset in Palantino by Photoprint Typesetters,
Torquay, Devon
Printed and bound in Great Britain by MPG Books Ltd,
Bodmin, Cornwall

A CIP catalogue record for this book is available from
the British Library

To Alison, Kevin and Colin

Prologue

Exactly half an hour after the phone call, I hear the swish of tyres on the forecourt of the Lone Harp Auto Repair garage. My companion and I are standing inside the car repair shop, facing the big vehicle door which I have set just wide enough for a person to walk through. This is the delivery we've been waiting for – a furtive delivery, in the dark hours that creep in after midnight.

Three shadowy figures get out of the newly arrived car, leaving the motor running, and move towards the door. Two of our visitors stop just short of the gap and shove the third one through it. A coarse voice says:

'All yours, mate, an' ye're bloody welcome.'

About five seconds later, the two escorts are back in their car and accelerating down the road in the direction they came from.

Even while sliding the door shut behind the newly delivered package, I am giving him the once-over. In spite of the dimness of the light from the single tube I have switched on in the workshop, I can see that he is tall and lean, with a stubbly haircut, and that his hands are clasped behind his back. He is wearing jeans and a rough black sweater.

When I go round in front of him, beside Petesy, I get a good chance to appreciate the depth of malice in the pale-faced looks he is throwing our way. Surprising, that, I think – you'd suppose that any man would be grateful for being sprung out of prison.

Petesy, my colleague for the occasion – not my choice by a long way – makes a bid for leadership of our team, by opening his mouth first. I let him.

'Hey, man,' he says to our new guest, 'you'll be pleased to know that we're gonna be moving you to a safe place just as soon as we get locked up here. What do we call you?'

The bloke snarls through twisted lips in a strong Glasgow accent:

'Ah don't give a shite whit ye call me . . . an' Ah don't seem tae have ony option but tae go wherever ye take me. Just let me have a pee first – Ah'm burstin', so Ah am.'

'It's back there,' I tell him, pointing to the back wall, where a narrow passage between two of the service bays leads to a small scullery on the left, and a toilet on the right.

'Right,' he says, 'who's comin' with me, then?'

Petesy and I exchange puzzled, and maybe slightly worried glances. Our visitor laughs like a maniac, turns sideways to us, and sticks his hands out from his back to show that they are tied together at the wrists.

'Did yer bosses no' tell ye? Ah'm still a prisoner. Some lucky bugger is goin' tae have tae get ma dick out and point it accurately while I take a leak.'

Bloody hell! It's beginning to sound as if this jailbird didn't actually want to be released from his cosy prison cell. Now I see that his ankles are also tied together – loose enough to let him take short steps, but he will go arse over tit if he tries to run. I also notice that Petesy has disappeared in the direction of my office.

'Forget it,' I say. 'You can just do without a pee for a while longer. It won't take long to get to where we're taking you.'

He grins at me with a lot of teeth. It makes his face look like a skull.

'Right ye are, then, Jimmy. Ah'll just have to let it go when I'm sittin' in your car. It'll take ye months to –'

He is interrupted by Petesy, back from his trip to the office.

'Shut your mouth and keep it shut.' Petesy is waving a gun in front of the bloke's face. Belatedly, he remembers to add, 'Asshole.' Then he starts to think constructively.

'Here's what we're gonna do. Kenny, here, will untie your hands. Then you go and take a leak with this gun in your back. Once you're zipped up again, the cord goes back on your wrists. What were you inside for, by the way?'

'Grievous . . .'

1

There was nothing very sinister about the day that the whole thing began. True, the first part of it was something I would rather have avoided, maybe even a bit unpleasant – but definitely not sinister. Anyway, it's where I have to go back to, so that I can explain how I found myself harbouring a fugitive from one of Her Majesty's prisons. None of it was my fault, as you will see.

As I said, the first part of the day seemed pretty harmless.

'That must be the "extensive landscaped front garden",' Aileen said, frowning at a patch of overgrown scrub.

We were sitting in the car waiting for the estate agent to turn up with the keys of this desirable country residence. Aileen was leafing through what she called the particulars, as if she didn't know them by heart. Personally, I couldn't see why we should move out of our rented maisonette. It was dead convenient, what with being right in Stratford-on-Avon and handy for both of us getting to work. But there's no point in reasoning with Aileen when she's got the bit between her legs. Anyway, here we were in what the particulars called the delightfully unspoilt hamlet of Boreham under Piddle.

She was still trying to get me interested by reading out the juicier bits.

'What do you think they mean by "fantastic scope for the buyer with imagination"?'

I was saved from having to guess by the arrival of a bright green Corsa in a spray of gravel. The estate agent erupted from it and hurried over to meet us. I could tell right away that she was one of those executive-style young women who think that being in a perpetual rush and talking brusquely gives them a businesslike image. She shook hands with Aileen and then turned her hand to me.

'You must be *Mr* Morrison. I'm Alison Steadfast, your residence location consultant. Let's get some details on the record before we go in. Then I can get the mortgage machinery started as soon as I get back to the office.'

Ms Steadfast swung her briefcase on to the roof of my car without seeming to hear me saying:

'No, I'm Kenny Madigan. We're not married ... not yet anyway.'

I should mention that Aileen and I talked about getting hitched, around the time we moved in together. About two years ago, that was. I was quite willing, but Aileen said no why don't we wait and see if you grow up and I said what did she mean by that and she said never mind she was only joking. Which I thought was a bit strange because Aileen hasn't got much of a sense of humour, as such. Not like me.

Anyway, there was this Steadfast woman already busy filling in forms.

'Occupation?' she barked.

Aileen told her that she works in Jonathan Phillips, the posh shoe shop in Sheep Street.

'Right! Retail assistant.' She turned to me with both eyebrows raised.

Aileen's got this annoying habit of replying on my behalf.

'Entrepreneur,' she said, just as I was saying, 'Motor mechanic.'

This caused some confusion until we got it sorted out that I was the owner of the Lone Harp Auto Repair garage. Lucky it wasn't six months ago – not that I would have admitted to stealing cars for a living, of course.

Eventually we were led towards the cottage with commentary provided by the estate agent.

'It's nearly three hundred years old ... these Grade 2 listed buildings are much sought after,' she said. You could tell who wrote the particulars.

I asked, 'Why does it have two doors at the front?' The path had split and we were heading towards the door on the right. The other one was maybe fifteen feet along the front of the building.

'Oh, that other one's the back door of course. It leads into the kitchen.'

I felt as if it was unreasonable of me to mention it, but I

pressed on anyway. 'Why isn't it at the back, if it's the back door?'

For the first time, a note of uncertainty crept into Ms Steadfast's voice, or maybe it was just because she was wrestling with a big black key in the lock.

'Well, there's a . . . another . . . er . . . structure joined on to the back of the residence.' She paused in her exertions long enough to deliver an evil glare in my direction.

'Does that mean all the windows look out to the front?'

That was Aileen getting into the act at last, but by this time I was off round the side of the house to see what was behind it. I got back just in time to hear Ms Steadfast telling Aileen:

'. . . and don't forget the sides. There are ample windows at both sides.'

'Are they double glazed?' I asked.

She looked shocked.

'Oh no! That would compromise the integrity of the edifice. Besides, you would never get planning permission to alter a Grade 2 listed building to that extent.'

By this time we were inside, looking at the crumbly stone floor. But I hadn't finished with the outside yet.

'That . . . structure round the back,' I said. 'I'm no expert, but it looks kind of like a pigsty to me.'

The confident hope was fading from Alison Steadfast's eyes, but she did her best.

'Well, I don't know anything about a pigsty . . . although I understand it may have been used for the purpose of animal husbandry at some time in the past,' she faltered.

'Never mind, love,' I said to Aileen on the way home. 'It just goes to show how comfortable we are in our little maisonette.'

But I could tell from the kind of silence she was using that this was a long chalk away from being the end of it. As luck would have it, fate went and struck a blow for Aileen's side of the argument, just as we arrived back at our maisonette. This blow came in the unpleasant shape of old Miss Downie, known to us as the Neighbourhood Witch.

Miss Downie took it upon herself to monitor everything that happened in our street, so there was little chance that she would fail to clock our arrival. Still, we were careful to keep quiet as we passed her door. Not that it helped this time, because the door flew open, and there she was, barring our way.

'Do you know what they're doing down there?' she screeched, presumably referring to the local kids, with whom she carried on a running skirmish. She didn't wait for an answer, just carried on:

'They're interfering with my wheelie-bin again. I want to know what you're going to do about it.'

'Just let us get to our house, Miss Downie. I'll come back out later, and look into it for you,' I told her.

The old bat didn't look happy, but allowed us to slip past and get to the safety of our own door. As we opened it, I heard her yell, 'I blame the Millennium Dome.'

With people like Miss Downie around, who could blame Aileen for wanting us to get out of there? My main problem was with the kind of place she wanted to move to. I knew I would be tramping over a lot more country cottages before Aileen was satisfied.

It's amazing really, when you think about it . . . you know, just a matter of months ago the idea of Aileen and me considering the purchase of any kind of house would have been unthinkable, not to mention bloody ludicrous.

Back then I was working for Quinn . . . well, not so much working, as nicking cars to order. Quinn was the previous owner of Lone Harp Auto, and he also had fingers in stuff that was a lot heavier than car theft, as well as turning out to be danger-ously unbalanced. In the course of some unpleasantness with another mob from London, various people got murdered, including Angus, who was the foreman at Lone Harp and a friend of mine. In the end, I managed to close down Quinn's operations, recovering a load of stolen jewellery in the process. The insurance companies paid out a reward which came to Aileen and me, though we gave a share to Senga, Angus's widow.

The police claimed all the credit, of course, and leaned their size twelves on me for a while. Anyway, when all the unpleasantness was over, Aileen and I used the reward money to buy the Lone Harp garage from the receivers at a bargain price.

* * *

10

Now that I was at the helm of a real business, I got no end of pleasure from just sitting in the office feeling that my hand was firmly guiding the pulse of Lone Harp Auto. Senga was turning out to be just as good a foreman as Angus used to be – I suppose I should really say fore*person*. The iron fist had been replaced by a half-pint redhead who could reduce an incompetent mechanic to jelly with a couple of Glaswegian sentences and a shake of her curly red mop. Senga had insisted on stepping into Angus's shoes after his death. I couldn't actually object, partly because she had a minority share in the business. But I kept myself in charge of the stores and ordering parts and supplies. Well, I had to find *something* useful to do.

Now and then I would open the door of my office and look out at the work going on in the workshop. Most days, I would be able to see the three mechanics doing mechanic-type things to several cars under Senga's critical gaze. It's a pretty well-equipped workshop, with ramps, inspection pits, and so on. Oil dispensers and other doodahs are built into the walls behind each of the three service bays.

Just inside the vehicle entrance there is a cubicle with a counter, where Senga charms the customers and dispenses their keys and bills. To get to my office, you have to walk through the workshop. There is also an inner office that is accessed through a door in the back wall of my office. This inner office contains a couple of computers that came with the business, and are hardly ever switched on. In fact, that room is only used one day a week, when Mrs Torrance, a middle-aged lady, comes in to do the bookkeeping.

The mechanics themselves are about the usual kind of mixture you get in any factory or workshop. Jeff is a hard-working but gossipy middle-aged Brummie who would tell his life story to the bus queue. There's Peasel, only about twenty, who is usually the target for the jokes of the others, on account of he will believe anything you tell him. I never have found out why they call him Peasel – his real name is Arnold Platt. Then there is the most recent addition, Brian Miller – a local bloke I've known since my schooldays, without ever being very friendly, as such.

So there I was, sitting thinking how I would have to be too busy to go with Aileen to inspect any crappy country cottage that might take her fancy. It was her day off and I knew that she would be round every estate agent in town like a ton of bricks before ten o'clock. She could be on the phone any minute. I was quite pleased when there was a knock on my office door, but when I saw who was there I stopped being pleased. I hadn't laid eyes on him for a couple of years but there was no mistaking that lumpy overcoat and nose – it was Kinnell.

I knew Kinnell from the old days when I was submerged in a life of crime, which I hated on account of the unsavoury characters you have to deal with – and this Kinnell was one of the shadiest. He had connections among the Birmingham criminal shit-pile. A bulky shapeless character he was, maybe in his fifties, and he walked in a kind of shamble, as if all his joints had been left a bit loose when he was put together. I've no idea what his real name was.

He came right in and sat down opposite me without any invitation. While he pawed the office with his eyes, his runny smile showed that the big uneven teeth had got even yellower since the last time I saw them.

'. . . 'kin'ell, Kenny,' he said, demonstrating how he got his nickname, 'you lands on yer feet every time. This looks like a bloody great front for business . . .'

When he said 'business', he tapped the side of his nose with a nicotine-stained finger. He went on:

'. . . and here I am to load your cup of happiness to the very dregs. See, I can put you on to a dead reliable supply of motor parts and stuff at a mere fraction of what you're paying for them now . . . a mere bleedin' fraction.'

Up to this point I'd had nothing to say, but I couldn't let it go any longer. 'Look, Kinnell,' I told him, 'my business is strictly legit and fair and honest. I'm a law-abiding citizen and I don't want your nicked gear even if it comes for free.'

He seemed to be thinking, but maybe he was just concentrating on the blackened fingernail that he was using to pick at a scab on his chin.

'. . . 'kin'ell,' he said finally, 'excuse me for breathing. That's what you gets for trying to help an old mate. But I knows you, Kenny – once a villain, always a sodding villain . . . I knows you.'

'We never were mates as such,' I said. 'I don't even know your first name, for Christ's sake. So go and peddle your bent canoe someplace else.'

If I had known then how soon Kinnell would cease polluting the local branch of the environment, I might have tried to be nice to him. On the other hand, maybe not.

As it was, I felt like being really nasty but it doesn't do to insult these kind of blokes ... they've got the kind of connections that can leave you with a permanent limp in both legs.

'... 'kin'ell, Kenny, you drive a hard bargain. OK, I'll see you gets a discount. Give us a bell when you come to yer senses and decide to place an order. This stuff is not yer average junk, you know – it's the real genuine original manufacturer parts an' whatnot. It just happens to be dead cheap on account of our overheads are sliced to the bone ... right down to the bleeding bone.'

I must have looked as if I still didn't believe him, because he sighed deeply, and said:

'... 'kin'ell, mate, what do I have to do? It's not jus' because you're a villain yourself. Most of our customers are solid respectable businesses, you know. Look, here's a reference.'

Kinnell had brought a card out of his pocket, and was writing on it.

'This is our company card. I'm putting the name of one of our satisfied customers on the back of it. You nip over to Evesham and talk to these geezers – dead bleedin' straight, they are.'

He flicked the card across the desk.

'Don't leave it too long.'

I didn't answer and he got up to leave. Before closing the door behind himself, he turned round and said:

'... 'kin'ell, Kenny. It's Sydney ... thought you knew that.'

All right, but I still didn't have a clue about his surname. When I was sure Kinnell was off the premises I threw his card in the bin.

It just goes to show there are worse things in life than helping Aileen to look at cottages in the country. I sat there for a while, thinking along those lines. And then I got Kinnell's business card out of the waste bin and put it in my desk drawer. Maybe the supplies he was flogging were the genuine article – or maybe he was right when he said that thing about 'always a sodding villain'.

* * *

13

Don't you sometimes get the feeling that troubles have got a way of coming along in bunches – like bananas? You know, you start thinking they must be somehow connected but they're actually just coincidences. As my Aunt Ursula used to say, 'When one door closes, you can be sure all the others are going to slam right in your face.' Well, that's what it was like for me that day. Kinnell was still rankling among my brain cells when I locked up for the night.

It was dark as I went towards my car, this being March, so I didn't see him at first. It was only when I heard my name called that I realised that a bulky figure had got out of a car parked in the street. When he came under the light, I thought for a moment it was Kinnell back again. But when I realised who it actually was I couldn't hold back a laugh.

'My God,' I said, 'I didn't recognise you inside that sheepskin coat. It's not like you to be seen wearing such a sad garment.'

It was Neil, the CID policeman who persecuted me and cheated me into solving a whole bundle of murders and rackets for him last summer. What made it more complicated was him being engaged to Sally, who is Aileen's best friend. So I have to meet him socially as well, though I must admit that he's quite a nice bloke in that capacity. And he usually dresses with a lot more style.

'All in the cause of keeping warm. It's bloody cold this time of year when you're doing a surveillance, which is what I've been on all day,' he said.

I was a bit surprised. 'What's a detective inspector doing surveillancing for? Can't you send one of your minions to handle stuff like that?'

Neil looked even more sheepish than his coat.

'Well, I'm still a sergeant ... my promotion hasn't come through yet. Some bureaucratic bungling ... but look, I didn't come here to discuss my career with you. I want a word.'

I sighed, but turned back and unlocked the door. 'All right, but we'd better go inside. I'm not freezing my balls off out here.'

Back in the office we sat down and Neil fixed his eyes on mine. Never trust a copper who looks you straight in the eye.

'I need a favour,' he said. I didn't react except for getting really interested in a job sheet in my in-tray. He went on:

'We've got a small problem that you might be able to help us with.'

Seeing me open my mouth, he went on in a rush:

'The villain community of the Midlands are flexing their muscles. They're feeding a stream of stolen goods on to the market and we need to get a handle on it. I hate to admit it, but we haven't got a clue where to start.'

I shrugged. 'What's new? There's always been bent TVs and camcorders and suchlike gear around. You can buy them in car boot sales or from a bloke in the pub.'

He shook his head. 'No, it's not like that ... this is different – well-organised. They carry out well-organised raids on ware-houses ... hijack delivery trucks ... things like that. And then the stolen stuff is marketed in a professional way and supplied to unsuspecting businesses. It's all goods like office equipment, carpets, building material ... you name it. They can undercut the legitimate suppliers. The thing is, all the police forces in the Midlands are co-operating on this, and I'm the contact point for this area.'

'Well, that should keep you busy for a while,' I said, 'but it's got nothing to do with me.'

'No, but ... with your past, you must know some of these villains. I mean ... what I would like you to do is use your underworld contacts to get supplies of whatever stuff you use. Like oil filters, plugs, exhausts – all the stuff you charge the earth for when you service your customers' cars.'

'Oh no!' I protested, 'I'm keeping well clear of all that bent stuff. Besides, if they found out I was grassing on them to the busies, they would have my balls for conkers. These are dangerous blokes to play footsie with.'

Neil shook his head. 'Sorry, Kenny, I'm not giving you the option. I'd hate to do this to you, but there are open files on quite a few things down at the station ... things like nicked cars for instance. And my super still goes around shaking his head over some of the unanswered questions left behind by that last escapade you were involved in. He's somehow got hold of the idea that you might not have been completely frank with us.'

Well, they didn't need to know every little detail, did they? Just so long as they solved the case. But I could see he had me by the proverbials.

15

'If I do my best to help you again, what's in it for me? I mean to say . . . there's got to be some kind of carrot at the end of the rainbow.'

'We'll see,' he said. 'Maybe some of those cases could become considered closed.'

I didn't believe a word of it. But then, it doesn't seem to matter what I might think. Once again the pincers of fate seemed to be closing in on me. I mean, the rozzers in the shape of Neil start blackmailing me into doing their dirty work on the very same day that Kinnell crops up to beckon me into the very same spider's web. It's almost as if they've got together and agreed on a joint course of action and they've got it all written down in a big book with the title *Let's Screw Kenny Madigan*. Faced with a coincidence on that scale, what choice have I got?

Kenny Madigan, the helpless straw in the wind.

2

When I got back home, I told Aileen the whole thing. All about Kinnell's visit . . . and Neil stepping in right on cue wanting me to get involved with the criminal element. See, Aileen's got this dead effective way of looking at problems. I think it's the kind of brain she's got . . . not that she's an intellectual or anything like that, though she has got some O-levels. No, it's more that she can take a problem and bend it into a different shape so that she can look right through it – and then she tells me exactly what I should do.

Anyway, from my point of view, there might be some extra advantage in getting Aileen to concentrate on my troubles – it might help to keep her mind off country cottages for a while.

When I finished telling my story, Aileen was still in the middle of making her weekly list of the health foods and vitamin tablets she needed, so she never said a word for a while. I just waited quietly, because she's really meticulous about her supplies of health food stuff.

Finally, she finished her list, her big brown eyes came round to me and I could see they had that foggy look they get when she's thinking. She flicked a strand of her fair hair away from her face and said:

'I'm not having you sucked into a life of crime again . . . not after the last time.'

'Aw, come on, Aileen,' I said, 'of *course* I don't want to do it, but Neil's got a poison pill pointed at my head. You know he could still put me inside for being involved in that car-nicking business and . . . well . . . maybe other stuff into the bargain.'

'Right then!' she said, trying to sound decisive. 'We'll need to have a board meeting.'

I groaned. When Aileen calls a board meeting it means that we have to sit down at the table while she does her dog and bone act on a problem till my brain cells start holding protest rallies. Still, I have to admit she usually steers us into the right decision in the end. I tell her she could manage just as well without dragging me all round the houses. But she always insists that it's vital to our relationship for us to talk everything over before she decides what we should do.

So we cleared our plates with the remains of the spaghetti bolognaise off the table and dumped them in the sink. Then we got sat back down. I bet not too many people have tilt-and-swivel chairs round their dining-table. It's because I was smart enough to furnish our maisonette from this place in Redditch where they auction off all the contents of the offices from firms that have gone down the grid.

That's how we've got all dead smart furniture at a fraction of the shop prices. Unfortunately I didn't manage to match the colours of the chrome-framed easy chairs with the leather sofa from some reception area. The dining-table itself was once a section of some company's boardroom table – so Aileen was not too far off the mark in calling it a board meeting.

This particular board meeting only went on for ten minutes before I was grilled to Aileen's satisfaction. After all, there was nothing very deep about it – not a complex issue, as such. She delivered her verdict.

'You haven't got any choice,' she said, putting on her really prim look. 'It's your duty as a good citizen to do everything you can to help the police and . . . Oh, rats! I forgot the seaweed

17

tablets ... after all, you'll not be doing anything that's actually criminal.'

I couldn't think of an answer to that. I just nodded as I watched her turn back to her list of vitamins. It didn't seem worth mentioning that receiving stolen goods is regarded as criminal in some quarters.

I let nearly a week go by before taking the matter any further. Not that I was weighing up the pros and cons; it was more like putting off a visit to the dentist. I had this feeling that once I got them started, the wheels would grind on and pull me further and further into the melting pot. All I want is a nice quiet easy life without too much hassle.

Anyway, something had to happen, because I was putting off ordering supplies for the business. Eventually, it became too much for Senga. She came steaming into my office to express her reservations about my working habits and business acumen.

'Ye're a lazy useless bugger, Kendall Madigan. You're supposed tae be in charge o' the stores, an' here I am having to send a man round to Halfords to buy oil filters at twice our usual price just because you canny be bothered tae get yer fat arse intae gear an' order the supplies I need so as I can keep this crappy business on its feet an' making enough money tae keep a fat cat like you in idleness ...'

By this time she was out of breath, and her face was almost as red as her hair, but she saw me opening my mouth, so she got her last word in first.

'Just get yer fucking finger out, Kenny.'

And she was through the door before I could say a word. I thought I was supposed to be in charge around here – but bugger-all chance of that when you're surrounded by bossy women. I sighed, got Kinnell's greasy business card out of the desk, and reached for the phone.

I didn't pick it up, though. My eye snagged on the card. I was looking at the back of it, where Kinnell had written the name of his reference customer.

Senga would definitely bollock the shit out of me if this gear turned out to be junk. It might actually be a good idea if I could see some of the stuff and talk to somebody who'd been using it.

It would also provide me with a good excuse to get out of the garage for a while. Or at least until Senga was ready to treat me like a member of the human race again.

Kinnell had written a name on the back of the card – Del Cotteridge – and the address, which was Five Ponds Garage, Evesham.

It wasn't hard to find. The Five Ponds area of the town is a sprawl of newish housing with a neighbouring retail park and small trading estate – and not a pond for miles. The garage was a slightly bigger operation than Lone Harp; probably five or six mechanics. I suppose being bang next door to a large pool of customers must give them a head start. The vehicle door was round the side, and at the front there was a separate person-sized door marked 'Reception'.

The girl behind the wooden counter was using one of those mouse things, to drive a computer screen. As she turned towards me with a welcoming smile, I could see that she was not what my Auntie Ursula would have called a slip of a girl, but a very attractive woman, probably in her late twenties. Her hair was cut short, and the row of teeth revealed by her smile looked even whiter than they probably were, on account of the contrast with her dark skin. Her shapeless tan-coloured overall and the height of the counter did a good job of concealing her figure. Still, the overall impression I got was of energy, vitality, and intelligence.

'Hi-ya,' she said. 'What can I do for you?'

I asked if I could see Del Cotteridge. She pointed over her shoulder, and said:

'Del's busy out in the workshop right now. Maybe I can help – I'm Sam Cotteridge.'

So I introduced myself and told her why I was there. We shook hands, and she told me:

'Well, you got the right person. I'm the one who does the ordering of supplies – as well as running the office and looking after the stores.'

'So you and Del run the garage between the two of you?'

'That's right, we're partners. Come on into the office, and I'll get somebody to bring us some coffee.'

It's great how being in the same line of business can get you instant respect and even friendship. Sam ushered me through a door and into a chair in the office. I sat there and looked around the room while she opened another door to shout an order for three mugs of coffee to somebody in the workshop. It was pretty much like my own office, except for being slightly bigger and having two desks side by side against the wall on the left.

'Right!' she said, sitting down and swivelling her chair towards me (neat ankle sticking out of her jeans, I noticed), 'so you want to know how we're getting on with our supplies from AutoSupCo – weird name, isn't it?'

'Do you mind if I ask how you came across them, as such?'

'Their salesman came round. I was out somewhere, so it was Del he saw. Del thought he was repulsive, and got rid of him as quickly as possible. That would have been the end of it, but for the fact that the salesman left a price list. When I looked at it, my first thought was that their stuff must be rubbish quality . . . but at these prices, I had to give it a whirl.'

Sam broke off as the door opened – the door leading to the workshop, that is. And Sam came in carrying a tray with three mugs on it. I looked at her, and then I looked at the other one of her who had just been talking to me. 'Hi-ya,' said the new Sam, smiling at my expression.

It was Del, of course. Twins, identical ones – at least, I couldn't see any way to tell them apart, except that the flame behind Sam's eyes seemed to me to burn maybe a little bit brighter.

I found out later that the garage had belonged to their father, who had trained both of his daughters as mechanics. When he became an invalid, the girls just took over. Another thing I found out later was that a mixture of Jamaican mother and blond English father had blessed them with that beautiful light caramel skin.

'I was just telling Kenny about our experience of AutoSupCo,' Sam said.

Turning back to me, she got back on track:

'I gave them a small order . . . and the stuff they supplied was fine, and delivered promptly, too. So we switched to them for all our supplies – well, everything that doesn't *have* to come direct from the car manufacturers, like engine parts and suchlike.'

When we finished our coffee, Del went back to the workshop,

and Sam took me into the storeroom so I could judge the quality of their stock for myself. I was impressed, and said so.

'Who would have thought Kinnell would ever get mixed up with a well-run operation?'

'Who?' Sam asked.

'Kinnell,' I told her, 'the bent salesman with the bloodshot eyes, nose, and life.'

'Oh, is that his name?' she said. 'I don't think that's what Del said he was called ... but what do you mean about bent?'

Well, I thought I owed her some of the truth, as I knew it, so I told her a little about Kinnell's murky connections in the Birmingham underworld. And I stupidly went on and mentioned that there was a fair chance of the supplies not being, you know, strictly honest, as far as their origins were concerned.

Sam got such a troubled look in her big black eyes on hearing that, that I was forced to assure her it was probably OK ... and whatever the facts, there was no danger to their business.

'Well ... shouldn't the police be informed ... even if it's only a suspicion?' she said, and then she frowned. 'Anyway, how do you know so much about it?'

Well, I couldn't leave Sam thinking that I was mixed up in something dishonest, could I? So I dropped her a hint of my role in the struggle of the goodies against the forces of darkness.

'Don't worry, the ... er ... police are well aware of what's going on – in fact they've asked me to try and help them get the evidence they need ... but I shouldn't be telling you this. I'd appreciate it if you'd keep it to yourself.'

On the way back to Stratford, my brain regained control, and let me know that I had opened my big mouth too wide, just to impress a woman. *And* it kept on reminding me about Aileen sitting at home, waiting for me – which wasn't strictly true, as she would still be out at work. I had to be quite stern with myself in the end, and point out that:

a. I am not the type of person who goes around womanising at random.

b. I might occasionally fancy some babe, but that doesn't mean I'll do anything about it – I practically never do.

c. I can't remember what c was, as such.

On the other hand, maybe I should keep in touch with the Five

Ponds Garage. You know – just in case they could help me to get more information about this AutoSupCo outfit.

Over the next few weeks, I was well pleased with the quality of the parts and supplies that were delivered to Lone Harp. Senga was quite pleased with the stuff too. Surprising that, since they came from an outfit that had Kinnell on its payroll. AutoSupCo not only undercut the prices of the usual suppliers by a good margin, it also delivered promptly in neat vans with efficient-looking drivers.

Just for the sake of courtesy, I telephoned Sam Cotteridge in Evesham, to thank her for making the recommendation. It was nice to hear her voice again.

When I passed the word on to Neil that I now had goods in my possession which might be regarded as suspect, he arranged to come round to Lone Harp one night after we closed. Don't ask me why, but our brilliant sleuth seemed to think that the sight of allegedly stolen gear would give him a hint as to who might have stolen it. I mean it's not as if he could throw an oil filter into a cell and beat a confession out of it.

Anyway, I didn't attempt to argue. I simply showed him the storeroom, and he wandered around a bit picking up this and that, to stare at for a minute and then put back.

'It's all genuine stuff,' I pointed out. 'You can't tell a thing from looking at it . . . not unless you're psychic.'

That got me a sharp look from Neil. 'What do you mean about psychic? What have you heard?'

'Pardon me for breathing,' I said. 'It was really just what you might call a shot in the tunnel.'

I hurried on before he could get even more annoyed at me.

'Why don't you chase up AutoSupCo? They deliver the stuff to me.'

'Do you think we haven't?' He shook his head. 'You know it's not as easy as that. The stolen goods are well laundered. Auto-SupCo buys from several wholesale suppliers, only some of which might be suspect. Also the stolen gear is almost certainly merged in with parts from legitimate sources. We can't prove a thing. There must be a whole network of companies involved –

some of them honest, others bent, and who can tell which is which.'

I was well aghast at this. Well, who wouldn't be?

'So why the bloody hell did you make me buy all this stuff instead of getting it from my usual suppliers? And what do you think you're doing here, pretending to look at it?'

'OK, OK, Kenny. Tell you the truth – I wanted to have a talk with you, but if I had come over to your place, Sally would have come with me . . . and then she and Aileen would have turned it into a holiday or hairdressing discussion.'

I noticed that Neil had partly answered my second question – which meant he was trying to avoid replying to the first one. If I hadn't known him so well, I would have thought he had an embarrassed look, the way he stood there fiddling with a box of spark plugs. He finally got round to it.

'You see, Kenny, I never really thought that your buying from these people would be much help. After all, they're probably supplying half the small garages in the Midlands. It just seemed like it would be a sensible first step – the thin end of the wedge, if you like. As a customer of these people, with your criminal qualifications, you might be able to get closer to the nerve centre. I bet they'll snap you up when you throw out a few hints that you are willing to make your talents available to their organisation.'

You'd think that the copper force would be the last people to discourage a person from going straight, wouldn't you? I hadn't the energy to rant and rave at him, for all the good it would have done. My brain cells could see Shit Creek beckoning, but I decided to play it cool for the moment, so I didn't even raise my voice when I said:

'You are definitely the most bastardly CID sergeant in the country, if not the world.'

'No, Kenny, you got that wrong.' He grinned at me. 'I am now the most bastardly CID *inspector* in the country. My promotion has come through.'

Christ, he was waiting for congratulations. I was dead careful not to offer any, and after a moment, Neil added:

'We must go out in a foursome soon – to celebrate, you know. I'll get Sally to fix it up with Aileen. OK?'

* * *

Aileen wasn't a great deal of help either. She was busy leafing through a bundle of estate agent's country cottage details when I got back, so when I told her about Neil trying to push me back into a life of crime, she didn't say anything. I thought she was turning it over and over in her brain, so I waited to hear some words of wisdom. I was disappointed by her eventual response; she flipped a sheaf of badly copied paper to me with the words:

'What do you think of this one? It's got these staddle-stone things like mushrooms all down the drive, and roses round the door.'

I decided that nobody else gives a shit about what happens to me, so I just sat there trying to think it all through in private, inside my head. As you know, I'm a very law-abiding person, and always have been. Even when I was relying on crime for my living, I only broke the law professionally, as you might say. It was just a job. In my private life, on the other hand, I was careful to obey all the speed limits, paid the bills on time, and always made sure I had a valid television licence.

My thoughts were interrupted around that point, by a ring of the doorbell. The bloke who bounced through the door was one of my favourite people. Peter, Aileen's dad. Tonight he was wearing perfectly pressed grey flannels and the navy blue blazer which sported an impressive badge that looked as if it might belong to an exclusive yacht club. He came in yukking in his own special chortle.

'Yuk, yuk, yuk ... that's a wonderful old biddy you've got next door ... what a character. She thought I was a wheelie-bin inspector from the council, so I gave her half a dozen duck eggs. That means there's only half a dozen left for you. Yuk, yuk, yuk. How are you, petal? You're looking lovely.'

The last bit was to Aileen, who got a kiss on the forehead. He handed me the box of eggs.

Peter lived – alone, since he and Aileen's mother parted about five years earlier – in an untidy bungalow right out in a very sparsely populated part of the country to the north of Warwick, not even in a village. Behind his bungalow was what you might call a very small-holding, where he pursued various country pursuits, including the keeping of hens, ducks, geese, and often lambs for a couple of seasons.

Peter was too sociable to spend all his time working in the fields; his now-grey wavy hair and RAF-style moustache were regulars in every pub within a radius of fifteen miles of Mousel End. In most of these places, he was known as the Wing Co. I doubt if he has ever been on a plane. To be fair, I don't think he has ever claimed any connection with the RAF (though Aileen once showed me a photograph of him sitting on a horse, wearing a very fancy uniform). I've always thought he would have made a great con man.

As it turned out, Peter was a great help to me. He looked at Aileen's cottage particulars, and made fun of them, with many a yuk. I would never have dared to do that, but have you noticed how a girl's daddy can get away with anything?

When Peter left, I got back to my thinking for a while. Then I tried to give up thinking, and suggested to Aileen that maybe we should have an early night. Having an early night is Aileen's code phrase for going to bed and having sex until I'm so knackered I can't move any more. And then Aileen takes over and does the moving for both of us.

Even as I lay on my back, with Aileen bouncing up and down on me, I was still thinking about the consequences of me getting hoovered into all that crime stuff. Maybe if I treated it just like a job ... After all, Neil should be able to keep me safe from getting my collar felt by his fellow coppers. Of course I might have to put up with the company of some pretty unpleasant types of people. Kinnell sprang to mind ... But surely I wouldn't be in any actual physical danger.

Kenny Madigan, the fool in paradise.

3

The street was called Tagley Road. It was in Shirley, branching off Stratford Road, one of the major traffic routes into Birmingham from the south. The kind of street which has a few busy shops that have leaked a short distance up from the main drag, before lapsing into more commercial premises and types of enterprise that nobody goes near unless they've got specific business there.

Number twenty-eight was a perfect example of that, on account of belonging to Condiment Brothers Ltd – a firm of funeral directors. I sucked in a deep breath and pushed through the plate glass door on to the plush burgundy-carpeted space of . . . a small, brightly lit reception area.

I looked around. On the right was a counter, tastefully done in walnut, with a single closed door behind it, and several chairs on the public side. On the left wall there were double white doors with a sign saying 'Sayonara Suites'. The wall opposite the entrance had two grey doors, both labelled 'Private'. There was a faint smell of vinegar hanging over everything. Very quiet music of a vaguely classical type oozed along on a tide of violins. No sign of any human being. I looked around again, and spotted a little brass bell on the counter top, which made a tinkling sound when I picked it up. After my third look around, I turned back to the counter to find that a man-sized black beetle had silently materialised behind it.

'Good day, sir,' it said in a deep voice with a strong Brummie accent. All right, not exactly a beetle, but this bloke was all in black and didn't seem to have any angles or straight lines. He folded his hands over his rounded belly, and chanted:

'Condiment Brothers extend our condolences. You have a departed?'

I ignored the question. 'I'm supposed to see Mr Anchovy.'

The beetle reached to press something on a shelf behind and below the counter, and without taking his eyes off me said:

'There's a *person* here with the anchovy word for the Wheel. Says his name is . . .' He jutted his chin forward and raised his eyebrows at me. I took the hint and told him, 'Kenny Madigan.' An intercom voice replied, 'All right, Joe. Send him up.' Joe pointed at the left member of the pair of private doors and told me, 'Through there – up the stairs – turn left – door marked "Embalming".'

The door marked 'Embalming' was whipped open about two milliseconds after my knock. I stepped forward into a comfortable, but quite plain, office. The man sitting in the swivel chair behind the big desk didn't get up to shake hands. Instead, he waved me towards a chair that faced him across the desk. I sat

26

down and looked him in the face. 'Nice place you've got here, Mr Anchovy,' I said with one of my best smiles, assuming that's who he was, and trying to show friendliness. He didn't smile back. Instead, he leaned back in his chair and said, 'I don't do small-talk, Mr Madigan. Remember that and we'll get on fine.'

It definitely wasn't any kind of Midlands accent. I think it was more northern, probably Yorkshire, but not really strong, if you know what I mean. He had a fair-sized mop of black hair which was a bit untidy – but it was the only untidy thing about him. The multi-coloured tie was silk, and was draped down an immaculate white shirt. The suit jacket I could see on a hanger dangling from a hook on the wall behind him was too good to have been bought from any High Street store. All in all, his dress was expensive without being the least bit stylish – and definitely not fashionable. This was a smooth bloke in his late forties, who carried an air of being not short of the price of a pint or two.

I tried again – straight into the big talk.

'I understand that Kinnell has told you about me.'

Anchovy leaned forward this time, and placed a pair of well-manicured hands flat on the desk. 'Well,' he said, 'that's where the first referral came from, but I would be in trouble if I accepted every one of Kinnell's recommendations at face value. However, I have compiled a file on you. It contains information culled from quite a lot of sources, including the results of some investigation by Basil, there.'

He nodded in the direction of something behind me and to my left. I had been aware of another presence in the room, of course – the shadowy figure who opened the door. But I hadn't had a chance to clock him yet. He was sitting on a small chair in front of a table over against the left wall. The table held a personal computer and the kind of phone that can be used as an intercom. Then I realised that the chair *wasn't* a small chair. The chair was normal-sized; it was just that, under Basil, it looked small. He was dressed in jeans and a shirt with no collar. It occurred to me that this was a clever choice, because he had no neck to put a collar round. Loads of bulk, but something told me there was not an ounce of fat on him.

Then I had to whip back round to face Mr Anchovy, who was starting to talk again.

'I know an awful lot about you, Kendall Madigan. Clean

licence, safe careful driver – no hotshot stuff, quite a competent practical engineer. You've got the instincts and habits of a pick-pocket and you've never been arrested. Am I right so far?'

He had me off balance. I kept my voice in neutral:

'No comment.'

'OK, OK! You are quite right to be cautious. You know nothing about me and my organisation. Your reticence confirms that you don't go around shooting your mouth off; so, we can add discretion into the plus side. It seems that you and I have something in common. We both like things to run very smoothly. In my case, because that's a sign of a profitable business: for you, it's because you enjoy having a trouble-free life. A kind of laziness, I suppose. I don't really care what *your* reason is. As far as I'm concerned, it just indicates that you will not rock the boat as long as things are going well, and you're unlikely to do the dirty on me. Incidentally, I also understand your distaste for violence . . . and I would like you to know that I share it.'

'So what?' I asked. 'Are you suggesting some kind of business co-operation or something?'

'Some kind,' he agreed. 'There are three good reasons why I'm interested in you, Madigan. One is that I need somebody on the ground in your area – a representative, if you like. My business interests are expanding fast, and I find I need reliable eyes and ears all over the Midlands. You would become my representative in South Warwickshire – Stratford, Warwick, Leamington, Evesham . . . all round there.'

I thought of pointing out that Evesham is in Worcestershire, not Warwickshire, but decided that discretion was the better part of vanity. Mr Anchovy was still talking – Christ, he could talk ten to the dozen, and it certainly helped to make him look and sound dynamic. No wonder he had no time for small-talk.

'My second reason is your garage business. It is an excellent front for all sorts of . . . illegal activities. For instance, you've got traffic coming and going all day . . . and that makes it a perfect delivery and pick-up point. You get, say, a van booked in for a service, and nobody knows or cares whether the person who collects it is the same person who brought it in. Right?'

I suppose he had to stop for breath. I said:

'You still haven't told me anything very specific, as such. What exactly are you asking me to do? And why should I do it

28

anyway? I haven't heard anything in it that's attractive enough to make me bust a gut.'

'You're quite right, Madigan. As you have correctly pointed out, I'm not asking you to do anything specific just at the moment. What I am proposing is that you become, let's say, an associate member of my organisation. I'll pay you a monthly retainer directly into your Abbey National account . . .'

Mr Anchovy flicked open the slim folder on his desk.

'. . . number 2582712. Let's say . . . um . . . seven hundred and fifty pounds per month for starters. Of course any time you do something specific for my organisation, you get an additional payment for that. All right?'

I thought about it.

'I'll think about it,' I said. 'Can I let you know?'

'Of course,' he said. 'You have until this time next week to get back to me. Basil will give you a note of his mobile number on your way out. Call him and just say yes or no.'

'Right!' I had started to get out of the chair when I thought of something. 'You said you had three reasons for being interested in me. What was the third one?'

'Ah yes!' he said. 'The third reason is the clincher – it's Sergeant . . . no, Inspector now . . . Neil Cornfoot.'

Bloody hell! All of a sudden, I felt like a cat in a Chinese restaurant. I froze, to give my brain a chance to pick the bones out of this.

Let me get this straight; if Anchovy knew that Neil had forced me to get involved, then surely I was no use to him. That could be good news for me – a rejection here might mean I could climb out of the frying pan and back into my backwater; hopefully without getting beaten up too badly. I sneaked a look at Basil, but couldn't see any increase in his menace index. It was the kind of situation that would have had my Aunt Ursula going on about a nil wind.

My hopes rose a bit . . . but on the other hand, why would Anchovy still want my services if he knew . . .?

He was starting up his mouth again.

'Don't look so worried, Madigan, I've got my own contacts in the force. That's how I found out that you don't have a police record. But having no record does *not* mean that they don't know about you. Apparently, your friend in the CID managed to lose or ignore certain evidence that could have convicted you a year ago. Now, I don't want to know how much of the insurance reward that bent copper screwed out of you . . . but it gives you a permanent hold over him. Anybody who has a policeman in his pocket is welcome aboard my organisation. My only concern arises from the fact that you mix socially with this Inspector Cornfoot.'

I drove back towards Stratford with my brain going round like a leaf in the tide. As far as I could see, my quality of life had just taken a dive into the pot noodle. The busies wanted to exploit my connections with the underworld, while the criminal brotherhood only wanted me because they thought I had my very own tame copper on a leash.

When I got to Henley-in-Arden I pulled into the car-park of a pub I know there. I needed to do some solid thinking over a half-pint of lager. What should I tell Neil? I bet he would be fascinated to hear that somebody thought he was just the monkey who was saddled with me as his organ-grinder. In the end, I decided that Neil could manage without that information. And that meant I had to be careful what I said to Aileen as well. I mean, I trust her completely to keep her mouth shut – but who knows when she might accidentally drop a wayward word to Sally.

Kenny Madigan, the notorious double agent.

I did tell Aileen all about my meeting with Mr Anchovy – except for what he thought about my relationship with Neil. I had no intention of doing a repeat of my last encounter with the criminal world. Aileen stood by me that time, but only just; and in the end she was the one who shoved me into getting the whole mess sorted out.

My other reason for being so frank with Aileen can be summed up in two words – country cottages. It provided me with a plausible reason for not being able to go with her to look at them. I mean, I'll have to stay close to the garage to keep an eye on whatever illicit stuff might be coming and going, so that I can report it to Neil. Well, won't I? Anyway, Aileen didn't like it very much, but she could see that my heart wouldn't be in the cottage hunt until I got my head through to the light at the end of the tunnel.

I used the number I got from Basil. When I said who I was, he just growled, 'Yes or no?'

'Yes.'

'Right, from now on, you will have a new regular customer. They're called Drennan's of Wellesbourne.'

'OK,' I said – but he didn't hear me; he had already hung up.

They started using Lone Harp garage the very next week. And from then onwards, we would get a Drennan's motor – usually an estate or small van – booked in maybe twice a week or so. Basil was right, it was just like getting a new regular customer, not that it would grab anybody's attention. I mean, there was no obvious connection between the different cars and vans that turned up; just that they went in the book under the name of Drennan's – and on the bills of course, which were always paid in cash by whoever picked them up.

I reckoned there were two things going on. There were genuine Drennan's vans – they had the company name painted on the sides. Drennan's of Wellesbourne was, to all intents and purposes, a legitimate business – I checked. A good front, I thought, for dodgy activities – like Lone Harp, I suppose. They were good customers too. And then there were the fake Drennan's vehicles; miscellaneous unmarked estates and vans on various shady missions for the Wheel's mob. I decided that their only connection with Drennan's was that they used the name when they booked in for unnecessary servicing.

Being dead nosy, as I am, I made a point of taking a close look at these vehicles, and sure enough they were usually carrying something. The problem was, I could never find out what the cargoes were, on account of they were always well packaged in cartons which were sealed in such a way that it would be obvious if anybody tampered with them. I suppose they were testing me as well, to see if I could be trusted.

Anyway, I tried to let Neil know what was going on, but that useless bugger can be a right Scarlet Pumpernickel at times. In fact it turned out that our own favourite copper was away for a while – a fact that had its repercussions on me.

Don't get me wrong; I really like Sally, and she's very decorative – but it was starting to do my head in, finding her in the maisonette night after night. She would drape her long slim body right across the part of the sofa that I usually sit on, and twitter on and on with Aileen about clothes, wedding preparations, what a cow that Marilyn in the hairdresser's is, and even about some bloke that fancied her at work.

Funny thing about Sally; I don't find her all that sexy, even though she does look kind of like a supermodel, and dresses to maim at least. She's got a good sense of humour, so she and I get on well with each other, on a kind of jokey sort of basis. Aileen and Sally have been close mates since school, and Aileen always used to feel sorry for her because of what she called Sally's constant problems in 'the trouser department', because she could always attract men, but couldn't seem to keep one for more than five minutes. Not until Neil came along, that is, and now they were engaged and heading for the big M, although they didn't have a date fixed yet.

So I sat there on the armchair facing the sofa, and tried not to look as if I was looking at Sally's legs which, on this particular night, had a miniskirt fringe round their tops. (I didn't want to be on the wrong end of one of Aileen's heavy glares which would be followed up, probably in bed, by a rant about what she would call my 'ogling'.)

'So where has Neil gone, exactly?' I asked.

'Oh . . . Neil? You mean where has Neil gone?'

'Yes,' I nodded. 'You know, Neil, the bloke you live with . . . the one you're going to marry.'

Sally was never a very good liar, even when she had been told what to say.

'Well, he's gone . . . er . . . on a course. You know how the police make their people go on all sorts of courses. Well, Neil's on one of these . . . er . . . courses.'

Her face brightened up a bit and she added: 'He phones me every night from the hotel, though.'

I thought about asking exactly where this course was, and when he would be back, but I could see it would be like paddling in treacle, so I just said:

'Well, the next time he calls, would you mind telling him that there's some activity at the garage now – he'll know what I mean.'

'All right, I promise. And we can arrange to go out on a foursome when he gets home. What do you fancy – Chinese or Indian? . . . Or we could try that Thai restaurant . . . the one on the Gyratory . . .'

But I had stopped listening. I don't know if she ever did pass my message on to Neil. Not that it mattered, because things started to get out of hand before he got back.

It started innocently enough. I got this phone call at work, and it sounded like a heavy breather at first, but turned out to be Basil, the professional gorilla. I remember thinking his voice was so deep that you couldn't tell what kind of accent he had. He grunted:

'The Wheel wants to see you . . . tomorrow afternoon. Crack of half-past four.'

I couldn't help my groan, but hoped it was silent at the other end of the phone.

'Will that be at his office in Condiment Brothers' place?' I said, thinking of the funeral parlour – and just checking.

'Oh, no, he's got loads of business interests. This is where you have to go . . . it's in Birmingham.'

He gave me an address I didn't recognise.

'OK. I suppose I should ask for Mr Anchovy again?'

'If you do, you'll need a crash course in walking with two broken legs. You ask for Cicada.'

The phone went dead. I hoped I wasn't getting into a bag of worms where I might do the same.

4

The Birmingham A to Z placed the target address near the centre of the city, not too far from the Bullring market area. But when I got there, it didn't look right. It was an old-fashioned natty gents outfitter's. Nothing the least bit stylish. You know, the sort of place that features rails of hairy sports jackets in assorted shades of vomit, and the kind of nylon trousers you see old men wearing in the post office queue. A tall thin shape with a tape measure dangling round its neck drifted out of the shadows, attracted by the pinging of the door as it closed behind me. Its brows were lifted in a question mark.

'Er . . . Cicada,' I said, feeling foolish; but he must have heard the word before, because he nodded.

'If you would kindly step this way, sir.'

I followed him to a door at the back of the shop. He opened it to reveal a garbage-infested backyard area. Opposite, I could see the backs of premises which must have their fronts on the next street over from the one the tailor's shop was in. Pointing to a door at the opposite side, my guide said:

'That green door . . . there.'

The door behind closed, to leave me standing among a regiment of overflowing rubbish bins. I made for the green door and knocked. When it opened to invite me in, I couldn't see a thing in the gloom after the bright daylight. But Basil's grunt and footsteps were there, and I managed to follow them through various corridors and doors until we emerged into a big space. Most of it was dim, but there was a puddle of fluorescent light with a round table in the middle of it. Two men were sitting at it with drinks in front of them. There didn't seem to be anyone else in the place.

'Ah, Mr Madigan, we thought you weren't coming. What would you like to drink?'

It was the bloke who was known as Mr Anchovy the last time I met him, though his sidekicks seemed to refer to him as the Wheel. For the first time, I wondered if maybe Anchovy wasn't his real name. Might as well be hung for a fish as a lamb, I couldn't help thinking (my Auntie Ursula has a lot to answer for). Somehow, I didn't fancy my prospects would be helped by addressing him as Mr Wheel – or Mr Cicada, for that matter. I moved myself carefully on to a vacant chair and admitted that a glass of lager would be fine. Basil faded towards a bar that I could now distinguish in the middle distance.

I thought maybe I'd better explain why I was five minutes late; keep my credentials intact, you might say.

'The traffic's diabolical out there – and the parking –'

The Wheel interrupted me with a dynamic snarl:

'No small-talk – remember? Well now, Mr Madigan, you will no doubt be pleased to hear that we have a little job for you. Not a difficult job, but quite an important one. In fact, it's so vital that I'm giving you a partner to share the responsibility.'

He flapped a hand to bring his companion into play. 'Meet your partner.'

I gave the other bloke a serious clocking for the first time, helped by the interruption caused by Basil arriving with my lager. This new bloke looked to be about my size and a few years younger than me – medium height and middle twenties. A very stylish dresser. You know, not just expensive clothes, but as bang up to the minute as a London securities trader who has just copped a large undeserved bonus. I was willing to bet that everything he was wearing was labelled in Italian. His black hair had a faint waviness that must have been put there in a glitzy salon. He was what the Cat in *Red Dwarf* would have liked to be.

While I was giving this flash git the once-over, he was doing the same act on me. If we had been bulls, we would have been circling each other warily; snorting and pawing the dust. Eventually, he stuck a manicured hand out towards me.

'Peachy Curtain,' he said. At least that's how I heard it. I grasped his hand for about a microsecond, being careful not to shake it or show any other sign of friendliness, and told him, 'Kenny Madigan.'

'OK, OK.' The Wheel was getting impatient. 'Now that you people know each other, let's get on with it. This job is all set up. You two are to be one of a number of links in a chain. You will have a brief contact with the link before you, when it delivers the . . . er . . . merchandise; and you'll certainly have no contact at all with the downstream link when you make your delivery. It's a bit like pass the parcel – in fact, I have designated it Project Parcel; just make sure not to be holding anything incriminating when the music stops.'

He threw a very significant look at Curtain when he said that last bit, and it made me wonder what extra meaning could be lurking behind it. But mostly I was reminded how much this bloke can talk. And he hadn't finished. He fixed his gaze on me.

'Madigan, you have influence with the constabulary. It's up to you whether you warn your contact to keep the Old Bill's eyes pointing in some other direction. I believe in letting my executives use their own initiative. You two just have to be in position at the ... Lone Harp garage isn't it? ... at half-past midnight, each night from next Monday until the job takes place. If you don't hear anything by one thirty, you can go home. On the night the job goes forward, you'll get a call from one of my people, and within the next half-hour the goods will arrive.'

His head swung round to point at the other guy.

'Pe ... er ... Mr Curtain, nearer the time, you will be briefed on where it has to be delivered.'

Then I was the target again.

'He'll pass that information on to you when you're about to do the job, Mr Madigan.'

The Wheel paused and leaned forward so that his face hung right in front of mine.

'If you foul up, then you foul up – I'll recruit somebody who doesn't, and your injuries will heal in time; but if you ever *deliberately* double-cross me, you won't live long enough to know what your injuries were.'

It didn't sound like a threat at all, the way he said it. Just like ordinary conversation, it was – dead matter-of-fact, in fact. That was what made it so frightening.

Then the Wheel leaned back and included both of us.

'Now you each know what's expected of you, at the end of the day?'

We both nodded, although I was a bit hazy about what was expected of me. At that moment my brain cells were too busy trying to work out why it had suddenly turned so cold in that place.

'Right,' said the Wheel, getting to his feet, 'I'm leaving now.'

He looked at his watch.

'The tailor's shop will be closing up now, so you'll have to go out by the front door. But take your time ... finish your drinks first – and try not to be seen leaving.'

He took a step away and then half turned back with a final reassuring message:

'Oh, there is one other thing you should know ... the

merchandise you'll be responsible for will be alive. At least I hope it will still be alive at that stage in the proceedings.'

And he was off – not the way I had come in, but more or less in the opposite direction. Peachy Curtain and I were left alone, Basil having merged into the background shadows after serving my lager. We sat silent until we heard a door open and close. Then I heard a deep sigh from my new partner, as if he had been holding his breath for half an hour.

'Peachy, do you know if there's a bog around here?' I asked him. 'I'm dying for a pee.'

And I *was* too. I had only just managed to keep my trousers dry when I heard that last remark from the Wheel. And now this guy was looking as if he was mad at me for some reason.

'Watch it, buddy-boy,' he said. 'I don't let any asshole make fun of my name ... it's Petesy – not Peachy. Petesy ... got it?'

Christ, what a terrible accent – fake mid-Atlantic on top of general South of England.

'OK, sorry,' I said, making light of it. 'It sounded like Peachy to me.'

'Awright, I accept your apology,' Petesy said, and added, 'Come on and I'll show you where the john is.'

It was a large men's room with a long row of urinals along one wall, and a long row of condom-vending machines along the adjacent one. Clean, though. We were standing shoulder to shoulder at neighbouring urinals, enjoying the facilities, when Petesy said, 'See that?' He nodded towards the sign on the wall facing us. 'NOW WASH YOUR HANDS PLEASE', it said, in big black capitals. He went on: 'I keep my dick so clean, I should wash my hands *before* I take it out.'

I couldn't think of an answer to that.

After washing our hands, we went back to the table for Petesy to pick up his handbag – that's right, he had one of these men's handbags in black leather with a loop that goes round your wrist. Of course – a bloke who dresses as snazzily as Petesy wouldn't want the lines of his clobber spoiled by carrying personal possessions in his pockets. Still, when he picked up the handbag, I got the impression that it was a lot heavier than you might expect of something that held a wallet, small change, handkerchief, and maybe a pack of cigarettes.

When we finally went out through the front door, I looked up to see if there was some identification on the premises. It was still too early for the neon tubes to be lit up, but the message over the entrance was clear – 'The Silver Cicada'.

Of course, when I got home I told Aileen all about my adventure at the Silver Cicada. It turned out that she had heard of the place because some of her workmates had been there. It was the kind of night-club that caters for block bookings for hen parties and office outings. There's a cabaret, and you get dinner thrown in – you know, prawn cocktails followed by overcooked rump steaks and chips, and they make most of their money by charging fifteen pounds a bottle for some of the worst red wine ever road-tankered in from the other end of Europe.

Aileen and I both had a good laugh over Petesy Curtain. She thought I was exaggerating how well he dressed, especially when I couldn't tell her what kind of gear he wore on his feet. I had to point out that it was only people who work in the shoe trade who notice a person's shoes. I think we were only laughing to blot out the scary bits. We finished up having to agree that the Wheel didn't trust me, else why would he saddle me with Petesy? (At that point, I still thought I was to be doing a simple one-man job, though I was right about him not trusting me – he didn't trust anybody.) Anyway, I was pretty determined not to cock it up, because the consequence of that was something I didn't want to think about.

Neil still wasn't around. We knew that from Sally, or at least Aileen did, so there was no chance of getting advice from that direction. Aileen offered to do anything she could – and there *was* something which could usefully be done. The trouble was, there was a slight chance that the person doing it might be in danger, so I definitely was not about to let Aileen in on it. Still, it set my brain cells off, trying to dig up somebody else who could help out. My mate Steve was ruled out, of course, on account of the danger, and the fact that he's a pillar of respect-ability. Then I had it – there was someone who I wouldn't mind too much if he got his fingers burned in the cogs of the Wheel's empire.

I would have to pay for his services, of course, but then Nick Pearson was anybody's for thirty quid. He used to be a reasonably competent breaker and enterer, although I knew that he wasn't too proud to turn his hand to anything for money. Except proper work, of course, and preferably if it was something dishonest. I called him and said I had something in mind that might be right up his street, and if he would meet me in the Cross Keys in half an hour, he might learn something to his advantage.

Naturally, I had to buy the drinks. We carried them to a table in a dim corner, well away from prying ears.

'It was good to hear from you, Kenny. Thought you'd forgot all about your old mates now that you've joined the fat cats.'

I don't know why he said that, because we've never really *been* mates, as such. In fact, I had occasion to teach him a sharp lesson a while back. But that's Nick Pearson for you.

'OK, Nick, enough of the pleasantries. I've got a little job for you . . .'

Nick Pearson's black curls always bob up and down, because of his habit of nodding constantly when anyone is speaking to him, and even more so when he's got his own mouth in gear. They were yoyo-ing like . . . well, like yoyos, I suppose, while I told him what I wanted, and handed over twenty quid with the promise of another twenty if he came up with the goods. What a bloody cheapskate.

In spite of my hopes, Petesy turned up in good time at the garage on the Monday night. After parking out of sight, round the back, he swaggered in through the partly opened front door, which I slid shut to hide the lights from outside view. I led him to my office, where I had a pot of coffee ready. I was hoping to pump him for information about this mysterious job, about the Wheel, and about the whole bent shit-heap he was part of.

Trouble was, Petesy had other kinds of information in mind.

'Hey, man, I came down to Stratford early – this afternoon in fact. It's a real neat place. Full of tourists and all, even at this time of year – loads of babes from all over the world. You must be fighting them off every day, man. I could of pulled anyone I wanted, of course, but I restrained myself because of having to come here tonight.'

Petesy took a swig of coffee, gave me an over-confident smile, and looked even more insufferable than he did at the Silver Cicada. He ignored my deliberately sour expression, and carried on:

'You gotta give me the guided tour, man. I just bet you know where to lay your mitts on the best chicks around . . . once this job is over, of course.'

I told him about Aileen, and how I couldn't possibly join him in chasing after stray nookie like a twitchy teenager.

Kenny Madigan, the sanctimonious git.

'OK, man,' he said, 'no sweat . . . you just point me in the right direction, and I'll scope out the action for myself. I can handle that – score every time, I do.'

Petesy's face brightened. 'Hey, why don't you bring your girl along? I'll turn it into a foursome in no time. Yeah, bring Eileen . . .'

'Aileen,' I corrected him but he charged on like a white tornado.

'. . . Yeah, whatever. It's time she saw a real action man in action.'

Not if I can help it, I thought, and then it struck me like a ton of bricks that Petesy, this flash sod, was as nervous as a chicken up a tree. He was chattering like a barrelful of monkeys to cover up how edgy he was. The other thing that tipped me off was how he couldn't take his eyes off the phone that was just sitting there on my desk, minding its own business.

Christ, coffee was the *last* thing he needed. I put my feet up on the desk, switched my ears off, and just nodded now and then, while he ranted on. This is a technique I've perfected for use on the rare occasions when Aileen really lets go at me. When Petesy's elastic band finally wound down a bit, I asked him about the Wheel.

'Great guy to work for. Fucking dangerous bloke if he thinks you're holding out on him. He's at the centre of every criminal web in the Midlands – and he's expanding as fast as McDonald's. That's why his organisation is a good place for an ambitious lad like me. In fact, I'm heading for the very top of the heap, if you must know.'

Then he gave me a sharp look, adding:

'And I'm well in with the Wheel – so you'd better not do anything to annoy me, mate, or you'll find yourself in trouble.'

'Yeah, you've got me really scared,' I said, and then wished I hadn't, because, as you know, I can never seem to make sarcasm work. Not the way Aileen does.

Petesy wouldn't say anything else on that subject, except to tell me that he knew the Wheel's real name all right, but I was too low down the scale to be allowed in on it.

On the other hand, he was more ready to talk about this job which was waiting to happen. I started to feel even more nervous myself, when I heard what it was – a sodding jailbreak for Christ's sake. My little friend didn't know who the jail-breaker was – not that it would have meant anything to me anyway – but he did know that it was some evil bastard who was being busted out of a prison somewhere in the London area. We had to move him on to somewhere that Petesy knew, but wasn't telling me yet.

I have to admit that the stage-coach system seemed like a good way to transfer that kind of merchandise to a safe place. Except that if I was in charge of it, I would be dead worried about so many people being in on the operation. And these people are mostly criminals, remember – and criminals are not famous for their high levels of intelligence, or for their reliability either. The only consolation would be that the police can be just as stupid and inefficient. Anyway, it made me realise that the Wheel might have chinks in his army, what with having to rely on a whole chain of society's outcasts – like Petesy for instance.

So we were starting to get on reasonably well, Petesy Curtain and me, by the time I noticed it was one thirty. Nothing doing tonight. I wasn't sorry.

5

At work in the morning, I was feeling OK. Not great, you understand, but on fairly friendly terms with destiny, and start-ing to hope that the jailbird transfer would take place that night, and then it would be all over and I could start getting on with the next bit of my life.

Like so many depressing pieces of information, it came straight down the phone and into my ear.

'Kenny, it's Sam . . . Sam Cotteridge. We've got trouble. It's all gone wrong, and Del's been beaten up, and I don't know what do, and –'

'Hold it, hold it,' I said. 'Are you at your garage?'

'Yes.'

'All right,' I told her, 'I'm coming over. Don't do a thing till I get there. I'll be about fifteen minutes.'

I've got this theory that everybody talks like a television drama when they're under pressure – and I had just proved it.

I went straight in through the little reception area, to the office. Sam jumped up from her desk, and came towards me. She had obviously been crying. I hugged her, just to comfort her and let her know she had a friend. It felt good though – I got the impression that the shape under the shapeless overall was as succulent as you could hope for.

After maybe half a minute, Sam got herself together, and pulled away. She took me by the hand, and led me through the door leading to the workshop, saying:

'Look at what they did.'

I looked. The car standing in the middle of the workshop was in a sorry state. If you met it in different surroundings you might have trouble knowing it *was* a car. It had been systematically wrecked. Every window and light was broken. All the body panels were bashed beyond any possibility of repair. When I peered into the open engine compartment, I saw that everything in there had been given a lot of attention by someone expertly wielding a very heavy metal object.

I raised my eyebrows in Sam's direction. She nodded.

'Yes, it's . . . was . . . a customer's car. It happened last night. Del came back about ten o'clock, to catch up with some paper-work. She walked in on them. I've sent the mechanics home for the rest of the day.'

'How badly was she hurt?' I asked.

'Bruises, couple of cracked ribs, concussion. She's in hospital . . . looks a mess, but nothing serious. She'll be out in a couple of days.'

'Do you know who did it . . . and why?' I asked.

'Haven't a clue who did it, but I think I know why it was done. Come on back into the office – it's too depressing out here.

'It's a warning,' Sam told me. 'After you told me there was something shady about AutoSupCo and their supplies, I got to thinking it's not worth breaking the law just to save a few quid. We don't want to get mixed up with these kind of people.'

I was nodding about as much as Nick Pearson, by this time. Sam paused to sniff and blow her nose.

'So I cancelled all our orders with the company . . . and I wrote them a letter to say that we would no longer use them as suppliers. That was when they turned nasty. We started getting letters that promised we would regret it if we did not buy from them in the future.'

'So you've got something to show the police. The letters.'

'No, they were clever about it. The letters were written in such a way that they sound like half the junk mail that we get from firms canvassing for our business – just a little more aggressive, that's all. Anyway, I tore them up. The phone calls were much more threatening. They were a lot more up front about putting us out of business on the phone.'

'And you didn't do what they said?'

'Not on your life.' Sam put on a defiant expression. 'I thought it was just empty threats – anybody would have thought that, wouldn't they?'

She looked straight into my eyes and said:

'Oh, Kenny, what am I to do?'

It was lucky I was sitting down at the time, because my knees melted and turned so weak that I wouldn't have been able to keep standing. As you know, I'm not a person who gets hot under the collar over women, but this beautiful, vulnerable creature was doing my head in – and not just my head . . . but back to the serious stuff. I had to give her an answer.

What I did was, I talked Sam into going back to AutoSupCo for her supplies, or at least some of them, on the grounds that she had to protect her business and the people who worked in it.

I persuaded her that when the police caught up with these

villains (with my help, of course), the crooked supplier would be shut down. And there would be no question of any of their customers getting into trouble for receiving stolen goods – after all, they were probably supplying half the small independent garages in the Midlands. She seemed to accept this, although it was obvious that she hated the whole idea. No alternative, really, when you think about it. It was just that she needed somebody trustworthy to tell her so.

Kenny Madigan, the well-known pillar of society. Well, pillock maybe.

I stayed on for a while, helping to clear up some of the worst of the mess in the workshop, but Sam's heart wasn't in it. She finally said:

'Oh, what the hell. Leave it, Kenny. I'll get the guys to do it tomorrow. Let's get some coffee and take it into the office.'

I don't know whether she meant it to happen that way, but when we got back into the office, I felt the need to give Sam another comforting hug. At least that was how it started out, but before I knew it, we were kissing pretty bloody passionately, and starting to move on to the heavier stages.

'Just a minute,' I said, moving back a little so that her tongue wasn't in my mouth for a moment. 'The reception door isn't locked. We wouldn't want anyone to come in and find –'

'Shut up and kiss me, you fool,' was her response. 'I slipped out and locked it a while ago.'

Suddenly I remembered how devious a woman can be. A bit later, I even wasted a microsecond or two noticing how lucky it was that the two desks were placed side by side, providing a good length of continuous flat surface. Hard on the elbows though.

Afterwards, Sam sighed and clung to me.

'Oh, Kenny, that was great. I feel so much better now. There's nothing like a good shag to make you feel human again after fate has trampled you into the dust.'

That would have made any bloke feel smug.

And Sam with her kit off was a sight my memory will want to bring out and look at in the long winter nights when I'm too old to do anything more than think about it.

I've heard it said that sex without a caring commitment is an empty and unfulfilling experience. On the other hand, as empty and unfulfilling experiences go, it's fucking marvellous.

It seemed that I had, not one, but two new things to worry about. The first was that I now had plenty of evidence that the Wheel's mob was about as full of compassion as Ghengis Khan. For a moment or two, I wondered why they didn't just run it as a protection racket, and to hell with all the bother of running a whole stable of businesses. But then I remembered my meetings with the Wheel. It was obvious that he saw himself as a successful entrepreneur – which he was, I suppose. So he didn't really *need* to do the criminal stuff, not from a financial point of view. And of course there's nothing else as good as having a legitimate operation, when it comes to laundering your ill-gotten gains.

What it came down to was that I had good reason to feel shit-scared. These were people who didn't hesitate to beat up a woman just because she was there. Could it have been Basil?

And then there was my second new thing to worry about – my little fling with Sam, and my relationship with Aileen. I knew I still loved Aileen, but Christ, Sam was exciting. And how about that great body, although that wasn't the only thing I found exciting about her – it could be a serious attack of infatuation on my part. I decided to put that one on the back steamer for the moment.

Coming back to the Lone Harp garage felt like coming home after a long holiday; I had to make an effort to remember what was going on – and to get Sam out of my mind.

Oh, yes! I now had to prepare myself for my second night of waiting for the escaped prisoner to be passed down the line. I got Aileen to check, discreetly, with Sally, to see if Neil was back on his home patch. No luck; no forecast of when he would get back. So there was no means of warning him about the prison breakout. I was on my own. If the sky fell in, and the Old Bill swooped on me while I was harbouring an escaped convict, I was done for. Unless ... but there was no other copper who knew anything about Neil's arrangement with me, and he always warned me not to talk freely to any of his police mates. I'm pretty sure that was because our arrangement was completely unofficial. And of course, who knows what whispers might get back to the Wheel, and I would stick pins in my eyes rather than be on the wrong side of that malicious bastard.

The second night, Petesy was still swaggering but seemed a lot more relaxed. It was me that had the bats flying around inside my guts. For a while, we sat there, gloomily pretending not to look at the phone. Any animosity there had been between us had dried up. I suppose we were both too busy willing the phone not to ring. If we were lucky, the jailbreak might fail and our involvement would be cancelled. We talked about everything except our role in the prison escape route.

In some ways, Petesy was a sad bastard. According to him, he had been working for the Wheel since sometime last year, and was now a trusted member of the gang. He had jumped at the chance to make a lot of money, and found that it was a lot more fun than travel agenting, which was what he did before. He spent all his money on clothes and his BMW, with the sole aim of impressing the girls who frequent the flashier clubs in Birmingham.

I made a detour round Petesy's night life, and asked him if Basil was the Wheel's bodyguard. It seemed that he had got to know the gorilla, and quite liked him.

'He's a Londoner. And he's the Wheel's accountant. I think he's actually a chartered accountant. He does the books for the Wheel.'

Christ, a great big accountant; a number cruncher as well as a bone cruncher – and he must have a good imagination too, if he keeps the crooked accounts.

'Is he also the one who smashes property and beats people up to keep them in line? I mean, the Wheel must need strong-arm stuff done now and again.' I was thinking about Del's injuries, and the damage at the Five Ponds Garage. 'It's just . . . well, Basil looks like somebody you wouldn't want to meet on a dark night.'

Petesy shook his head. 'No, he's not like that. He's a nice guy really, when you get to know him . . . kinda shy, that's all. When the Wheel needs what you call strong-arm stuff, he usually hires a couple of no-brain muscles from Rent-a-Thug, just for the occasion.'

I sat back and tried to think about that for a while, without much success. It was Petesy who broke the silence, finally.

'Sorry if I gave you a bit of hassle last night, Kenny,' he said, sneaking another look at the phone. 'I'll find the local chick hang-outs for myself.'

It turned out to be another blank night.

On the third night, Petesy turned up looking twitchy. I have to admit that the waiting was getting to me a bit as well. We settled down to our usual routine of coffee, clock watching, and phone stalking. Conversation didn't exactly flag – it just never got unflagged. Eventually, Petesy said:

'Fuck this for a game of soldiers. I almost wish I was back at Sunshine Tours.'

'I know what you mean,' I told him, 'but we've made our bed, so we'll just have to lump it.'

'Lie in it,' he said.

'What?'

'Lie in it.'

'What does that mean? Lie in it? What are you on about?'

'You said we made our bed, so we'll have to lump it. But the saying is, we made our bed, so we'll have to lie in it – not *lump it*.'

'Don't talk such crap,' I told him. 'That was one of my Auntie Ursula's favourite sayings, and she always said lump it.'

'Well, you can tell your Auntie Ursula from me that she got it wrong.'

Petesy was getting a bit heated now. His accent had lost any pretence of Yankee-hood. He had his horse in mid-stream.

'Look, you moron. How can you lump a bed? That doesn't mean anything; you *lie* in a bed. That's what it's for – lying in.'

'You stupid bastard.' I was willing to teach him a lesson if he would only listen. 'It doesn't *have* to make sense. It's just a . . . a crappy saying . . . like a stitch in time has got nothing to do with sewing. It's definitely lump it.'

'Lie in it.'

'Lump it.'

'Fucking lie in it.'

47

'Sodding lump it.'

We were standing nose to nose, glaring at each other, red-faced – at least his was. Both our hands were clenched at our sides. We were nearly ready to cross the rubicund for the sake of some stupid proverb. I said:

'Anyway, my Auntie Ursula's dead, so I can't make her change it.'

Petesy opened his mouth to say something, but he never got it out.

We both nearly jumped out of our skins at the sound of the phone.

The message was short:

'This is it, mate, they're on their way.'

It was followed immediately by the dialling tone. The caller didn't need to identify himself. Project Parcel, or at least our bit of it, was under way at last.

I turned to Petesy.

'You better tell me now. Where do we take this fucking jail-bird?'

'Right, well, there's this storage place . . . warehouse, I suppose, that belongs to one of the Wheel's companies. It's in some place called Alcester, not far from here . . . I've got directions and the keys. It's sometimes used for storing hot merchandise in. We're to leave the escaped guy there, to be picked up later by somebody else.'

By this time, nearly all of my brain cells were ringing bells. I was willing to bet that the place in question was the same one where I had an unfortunate personal experience of kidnapping the previous year. Its existence was one of the things I 'forgot' to mention to the police when I cleared up that whole mess for them.

'OK,' I said to Petesy, 'I can show you the way to Alcester, but we'll have to use your directions to find the warehouse.'

No sense in telling Petesy anything unnecessary, either.

Somehow, we both seemed more relaxed, now that it had started and we had something to do. Well, I certainly felt better.

As I said before, it was dead on half an hour after the phone call, when we heard the wheels on the forecourt of Lone Harp Auto.

6

Up to this point, it was as if I had been wading into the sea on a gently sloping beach. You can see how gradually I had got immersed in the criminal underworld. And now it was closing over my head.

'Grievous . . .'

It was our prisoner's one-word answer to Petesy's question about what he had been inside for – but not one that made me feel secure. Anyway, Petesy had put himself in charge. He sounded dead confident when he said:

'OK, that's what we'll call you from now on – Grievous.'

It's amazing what a gun can do for the man who is holding it.

I loosened the cord that tied the escaper's hands together, and Petesy took him at gunpoint towards the toilet.

So there I am, in the workshop, looking into the brightly lit passage where Petesy is standing outside the open toilet, pointing his gun at the prisoner inside. After a suitable interval, I hear the sound of the toilet being flushed – and then there's an almighty commotion. Petesy is snatched into the bog by his gun hand, there is some shouting and grunting, and a struggle which seems to go on for a long time, but is probably only a few seconds.

But it's long enough for me to think, first: Shoot, you fool, and second: Don't shoot, you fool.

There is also enough time for me to wonder if there is anything I can do to help. But it's all happening in a confined space – there is hardly enough room for the two people already there, without me leaping in to increase the sardine factor. I decide my best option is to move to a position against the back wall of the workshop, just to the left of the passage. I can peer round the corner if something with a more encouraging sound starts to happen.

Silence. Then some more silence. I'm just about to take a look, when I hear:

'Hey, you! You oot there. Just in case you've got a gun as well. We're comin' oot. An' Ah've got your mate in front of me, so you wid hit him furst.'

I think about sneaking a look. They probably wouldn't see me because of looking from a bright place into a dim place. In fact, that very thing might be my best weapon. I snatch the nearest built-in dispenser on the wall beside me. This is a trigger-operated nozzle on the end of a spring-loaded retractable hose. Its purpose in life is to dispense engine oil. I use it now, to dispense a good-sized puddle of the stuff on the workshop floor, right in front of the entrance to the passage – or in this case, the exit from it.

It only takes me about five seconds, but that is long enough for Grievous to get impatient. He shouts again:

'Ah want tae hear your voice oot there. Tell me you'll behave yourself.'

Now I sneak a look. He has Petesy held close by an arm round the neck, squeezing. He must be holding the gun at Petesy's back with his other hand. Petesy looks shit-scared – as you would – and is carefully making no movements at all. I try to prevent my voice from shaking, when I answer:

'OK, I'm not armed. Come on out and we'll discuss where we go from here.'

'Nae discussions necessary, Jimmy. I'll decide whit to dae wi' you pair o' chancers – an' you don't get a vote. Here we come.'

By this time, I've got a hold of a car jack. It's one of those big jacks on rubber wheels with a long handle, that you roll under a car, and a couple of pumps of the handle lifts the car by hydraulic magic. As they step out of the passage, I push the jack gently across their path. It is quite difficult for anybody who steps into a puddle of oil to stay upright. When people do it with their balance already unsteady on account of being frog-marched, or having their ankles tied together; they've got no chance at all. Especially if something heavy comes along and delivers a sideways nudge.

The two of them are thrashing around in the oil, not knowing exactly what's going on. That's when I nip smartly in and make

50

the bloke our prisoner again, by means of a sharp tap on the head with a handy adjustable wrench.

Emergency over.

Kenny Madigan, the new James Bond.

You'd think that Petesy would be grateful to me for getting him out of the clutches of that evil sod. No such bloody luck – he was determined to shoot his gift horse in the foot. Even while I was attending to the first priority – getting Grievous really thoroughly tied up before he could regain consciousness – Petesy was going on at me about how the motor oil had completely ruined his blue suede Versace blouson and his best Armani jeans.

Of course, I was not much inclined to hand out any sympathy, now that I was firmly in the saddle of the whole shambolic operation.

I broke into Petesy's whinging: 'Where's the gun?'

'What?'

'Your bloody gun! Didn't our friend here take it off you, and march you out with it stuck in your back?'

'Oh!' he said. 'No . . . it fell into the toilet in the struggle, so it wouldn't have been any use anyway. Would it?'

I refrained from making the obvious crack about the gun being no more use than a pee-shooter. Instead, I sighed and sent him to fish it out of the bog. We dried it as well as we could, and locked it away in my desk, wrapped up in a duster. Then I dug out a pair of garage overalls in roughly Petesy's size for him to change into. While he was trying to wash off some of the oil, and putting on the overalls, I made a quick call to Nick Pearson. I told him to get into action – and made a slight change to his instructions.

Now we could get ourselves back on track, and deliver the package. I allowed myself a bit of a shudder; despite what Petesy said about Basil, I was pretty sure that he would have been sent to hand out the punishment if we had dropped the parcel.

We rolled Grievous up in a sheet of polythene to protect my car from the worst of the oil, bundled him into the back seat, and headed for Alcester, with Petesy now out of his designer camouflage, and sounding a bit more thoughtful and subdued.

'Er . . . thanks, Kenny . . . for what you did back there. I . . .'

'Forget it,' I told him, 'and stop talking like a TV soap. Anyway I didn't do it for you, as such – I just decided I wasn't going to get killed on account of your sodding incompetence.'

'OK, OK,' he said gloomily. 'I just wish I had been wearing some crappy old clobber when I fell in that oil.'

I couldn't help grinning when I said:

'Well, if you don't like it, you can . . . lie in it, I suppose.'

By the time we reached our destination and got the door unlocked with the keys I had remembered to get out of Petesy's greasy jeans, our prisoner was awake and taking notice of his surroundings, so we made him walk into the warehouse. Petesy had been given detailed instructions. Inside, we walked about eighteen feet down a wide corridor helped by the flashlight from my car, where we found the door into a storeroom on the right. Once again, I refrained from mentioning that I could have done it blindfolded, having brain-curdling memories of this place. We ushered Grievous in and let him sit down on a pile of old sacks. Since he was going to be locked in, I decided to remove the cords from his wrists and ankles. It seemed the humane thing to do. Anyway, he was still quite groggy, and must have had a humdinger of a headache. At least he was no longer desperate for a pee.

'Right,' Petesy said, 'let's lock him up and get the fuck out of here. This place gives me the creeps – and it's bloody cold when you're wearing nothing but dirty overalls.'

'No, hang on a minute,' I said and turned to Grievous, thinking he might just be confused enough to say something he might regret later.

'Why would somebody want to get you out of stir?' I demanded.

'It's no' me they want. It's whit's in here.' He tapped his head.

'Do you mean they're afraid you'll grass on them?' I asked, wondering who exactly 'they' were. Was the Wheel in charge of this operation, or was he just obliging some other bunch of crooks by helping to move this sad punter through his territory?

'Naw, I would have did that two years back if I was goin' to. And anyway it would only be my own mates that got grassed up. The blokes at the top o' the tree wouldnae care if I grassed, 'cos I dunno who they are . . . not exactly.'

'So, what . . .?'

'Let's just say Ah've got some information that they want – like . . . I know where something is and they don't know where it is and they would like me to tell them where it is . . . An' Ah'm not *gonny* tell them where it is, by the way.'

'Right,' I said.

We left Petesy's car where it was, behind Lone Harp, and I took him straight back to the maisonette. On the way, I tried to pump him for anything he might know about the next stage in the escape route for our reluctant jailbreaker. Nothing, really. I didn't bother speculating about who Grievous actually was, or what he had been put away for. I reckoned some close attention to tomorrow's news headlines would answer those questions. It might even give me some clues about what kind of information Grievous was trying to keep to himself.

Aileen had gone to bed, so I just dug out a few of my old clothes for Petesy. When he started to pull on my old paint-stained baggy jeans, I stopped him:

'Look, mate, you better just crash out on the floor in here, 'cos there's no way I'm going out again, to take you back to your car. You've caused me plenty of trouble for one night already. See you in the morning.'

I threw him a couple of blankets, and took myself off to the bedroom. When I crawled in beside Aileen, she muttered something about how cold I was and snuggled up beside me. I shook her more awake and warned her that we had a lodger, just in case she wandered into the living-room in her undies, or worse. It would be bad enough having to listen to Petesy chatting her up in the morning, without him trying to drag her in between his blankets.

When I woke, Aileen was already up and about. I threw on some clothes, staggered out of the bedroom, and followed the smell of coffee and bacon. Petesy was sitting at the table fully dressed in my old clobber, though this was dressing down as far as he was concerned. Aileen was just bringing a pan with three fried eggs out of the little kitchenette.

'Oh, good. You're just in time, Kenny. Breakfast is ready.'

53

'You two have met, then?' I grunted, still trying to scrape the cobwebs out of my voice.

Petesy looked up at me.

'Morning, Kenny. You never told me what a great girl you've got here. Aileen, here, has been telling me all about a new kind of super multi-vitamin tablet from the US of A, with extra beta carotene and ginseng and –'

Jesus Christ, another health pill freak. I cut him off and said to Aileen:

'Has this low-life been bothering you?'

'No,' she said, all smiles, 'he's been very charming. You shouldn't say things like that about your friends. And fancy you not noticing that he wears Timberland boots – they're just about the best you can get. I don't know why you won't let me get you a pair with my discount.'

So I silently ate my breakfast, while the two of them chewed over the latest rumours about niacin and riboflavin. The only information of any interest that came out of the conversation was Aileen revealing that she was thinking about getting into holistic medicine – you know, all that aromatherapy and reflexology mumbo-jumbo. I was enjoying my bacon and eggs too much to pay attention – usually we only have coffee and toast, or even coffee and no toast.

After breakfast, I managed to get Petesy out of there and up to the Lone Harp garage before any of the mechanics arrived for work. Once he had driven off home in his flash car, I swept last night's oil spillage – squirtage would be a better word in this case – into one of the used-oil drainage holes in the floor of the nearest service bay.

Now there was just one loose end left over from the previous night's operation. I tried Nick Pearson's number, but, as I expected, it was still too early for Stratford's criminal aristocracy to be up and about. It was about eleven before Nick Pearson was ready to answer his phone. We agreed to meet in the Queen's Head at lunch time. I wasn't looking forward to spending time with him, but I knew he would tell me nothing until I handed over the money. It was a game of butter my fingers, and I'll butter yours.

Oh, yes! The other thing was what I learnt from the news on the radio I keep in my office. A desperate and dangerous criminal was on the run, having broken out of prison the previous evening, obviously with outside assistance. The fugitive was one Cameron Dalgetty, who had been convicted of GBH on the driver of a security van while relieving the van of its cargo of used banknotes. This had happened two years earlier, and the police had never discovered who Dalgetty's accomplices were – nor found any trace of the money, either. They were confident that the escapee would soon be back in custody – but then they always say that. In the meantime, anyone who identified him (apparently, the television news was carrying pictures of the runaway) should not approach him, seeing as how he was regarded as extremely dangerous.

I had just one more call to make before leaving to meet Nick Pearson – it was to Sam at the Five Ponds Garage in Evesham. I started with.

'Hi, there. Just calling to ask how Del is doing. Is she recovering all right?'

'Oh, Del? Yeah, she's going to be just fine. Is that the only reason you called, Kenny?'

'Well, no,' I said, 'of course not. I wanted to speak to you – and ... er ... thank you for your ... er ... hospitality the other day.'

'That's more like what I wanted to hear. And it's me who should be thanking you. You made me feel better when I was really down.'

I couldn't help being a bit embarrassed at that. Embarrassment always makes my brain cells freeze up, and causes me to say some pretty foolish things. This time wasn't one of my worst, but still, the best I could come up with was:

'Well, if there's ever anything I can do ...'

'Thanks, Kenny.' I could hear the smile in her voice. 'I'll take you up on that. Sorry – I've got to go now.'

She made a kissing sound down the line, and was gone.

Jesus Christ! I thought. I'm getting in too deep in *every* direction.

Then it was off to the Queen's Head to meet Nick Pearson. Right away, I could see that his nodding seemed a bit subdued. There was a funny look in his eyes, and he was not too well pleased with me.

'Here, mate, you might of let on that this was heavy stuff you was gettin' me into. The price has gone up to cover the risks I took for you.'

Surprise, surprise!

'Maybe, maybe not,' I said. 'We can discuss that *after* you tell me all about your dangerous mission. So let's just get on with it.'

You've got to be firm with people like Nick Pearson.

'Right! Well, I does what you tell me . . . I comes in from the town side of Alcester, and I parks at that second-hand car place, among a row of cars, mostly with price stickers on the windscreens – brilliant idea, that, ain't it – well, that's what I thinks at the time. I can see right down the road from there – there's a street light just outside that warehouse – and I'm only in position a couple of minutes when you and your mate arrive from the other direction and help that bloke . . . the one who was staggering . . . into the . . .'

'Yeah, I know what I did. And you saw us come out five minutes later. Right?'

It was like shoving a stick into the spokes of his back wheel. But you need to do that when Nick Pearson is in full throat.

'That's it, just the two of you comes out. And I waits. And as soon as you're out of sight, a car that was parked about three spaces along from me starts up. And it goes down to the warehouse place you've come out of. And two blokes from the car go in with their own keys. And one of them is a great big bugger . . . and the other one is somebody I recognise. You remember Kinnell, don't you, Kenny? Dirty fucking ugly bastard.'

He stopped for breath, and to take a long swig at his pint. I was starting to get a fluttery feeling somewhere low down, as if my intestinal bats were waking up. Not that I had thought it through yet – not enough to put my finger on the chink in my dyke. But somehow I knew there was one, and it hadn't been there till Nick Pearson got involved.

'So what happened next?' I prompted.

'What do you *think* happens? They comes out three-handed, with the other two having to help the lame bloke, and they drive

56

away. I don't follow them on account of you telling me not to.'

Bloody right, I did tell him not to follow anybody. I had experience of Nick Pearson's tailing skills, which make him stand out like a giraffe that's been brought up by a family of ants.

'Look,' I said, 'these punters must have clocked you when you came along and parked near them.'

'Yeah, I was wondering about that. I suppose they saw me right enough ... my car, anyway, but it was quite dim there. They couldn't of recognised me. Could they? Surely they couldn't? Ain't that right, Kenny?'

Pathetic, or what? Now I understood what that funny look in his eyes was – it was fear.

It would have been cruel to point out to Nick Pearson that his car registration must certainly have been noted, and that the organisation whose minions he spied on had enough pull with the cop force to have it traced back to him. So they would be on to him even if he had not been personally clocked, as such. I wished he had used a stolen car; but he didn't have the necessary skills to do that without alerting the whole neighbourhood.

I gave Nick Pearson fifty quid, out of compassion, which made him stop worrying, but probably only until the money reached the bookie's till.

He finished counting the money, and stuffed it into the back pocket of his jeans. Then he looked up at me and said:

'Like I said, I don't follow them, but some *other* bugger does.'

'Come on then, let's have it – and don't even think about asking for more money. You've just trousered all you're going to get, and you don't deserve that.'

I scowled, so as to look menacing, when I said that. It seemed to work, because Nick Pearson's nodding got souped up a bit and he started talking again.

'Well, there I am, sat there watching Kinnell and the others, like I said, and them driving away in their Scorpio, right? ... An' I'm busy thinkin' did they clock me or didn't they? ... An' I sit there for a while wondering ... and just as the Scorpio is about to go out of sight down at the roundabout, this other car starts up across the road from me, and goes off in the same direction without too many lights on . . .'

'Is that it?' I said, thinking that was actually plenty. 'I expect you clocked its registration, though, didn't you?'

'Nah,' said Nick Pearson. 'No lights on the number plates.'

Silently, I wished *he* had taken that simple precaution – or that I had told him to.

When Nick Pearson left, I sat on in the Queen's Head for a while, thinking. It would not be long before the Wheel's organisation – *our* organisation, come to think of it, as I was definitely in it up to my Adam's apple – before that mob put a name and address to the driver of a certain scruffy eight-year-old Escort. Once they questioned Nick Pearson, it would take him about three microseconds to come up with my name.

And all these same thoughts applied equally to the mystery bods who followed the Wheel's guys. They must have clocked Nick Pearson too, and who knows whether they could trace through him to me?

Kenny Madigan, target for the mob's next contract.

7

Saturday, and I was absorbing the morning very gradually, while Aileen was tarting herself up ready to go to work. She brought me a mug of coffee. I said, 'Thank you, gorgeous,' and tried to drag her back into bed. It's always worth a try, though I know I don't have much chance, because Aileen has this horror of being late for work. So it's very hard to derail her morning routine. Instead, *she* derailed *me* by saying:

'Oh, I forgot to mention about Neil.'

'What *about* Neil?' I asked, nookie quickly forgotten. Aileen's diversions always seem to work better than mine.

'He's come back home. Sally phoned me last night, while you were out to collect the Chinese takeaway. She said what about going out with them for dinner sometime soon. What do you think?'

'Sure, why not?' I said. 'Did she mention where he'd been exactly, or what kind of course he was on?'

As you know, I believed Neil's course was about as real as Santa Claus, so I was just going along with the story in the hope that Sally had accidentally let something drop.

'Well, that's the funny thing. Sally says Neil is so embarrassed about it that he doesn't want anybody to know – that's why she was so evasive before. Anyway, Neil thinks it would make the police into a laughing stock if everybody knew, but Sally thinks it sounds very sensible, so *she* doesn't mind telling me what it was about. And I must say, I agree. It sounds as if they really *want* to catch criminals for a change . . .'

At this point, Aileen switched her hair drier on. I could hear she was still talking, but I hadn't a clue what she was saying, so the rest of her speech fell between the cracks as far as I was concerned. No use shouting to ask her to turn it off. I just had to wait until her hair was *completely* dry; Aileen was very fussy about that.

When the noise level went back to normal, I tried to get back to the subject:

'What was that you were saying about Neil?'

'Weren't you listening? I said he's back home now.'

'No, not that bit. I heard that. It was what you were saying while the hair drier was on that I couldn't hear. The bit about what he was doing when he told everybody he was on a course.'

Aileen looked at me as if I was several biscuits short of a shilling.

'Well, he *was* on a course, of course . . . I said so . . . that's what Sally told me. I don't think you've wakened up yet.'

I decided to humour her. I pleaded, 'OK, Aileen, I'm sorry, it's my fault – but I missed the bit where you told me what it was that Neil was so embarrassed about. Please tell me again.'

'Oh, I see!' she said, as if the sun had just come up. 'No wonder you didn't hear that part – I haven't told you it yet.'

Aileen can be really hard work. A person who didn't have my gifts of patience and understanding could get very pissed off at her at times. But I must admit, she's worth it. She went on:

'I was saving the best bit for last. Neil's course had a title something like, "Harnessing the Paranormal". It seems the

59

police are getting so desperate to catch more criminals that they're willing to try anything. Neil was being taught how to use astrologers and fortune-tellers and telephanth . . . telepaths and all these kinds of people to help in solving crimes.'

Jesus Christ, I thought – this is bound to get out. The whole country will be flooded when all the villains wet themselves laughing. I couldn't help chuckling a bit myself – maybe the Wheel would fire us all and employ his own gang of astrologists.

'What a load of old crap,' I said, enjoying the joke.

'Well, you would think that,' Aileen said, 'what with you being a Capricorn. Capricorns are always septic . . . sceptical. Anyway, I don't know what you're grinning at.' Aileen frowned at me through the mirror. 'I think it's a great idea – and so does Sally.'

'What about Neil, though? I bet he'll hate having to pretend to go along with such a crackpot scheme.'

'Well, Sally says he sneered at it at first – just like you. But he was quite impressed by what he learned about the pilot studies. Apparently in one case, a fortune-teller was able to tell the police where to look for four dead bodies they had been trying to find for years. Just by using her crystal ball.'

That kept me amused until Aileen had left for the shoe shop. Then my troubles all flooded back. I didn't think it would be too long before the shit-pile reached out its tentacles, first for Nick Pearson, and then for me. No great urgency to fill Neil in on the prison escape pipeline; all the action was over now, anyway. And he couldn't help me to avoid the backlash from the Wheel – and wouldn't even if he could. So I would have to look out for myself, the best I could.

After juggling with that thought for a while, I came to the conclusion that it was time I took steps to protect myself. Quite often on Saturday mornings when Aileen is at work, I go to the garage just to check that everything is in order, and ready for action on Monday morning. So that's what I did. I headed for a part of Stratford-on-Avon that the tourists never see – where the industrial estates are – up Compass Road and turn into Anthony's Bridge Road, the cul-de-sac where the Lone Harp Auto Repair business is located.

My real reason for going there was to get Petesy's gun, which we had left for useless in my desk, after it fell down the toilet during the struggle with Grievous. Petesy hadn't mentioned it since, so I thought I might as well grab it while I could. To be completely frank, I couldn't really see how a handgun would give me any real protection, but I didn't fancy the idea of Petesy having it back. So I was really doing this for his protection too. Right?

Anyway, I got it out and put it down on the desk. I should mention at this point that I hate guns more than almost anything – thanks to my Auntie Ursula. You see, my mother and father were both killed in a train crash when I was hardly more than a baby. Auntie Ursula was baby-sitting me when it happened, so she was more or less stuck with having to bring me up. She was married to Uncle Ron at the time, and they lived in Henley-in-Arden, about ten miles north of Stratford. Well, I think Auntie Ursula needed me as much as I needed her, because Uncle Ron died of a heart attack when I was about seven years old.

So we became a single-aunt family, and Ursula did her best for me. Of course, she wanted me to have a good career in a safe job, but just in case, she passed on to me all the knowledge and expertise she possessed. And Auntie Ursula's wisdom wasn't limited to her vast stock of (sometimes dodgy) proverbs and sayings – she had a few other abilities tucked up her sleeve. For instance, that was how I inherited my kit of lock-picking tools, and the skills needed to use them. (Though, of course, I must be pretty rusty by now, and would need a lot of practice to get back my old expertise.) It seems that she and Uncle Ron had been a right pair of Bonnie and Clydes before they got lumbered with yours truly. Aunt Ursula insisted on them giving up their life of crime when they got lumbered with me; she was afraid that I would be left alone in the world for a second time if she and Ron went to prison.

So it was my Auntie Ursula who encouraged me to have such an active dislike of guns – but it wasn't because of fear and ignorance, more a wariness arising out of understanding, because she taught me a lot about guns, and especially hand-guns. For instance, this one lying on my desk was what a knowledgeable person would call an automatic pistol with tradi-tional double action. A high-quality American one, too, with a very reputable name stamped on it – Smith and Wesson. When I slid the magazine out, I discovered it was full – six rounds –

and its calibre was .380. Anyway, not to get too technical, I took it to pieces, gave all the bits a well-needed cleaning, lubricated all the moving parts with the lightest machine oil I had in the stores, and reassembled the whole thing. After I finished, I couldn't honestly claim to feel much safer than I had before.

It was so quiet, sitting there alone in my office on a Saturday morning; ideal for having a bit of a think, and . . . you know, sifting through my problems, and trying to work out what might happen, or even what I could do about any of it. It was no longer a simple matter of taking delivery of a few supplies that might be a bit dodgy.

I was up to my neck in crime, at the insistence of the law. In fact, I had become a cog in the Wheel's crooked empire – a position that had me feeling pretty bloody uncomfortable. What made me feel even worse was the likelihood that the villains would turn on me for spying on them. Maybe my copper friend, Neil, could give me some protection, but I doubted it – he's never been known to do anything in my interests. Anyway, he was too busy poncing around having his fortune told, for Christ's sake.

Then there was the stolen jailbird. I still thought of him as Grievous, though I now knew his name was Cameron Dalgetty. Why didn't they just have Petesy and me pass him on to Basil and Kinnell? Well, that was easy – they wanted to make sure that their escape route was secure; that their parcel hadn't picked up any new followers as it was passed up the country. And if Nick Pearson was to be believed, they had failed in that, so there must be some leak in their security.

Another reason for being devious could be that they didn't trust me yet – and I was stupid enough to go and prove them right, by sending Nick Pearson into the crow's nest to spy on them.

What did the Wheel want Grievous for? Where did Basil and Kinnell take him? Would he end up dead in a ditch somewhere, once they had filleted him of whatever dangerous information he was trying to keep to himself? I was forced to jump to the obvious conclusion – that Grievous had hidden the proceeds of the robbery that got him put away, and thought he just had to wait for his release to have it away with four hundred thousand pounds, give or take. The Wheel didn't seem to have that much patience.

My main worry was how I could manage to keep my skin intact in face of whatever shit might be kicked up by the Wheel. I sighed and locked the gun away in my desk – Petesy could have it back if he was stupid enough to want it. That was definitely not the answer.

I dragged myself off home and switched on the television, only to find it obsessed with people swimming, skating, snooker-ing, rugby league-ing, golfing, and taking part in twenty-three other pointless ways of showing off useless skills. I suppose it keeps them fit; it certainly wasn't doing anything for me. I switched it off and went out into the spring sunshine.

See, I've got this flaw in my character – it's the one that makes it impossible for me to stay miserable or worried for more than a few hours at a stretch. So I was feeling a lot better by the time I had taken a walk by the river, and watched the swans squabbling for the tourists' sandwiches. It's a funny thing, but only a few years ago the usual gloom and doom merchants were saying that there were only about three swans left on the Avon at Stratford, and they would soon be wiped out. Now we've got a plague of them – at least two hundred, and increasing every year.

Nice to think about something other than my own troubles.

I got back home feeling quite cheerful. Then, at five fifteen, the phone call came, and the sound of Basil's voice brought the dread flooding back.

'The Wheel wants to talk to you. Hold on.'

I sat down, thinking that might stop my voice trembling too much, while various clicking noises took place down the phone. Then the smooth voice of the Wheel:

'Hello, Kenny. Sorry to disturb you on a Saturday evening.'

Christ, it's Kenny now. I never thought the Wheel would bother with the tradition of being nice to the condemned man. 'Yes ... hello,' I managed.

'I want to offer my personal thanks for a good job well done the other night. Not only did you retrieve a tricky situation, but you also saved young Petesy after he made a complete fool of himself – and taught him a lesson into the bargain.'

'Oh . . . Right.' I was still trying to catch up with the change in climate, and hadn't quite made it yet. '. . . Er, no problem.'

'Yes, well, if he fouls up like that again, I'll have the shit beaten out of him – even though he *is* my sister's boy. Have you any idea how much it's cost me to get the oil off the seat of that Scorpio?'

Sister's boy – Christ, that explained a lot. And it looks like I've become the blue-eyed boy on account of having saved the family honour. Would that be the Wheel family? I wondered, not too seriously. But what about the Nick Pearson thing? . . . The Wheel couldn't *not* know about Nick Pearson. My brain cells were still chasing half a dozen questions around my head when I realised he had started talking again.

'. . . assigning him to work with you on a regular basis. You will be his mentor – keep him away from guns . . . curb his enthusiasm a bit. No, channel it . . . that's it, channel his enthusiasm. And for Christ's sake try to get him to dress and act like a normal human being.'

Kenny Madigan, baby-sitter to the criminal aristocracy.

I groaned and said, 'Well, I'm pretty busy, you know . . . what with running the garage business and –'

'A word about your friend, Pearson, while we're on the subject of . . . the other night. It was a smart move on your part, and I don't blame you for trying to get some kind of leverage, or covering your arse, or whatever you thought you were doing. Just remember this – I've had people blown away – permanently – for trying on something like that.'

He stopped to let that sink – to the base of my sump – before going on.

'I'm giving you the benefit of the doubt, Kenny, because it's such a refreshing change to find a villain as bright and resourceful as you are. I need people like you in my management team. So I'm letting it go this time. You'll go far with me, Kenny, if you just keep your nose clean. We're going to be the biggest and best in the country. Right?'

'Nick Pearson's not my friend, as such, and I was only –'

'Dump him – he's not in our class . . . my people spotted him watching your delivery, and they lost him easily when he made his clumsy attempt to follow them. Anyway, who knows how much longer he'll be around. You'll be hearing from me in due course.'

'I've got a question for you,' I said quickly, before he could put the phone down. Might as well be hung for a wolf as a lamb.

'Go ahead,' he said.

'Is it AutoSupCo company policy to beat up innocent women just to make them buy your products?'

'Look,' he said, 'I don't take an active role in the running of that company; I just give them sales and profit targets, and the management has to ... anyway, AutoSupCo is a straight business except for some of their streams of supply. They wouldn't put the knuckle on anybody.'

So I told him about Five Ponds, and Del's injuries. He was astounded – not to mention furious. It seemed that the Wheel was just like any top management boss – not a sodding clue about what's happening lower down the organisation.

'Leave it with me,' he said, 'I'll look into it right away. That's no way to run any fucking business. Some bastard is responsible, and I'm going to make sure he gets it in the fucking neck.'

The phone went dead. I hoped someone was going to get fired.

I should have been relieved at being off the hook over the Nick Pearson thing – and actually I *was* relieved, but there was a barrow-load of other feelings chasing each other round and round as if my brain was getting on with its own version of Pass the Parcel. I recognised one of these feelings as the one I always used to get in the lawn-mower factory whenever I was about to get screwed by the bosses. Five years I worked there, and I was one of the best engineers in the place, though I say it myself. They forced me out when I wouldn't take their rotten 'promotion to the management team'. Sooner or later they always want you to take responsibility – and as far as I'm concerned that usually means blame.

And the union was even worse; they wanted me to join so they could force me to be treated the same as the whole herd of brain-dead incompetents who go to the factory every day to read the *Sun* to each other.

Bastards.

The Wheel had used one of my trigger-words when he mentioned his management team, thereby revealing himself as something even more offensive than king of the underworld – Management.

I suppose what I most object to is the insulting way these kind of people always think they can make me do anything they want by using carrots and sticks – a mixture of threats and vague promises.

Another feeling the Wheel left me with came from knowing that he could carry out the threats he was making; he really could have people 'blown away'. I wasn't ashamed of the chilly feeling that always crept down my back after a conversation with the Wheel. And then there was the feeling of being hoovered into a one-way street leading right up Shit Creek.

I hadn't yet got around to thinking about how unpleasant it would be to have Petesy lurking around like a spare dick. I suppose he was really what my Auntie Ursula would have called a lamb dressed in wolf's clothing. Him being a member of the Wheel's family was a right turn-up; I could be dead certain he would be expected to report back as much as he could find out about me. It would make it harder for me to report developments to Neil – though that was never easy, especially recently.

But when I really thought about what I could learn from the Wheel's call, I realised he had told me something without meaning to. What I'm getting at is this – left to himself, Petesy would definitely not have come clean to the Wheel about what a pig's arse he had made of managing the escaped prisoner. As the only other witness was Grievous himself, it must have been from him that the Wheel heard of Petesy's cock-up, and my pulling the cat back out of the bag. If Grievous was just being passed on down the line to somewhere else, the chances were that he would never have met the Wheel. Therefore, it had to be the Wheel who wanted him. Grievous must by now be enjoying some pretty doubtful hospitality.

The Wheel's call also made me late at the Jonathan Phillips shoe shop to meet Aileen, which didn't do much for my standing in that direction – especially as Sally had also turned up to meet her. I found the two of them in Falstaff's Wine Bar, arranging for Aileen and me to go out in a foursome with Sally and Neil later that night.

That was on the Saturday, as I'm sure you remember.

8

Neil was very interested to hear about the adventures I had while he was away being groomed for stardom. Well, that's not exactly right; he didn't seem to give a bugger about the problems I had been wrestling with, he was focusing in on the escaped convict, Cameron Dalgetty – better known to me as Grievous. It sounded to me as if Neil wanted to get a lead on this Dalgetty, in order to help his own career in the police force. He questioned me closely about where the escapee might have been taken when he left Lone Harp.

You see, I wasn't ready to let Neil know about that warehouse in Alcester, so I let him think that Kinnell and Basil had picked up Grievous at the garage. I didn't bother to let him know about me sending Nick Pearson into the lion's den to watch what happened. Oh – and of course, I didn't feel the need to mention the gun; but apart from that, I was pretty free with all the information I thought he could be trusted with.

We were having preliminary drinks in the Lamplighter at the time. Aileen and I had arranged to meet up with Sally and Neil there, prior to going round to the Bombay Duck to check up on the corrosive properties of their curry. Seeing as how he didn't have me in a cell, Neil wasn't in any position to beat me up to make sure I was holding nothing back, but he did get insistent beyond the call of duty, not to mention unnecessarily shirty. The girls never noticed, of course, being in the middle of a serious gossip comparing that Marilyn from the hairdresser's with the Eiffel Tower (there are still some men who have never been up the Eiffel Tower).

Anyway, in the end, Neil contented himself with giving me a repeat performance of his warnings about letting him know the minute I laid a finger on any information that might be useful to him. The subject didn't come up again that night, although Neil did seem more thoughtful than usual. I should have known that was a bad sign.

The next Monday, I was enjoying an ordinary morning at the

helm of the Lone Harp Auto Repair garage, thinking it was about time I changed its name. After all, it's not as if I was an Irishman who used to live in Texas, like the original owner of the place. I printed 'Madigan Motors' on my desk pad. That looked quite good – somehow, it gave me the idea that maybe it would be worth displaying a few second-hand cars for sale on the forecourt. I was still admiring that idea, when a knock came to my office door, closely followed by Petesy Curtain. That's all I need, I thought.

'I've brought your clothes back,' he said, holding out a plastic Tesco bag. He was back to his well-dressed self in dark blue chinos and an expensively wrinkled cream linen jacket. His leather handbag dangled from his wrist. It looked a lot lighter now that it no longer contained sixteen ounces or so of Smith and Wesson automatic pistol.

'Thanks,' I said. 'Put them down over there in the corner.'

He did so, and I waited, expecting him to leave, but he just stood there like a spare candle in the wind. I raised my eyebrows at him but he went on just standing there. I said:

'Right! You'll be wanting to get back, then.'

'No, Kenny, I'm here to start working with you. My . . . the Wheel told me I have to learn everything I can from you. What do you want me to do?'

'Look, mate,' I told him, 'I can't afford to pay another employee. Especially not one who knows bugger all about fixing cars. So as far as I'm concerned, you're unemployed – not to mention unemployable.'

'No, that's all right. You don't have to pay me. I get paid by the Wheel's organisation, and I get extra whenever I do any particular job for him – like that one we did together.'

So that's how it came about that Petesy ended up being my shadow. From then on, he stayed as close to me as a verruca, and was about as welcome. I introduced him to Senga and the mechanics as the nephew of a friend who was here to learn about running a garage business. In other words, it was a favour for a business acquaintance, which I suppose was true, in a twisted kind of way.

I put Petesy in charge of the stores until I could think of something else to do with him. At least that way I could give him some training in stock control. That would meet the Wheel's requirement that he should learn something from me, although he was probably thinking of criminal skills. But then, when I thought about it, I decided that the Wheel didn't give a damn whether I taught Petesy anything or not. He just wanted to get the young sod out of his hair, and I was elected. I started to wonder how I could comb him out of *mine*.

Of course, as my Auntie Ursula would have said, troubles are like trousers – they never come singly, always in pairs or threes. There was me thinking that Petesy was my half-trouser of the day, but I was wrong; the next leg of my troubles swooped down on me that same afternoon. It showed up in the shape of my 'friend', Inspector Neil Cornfoot of the CID – and he was not alone. I did wonder at the time why he had a woman copper in tow. Actually, it looked as if she was just there to carry Neil's handcuff collection, as she was lugging a canvas bag full of bulges. At least he wouldn't be able to threaten me as long as someone else was present.

Neil was all businesslike. 'Can we go someplace where we won't be disturbed?' He nodded towards the back office as he said it. I shrugged and led the way through, feeling thankful that I had left Petesy counting parts in the storeroom, a job which would keep him occupied for at least another hour.

In the inner office, I gave one of the tables a quick dust, and we sat around it on the rickety old chairs. Neil introduced his companion as Miss Thomson. She smiled nicely at me and said:

'It's Heather Thomson.'

Then she glared at Neil and told him firmly:

'And it's Ms – not Miss.'

'All right then, Ms,' Neil said and turned to me. 'Let's get down to business, Kenny.'

He was starting to look a bit . . . well, kind of shifty, or maybe even a bit embarrassed. He went on:

'It's about Cameron Dalgetty, the escaped prisoner.'

He turned to the Heather woman and said, 'Would you like to get yourself set up now?'

Whereupon she opened her canvas bag and started taking stuff out of it. A thick Filofax was first; then a circular cloth which went on the table. It had designs all over it, mostly in strong blues, reds, and blacks. It was the signs of the zodiac all round the edge that finally led me to suss out what was going on. Christ, I must have been having one of my bad brain days.

'Who'd have thought that somebody called Heather Thomson could be a fortune-teller?' I muttered.

She didn't *look* much like one either, being a thin, brown-eyed, brown-haired woman in her late thirties. She was now bringing out a glass globe – crystal ball, I suppose, complete with a little black base thing for it to stand on. As she placed it at the centre of the cloth, she answered me:

'No, I could hardly use that name in my kind of work. I am well known professionally as Madame Kazzandra – seances and personal prognostications at reasonable rates – romantic predictions a speciality. Sittings by appointment. Here is my card –'

Neil broke in at this point:

'All right, Kenny, you can stop distracting Madame . . . er, Ms Thomson. The force is paying for her time, you know.'

Well, I wasn't the one who was trying to get a commercial across. Anyway, in my case her words fell on stony ears. She had now folded a piece of black velvet, and placed it on her head. A similar piece went to cover the crystal ball.

Neil cleared his throat.

'The idea here is to bring . . . er, Heather to a place where the escapee is known to have been, and to be in the presence of someone who had recent contact with him – that's you – so that she can detect his aura, or some such er . . . well, maybe her crystal ball can tell us where he is now. You have to concentrate on him as hard as you can. Maybe it will help if you look at this while you concentrate.'

He produced two prison photographs of Grievous with a serious scowl on his face. I took mine, and stared at it while I concentrated hard on something I see every day while I'm shaving – Aileen's bottle of seaweed tablets that she keeps on the bathroom shelf. I didn't believe in any of this crap, but I thought a little experiment couldn't do any harm.

'Don't we all have to hold hands, or something?' I asked.

That got me a withering look from the soothsayer. She snapped:

'Of course not. We only do that when we're trying to contact our loved ones who have passed through the vale of sorrow to the next world. Just keep quiet and concentrate on the picture.'

She rolled back the velvet cloth from the crystal ball, leaned forward, and looked as if she was nodding off. I expected this phase to go on for a while, but it was only about half a minute before she raised her head and said:

'I'm getting contradictory input here. On the one hand, I'm absolutely certain the subject is not far away; on the other, there's a strong impression of waves on the ocean and a smell of ozone ... and I seem to be hearing a sound like the cries of sea-gulls.'

'How far is "not far away"?' Neil asked.

The fortune-teller was quite definite: 'A twenty-five-mile radius.'

'And we're more than sixty miles from the sea in every direction. Right?' said Neil. 'Have another go, maybe something messed up your vibrations or whatever.'

She gave him a look loaded with sincere loathing, but bent her head over the crystal ball all the same. I decided to give it a chance, and contributed a genuine spell of hard thinking about Grievous – distasteful as it was. Heather went on staring into the glass ball for a whole minute this time, although at one point I caught her sneaking a look at her wrist-watch. At the end of the minute, she gave a satisfied nod, and started packing her equipment back into the canvas bag.

'All right,' she said firmly, 'I am able to confirm that he is not far away, and now I am also receiving an interesting mixture of impressions. But you will find all the details you want in my report.'

Neil protested at this:

'But he may have been moved by the time we get your report. You're supposed to tell me now.'

She got up, having finished her packing, and said:

'Sorry, but I'm running a professional business. You'll get my report in a few days, when it's been word processed. Come on, I can't stay here chatting all day – I have to go. My diary is absolutely packed full as far ahead as I can see. You've got five minutes to get me back to my consulting rooms. Your office will receive my invoice at the same time as my report.'

'You should have asked her to examine the tea-leaves,' I told

71

Neil as he trailed out after Ms Thomson. You could see that he was seething with anger, but I thought the whole thing was hilarious. I suppose even the psychic industry becomes brisk and businesslike when its self-employed professionals decide to maximise their earning potential. Now they could join the lawyers, dentists, and business consultants who live by the slogan: 'I've upped my hourly rate – so up yours.'

Aileen enjoyed hearing about my day while we chomped our way through our takeaway pizzas. She laughed at the idea of Neil being bullied by what she called a gypsy, but thought he had probably brought it on himself by failing to take the psychic thing seriously. For once in my life, I was more in agreement with Neil than Aileen.

When I told her about me being lumbered with Petesy, she was quite thoughtful for a while, so I knew she was boiling up some scheme in that gifted brain of hers. It came out while we were dumping the dishes in the sink, and preparing to do the washing-up.

'So you're supposed to be teaching Petesy all about how to be an expert criminal. Right?'

'Er . . . I suppose so . . . something like that,' I said. 'The Wheel talked about teaching him some common sense. Anyway, Petesy is so desperate to live a life of crime that he's bound to spend most of his life behind bars. He'll soon find out that there's nothing glamorous about breaking the law. So I don't see what I can teach him.'

'Well,' she said, 'I was thinking maybe you could teach him about cars instead, and he might get interested in that. He's a really nice lad; it would be a shame if he went further off the rails and –'

I didn't think he was such a nice lad, but didn't mention it. Instead, I kept to the subject under discussion.

'Look, Aileen, it takes years to become a good mechanic, and I haven't got the time to nursemaid that flash git through an apprenticeship.'

'No, that's not what I meant. You didn't give me time to finish.' She wasn't stamping her foot, but she *was* putting it down firmly – on my neck, as usual. Giving me the benefit of her stern look, she went on:

'I've been thinking for some time that you could sell used cars at the garage – you know, display them out on the forecourt. There's a lot of wasted space there. Anyway, the point is that you could put Petesy in charge of the second-hand car part of the business.'

I agreed to consider it. As you know, I'd already had the idea of selling used cars, so it wasn't hard to get my brain to swallow that. As usual, Aileen had come at it from a different angle – one which would never have occurred to me. Actually, it wasn't a bad idea to get some buckshee use out of Petesy, him being a freebie in the bush, as such. And – this was a great idea – I would finance the second-hand car operation out of the money that the Wheel was paying me.

On the other hand, I would have to take Petesy to car auctions to train him in what points to look out for, and what prices to pay, and all the other details of running a used car operation. Some things I would have to do myself – like setting up an arrangement with a finance company to provide loans or hire-purchase agreements for our customers. But Petesy could attend to lots of the other stuff.

I was starting to make lists in my head, of all the things that would have to be attended to. This would give me some real work to do, and it should be a lot more interesting than looking after the stores, which, I must admit, took me about half an hour a day on average. The whole idea of a new direction for the business was making me feel better. It provided me with a direction to point the next bit of my life at. In fact, I felt so much better that I quite forgot about the pack of wolves whose main ambition was to blight my life.

Which only goes to show that the brightest hour comes just before the thunderstorm.

9

Seated comfortably at my desk in the garage, I was starting to enjoy myself, getting some of my mental lists down on paper. One thing I had definitely decided; that was that the used car operation would be called Madigan Motors. We would have to start quite small, because of finance; just three or four cars at first, of the most popular types. I had just made a note to investigate numbers – you know, the ones to make up the price stickers that would be fastened to the windscreen – when the phone rang. I was actually annoyed at the interruption. I picked it up and answered it.

'Got a little treat for you and the lad. What you might call "on the job training". We'll pick you up at your garage – half-past nine tomorrow night. OK?'

The voice belonged to Basil, and he was making an offer I couldn't refuse. It seemed that Petesy and I had to join him and God knows who else, in some piece of crookery. All at once, my enthusiasm for selling second-hand cars went swirling down the drain. Uncertainty and dread were back in the driving seat.

Before I had time to get properly worried about tomorrow night's ordeal, the phone shot me in the foot again. This time, it was Aileen. It was her day off work, and she had already done her rounds of all the estate agents in town and as I had the car today would I please pick her up at one thirty and take her to Hampton Lucy where she had arranged to meet an estate agent so that we could look at this lovely cottage to judge from the picture and we would kick ourselves if we missed this one if it's half as good as it sounds in the particulars.

When she ran out of breath, she stopped and waited for my reply. What the hell, I thought, it'll get me out of this place for a while. So I sighed and agreed to do what she asked.

Unfortunately, the phone still hadn't knocked off for the day; it was determined to kick me when I was down. At exactly one fifteen, just as I was locking up my desk, to go and pick up Aileen, Nick Pearson called. He sounded pretty agitated, and said he needed to see me right away. At first, it was hard to understand what he was trying to tell me. Apparently, he had been contacted by somebody I couldn't get a handle on.

'Hang on, hang on,' I said. 'Slow down to a gallop and tell me all that stuff again. I didn't get it.'

'It was about the night you got me to watch that warehouse in Alcester,' he said. 'You remember how I told you about the blokes what followed the other blokes what took the bloke out of the warehouse after you put the bloke in there.'

I squeezed the bones out of that. 'You mean the mysterious ones in the car with no lights?'

'Right! That's what I've been telling you.'

'Yeah, what about them?' I asked, in the hope that he would get to the point eventually.

'Well, they've just been on the blower to me . . . not the both of them of course. Just the one of them was talking, but he kept saying "we", so I can tell he's talking, like, on behalf of –'

I jumped into the floodgates.

'Never mind the bleeding semantic analysis, mate. Just tell me what they said.'

I wasn't absolutely sure of what 'semantic analysis' means, but it sounded good – and Nick Pearson wouldn't understand it, for sure.

'What?' he said. 'Oh yeah, all right. Well, they were offering to pay me . . . er . . . forty quid to tell them what I was doing there that night and who I was working for.'

'Did you tell them?' I asked, feeling kind of exposed.

'Not on your nelly, mate. Not without I've got the dosh in my hand first. It's just, I wondered if you might be ready to pay fifty quid for me not to tell them.'

'All right then,' I said, not very convinced. 'Meet me in the Queen's Head tonight, and we'll see. But I'm not making any promises.'

'Nah, Kenny, that's no good, mate. I'm off in a couple of hours . . . down to Southend to look after my mother's place for a couple of weeks. She needs me to run the whelk stall while she's in getting her bunions done.'

Christ, fancy Nick Pearson having a mother.

This was the point where I should have got smart enough to tell him to bugger off. Instead, I suggested that we meet right away; not in the Queen's Head, because of how hard it can be to find a parking space in the town centre in the daytime; but in the Salmon Tail in Evesham Road, which has its own parking area.

'No can do,' he said. 'These blokes are coming to see me in about an hour. If you come round to my place right away, you'll get in before them . . . and I'll get away to Southend early just in case they get annoyed at me clamming up.'

I sighed and agreed. Now even the dregs can get away with threatening Kenny Madigan.

Of course, it meant I would have to let Aileen down as well, and I hate to do that, but she's very understanding, as a rule. So what I did was, I told Petesy I had to go to Evesham unexpectedly, and sent him to give her my apologies and take her out to the village of Hampton Lucy so that she wouldn't miss her examination of the latest irresistible country cottage.

On the way to Nick Pearson's humble abode – and they don't come much humbler – I stopped off at the cash dispenser to pick up the necessary fifty pounds.

Nick Pearson lives in a caravan – the kind that never goes anywhere. It sits on blocks in its own little plot in the caravan park at Loxton, out the Warwick road. I only know this on account of I took pity and gave him a lift home one night a couple of years ago, when he got rat-arsed in the Queen's Head.

The caravans at Loxton were mostly neat and well maintained. Many of the residents (I don't know if they were owners or renters) had turned their plots into flower gardens, which bristled with colour in the spring sunshine. Nick Pearson's mobile home stood out in this company – it was the shabby one with the four-foot weeds and flat-tyred rusty bicycle outside.

It looked as if his neglect extended to the door lock; it didn't seem to work.

The door swings back from my knock, bouncing open towards me. No sound from inside. At that moment I feel a shiver down my back, as my brain cells start shouting to warn me that I am liable to find something nasty here. I knock again, and call out Nick Pearson's name with no result. After a decent delay, I go inside. Looking left into the tiny kitchen area, the first thing I register is that Nick Pearson's housekeeping is no better than any other department of his life. I slide open the plastic curtain on the right, and go through the narrow dining and living section – still no Nick Pearson.

What I really want to do at this point is get the hell out of that depressing dump – but I've come this far. I take a deep breath, and reach for the next curtain; the one that I assume will reveal the sleeping quarters. I'm starting to feel afraid of what I might find here. The short hairs at the back of my neck are trying to crawl away to a safer place. If Nick Pearson is lying in there injured, or even dead – if he is, then it might be partly my fault. I got him into this, after all. And whoever got to him could be coming after me next. That last thought makes me check behind my back and out of the window. Still nothing there. I force myself to flick the curtain aside . . .

The manky bugger hasn't even made the bed. And judging by the sweaty pong, he hasn't been to the laundrette for a long time, nor used the shower either. But I am very relieved to see that the manky bugger himself is not present. I get out of there as fast as I can, only stopping long enough to glance into the empty toilet cubicle, just in case.

Outside, the sunshine seems unnaturally bright, and the colours of the flowers seem exaggerated. I let out the deep breath I hadn't realised I am holding, and look around. Now I see Nick Pearson's old Ford Escort parked just beyond the caravan; so he hasn't left for far-flung whelk stalls yet. I peer into the car, just for the sake of thoroughness. Then I go back and wipe the parts of the caravan door I might have touched, while pretending I am trying to make the door stay shut. Inside, I know the only things I put my hands on are the curtains, which wouldn't hold a print.

The cops don't have my prints on record, of course, but won't hesitate to take them if I should ever come under suspicion for anything. Better to be safe than sore, as my Auntie Ursula would have said.

For some reason, I can't get the idea out of my head that there is definitely something sinister going on here.

I took another look around, then went over to the next-door caravan, where I had clocked a twitching net curtain on one of the windows. The door opened within a microsecond of my knock. She could have been Miss Peroxide, 1969, still wearing her winning make-up.

'I was looking for Mr Pearson,' I said, a bit unnecessarily, as she had been watching me since I arrived on this side of the horizon.

She leaned forward out of her caravan door, and shot a piercing glance, first left, and then right. Once she was satisfied that there were no Miss Peroxide judges lurking in the neighbourhood, she directed her attention back to me.

'You've missed them,' she said.

I could see it wasn't going to be easy.

'What do you mean? Who have I missed? It's Mr Pearson I'm looking for. Nick Pearson that is.'

'That's right. You're too late. They've gone.'

'Who has gone?'

'Your other two mates. They got here before you, and Mr Pearson went off with them. They looked as if they were in a bit of a rush, so you'll need to hurry if you want to catch up with them.'

She started to pull the door shut.

'Wait a minute,' I protested. 'Where did they go?'

She spread out her hands, palms up, in the universally understood buggered-if-I-know gesture.

'Well, what did these two blokes look like?'

'Oh, they were fine-looking chaps. Very much like yourself.'

She leered at me. I ignored that, and asked her:

'Did you see what kind of car they had?'

'Oh yes, I noticed that particular. It was a very nice big blue one . . . dark blue.'

What Neil would describe as a reliable witness, then. I thanked her and left in the direction of my own car.

'*Very* dark blue,' she yelled after me.

Back at the garage, I sat down and had a think. I was scared back there in that caravan of Nick Pearson's – but I wasn't sure exactly what I had been afraid of. I mean, it was beginning to look as if something very unpleasant had happened to Nick Pearson, but why should that scare me?

My brain cells were racing ahead of me there, but I broke into a mental trot to catch up with their logical processes.

Right! Obviously the Pearson-snatchers never had any intention of paying for information. They only phoned to make sure he was at home – and then they just said whatever was needed to make him stay there until they arrived.

The next thing I realised was that the blokes who had taken him would very quickly find out that he knew nothing, and was only working for me that night. They would choose me as the next stepping stone to get stepped on. Not that I would be able to tell them much, of course, but I might have to absorb some violence to prove that. And then all I could do would be to point them towards the next stepping stone down the line.

That was an interesting thought. I might be able to aim these hard men at the Wheel's organisation. Basil would be able to sort them out, no bother.

There was just one more thing I had in mind to do. I called the local CID number and, for once, got straight through to Neil. I told him all I knew about the operation I would be involved in the following night, which was very little in fact, since I hadn't a clue about where, when, how, or what. Neil just went sarcastic on me, thanking me for the valuable information, and saying there was no chance of having us tailed, what with the staffing levels he was having to put up with. No point in telling him about the disappearance of Nick Pearson – not yet, anyway.

When I parked in the street outside the maisonette, I noticed that Petesy's BMW was there too. So they must have just got back from Hampton Lucy, I decided, and went on up the stairs. I was not surprised to see old Miss Downie's door fly open just before I got to it, and there was the Neighbourhood Witch in person, barring my way.

'About time you got back. She's had 'im in there for the last hour at least, and he looks to me like him as has been playing silly buggers with me wheelie-bin.'

'I don't think he's touched your bin, Miss Downie,' I said. 'He's Aileen's cousin.'

She was opening her mouth for a new screech, when I derailed her by saying, 'Have you seen what these kids are up to now?'

This was a reference to her main enemy, the kids who played on the rough grass behind the maisonettes, and it had the effect I was hoping for – it made her push past me and waddle down the stairs hoping to do battle. Which left me free access to my own door.

Aileen and Petesy were sitting at the dining-table, counting out vitamin tablets. It looked like the two of them had stopped off at the health food store on the way back, for Aileen to get stocked up with her weekly supply of yeast pills and whatnot. She's dead meticulous about her health food stuff, and always packs them up into little daily bags as soon as she gets them home, so that's what Petesy was helping with. For some reason which I couldn't figure out at the time, Aileen seemed less pleased to see me than Petesy did. That was why I decided this would be a good time to give her some special attention.

'Hello, love,' I said, leaning over to give her a peck on the cheek. 'When are we moving into that cottage in Hampton Lucy, then?'

She gave me a look full of daggers, and opened her mouth to say something which I never found out what it was, on account of Petesy choosing that moment to jump into the ring.

'It's very nice in some ways, but no good for you, I'm afraid,' he told me seriously. 'It's got a septic tank ... and you know how Aileen feels about anything septic.'

Aileen's mouth was still open, but she nodded, rather than say anything.

'What a shame, you must be really disappointed,' I said, projecting a look dripping with sympathy straight at Aileen, and trying to telepathically transmit into Petesy's head the idea that he was not part of this conversation.

The two of them got on with the pill counting, while I glared at Petesy. He must have got the message, because he decided to be on his way as soon as the job was finished.

As soon as Petesy left, I felt the temperature heading towards the basement. Aileen has this talent for radiating cold, you see; it's how I can tell she's mad at me. Quite often it doesn't inform me about the reason *why* she's mad at me, though. However, on this occasion I had a shrewd idea, so I bravely jumped into the male storm.

'Look, love, I'm awfully sorry about this afternoon,' I said. 'Something important came up ...'

I paused, to sample the atmosphere. No change. I tried again:

'See, I got this call from Nick Pearson and ...'

That got her going.

'Well then, maybe you'd like to go to bed with Nick Pearson tonight, instead of me,' she said. 'I'm giving you fair warning, Kendall Madigan. I'm not going to be played ducks and drakes with, by you ... or anybody else for that matter, and if you think you can get away with just shutting your eyes to my needs, and

... and ... running to the beck and call of the likes of Nick Pearson ... well, you can go and take a running ... you're going to end up bonking your fist for the next month ...'

Aileen's voice became a bit muffled after that, because I was hugging her tight, and kissing her neck. Over her shoulder, I looked at the wall calendar. Yes, there it was – a little red circle beside today's date. Her period must be starting.

It took quite a lot more cuddling to bring her back to normal. But I'm no shirker – I sat patiently on the sofa with my arm round my loved one, right through the television news. But it wasn't until the local Midlands news came on that I heard anything of interest.

The screen showed a Jaguar in a lay-by near Coventry. It had been found there in broad daylight with its engine running, hoses from both exhaust pipes pumping carbon monoxide to the inside of the car, and the asphyxiated owner dead in the driving seat. The poor man's family and colleagues were at a loss to account for the suicide of someone who had as much to live for as he had. He was a successful businessman – managing director of a fast-growing Midlands company, for goodness sake. It would not be easy for AutoSupCo to find a replacement chief executive who could fill his shoes adequately.

It was amazing how quickly Del had been avenged. I mean, it was only Saturday when I mentioned it to the Wheel, and today was Tuesday. Obviously, it was down to me that the bloke who was responsible was murdered by the organisation he was trying too hard to serve. I suppose I should have felt guilty – but bugger it, I didn't.

Later that evening, we had just switched off the television for half an hour – I can't stand watching *The Bill* – when Aileen said:

'That Petesy was very helpful; couldn't do enough for me. I suppose you know why?'

'I don't know. Oh ... do you think he fancies you, as such? He certainly goes after the chicks ... if he tries anything on with you ...'

'Don't be silly,' she said, 'he's always a perfect gentleman with me. And the reason I was referring to, is that you're his hero. He looks up to you, you know, so you have a responsibility to set a good example.'

That made me feel quite pleased with myself for a minute or two. I've never been a role model before. But then I thought, Get real, Kenny, you pillock. I put on my most satirical voice and said:

'Yeah, he wants me to teach him breaking and entering, advanced car nicking, and A-level lock picking. What a great example that is.'

Aileen sounded thoughtful when she said:

'Right! That's true. Perhaps it would be better if he *did* fancy me. Maybe you're right, Kenny. Perhaps it *is* because he fancies me that he's being so nice and helpful.'

Well, that was too ridiculous for me to bother answering. On the other hand, Aileen and Petesy do seem to get on quite well together – and they're about the same age.

Nah!

10

The next day was a fairly normal one at the garage. I went on initiating Petesy into the rudiments and principles of stock control, even though the garage wasn't a big enough operation to need most of the techniques I was telling him about. Still, knowing about things like ABC parts classification and EOQs might help him to get a job in a factory sometime. Neither of us mentioned the fact that we were going out with Basil that night, presumably to do some serious breaking of the law.

Given the timing of nine thirty for Basil to pick us up, I had no alternative but to take Petesy home to the maisonette to share our microwaved lasagne. He was looking more like a normal person in jeans and sweatshirt, mainly because I had told him to stop wearing his fancy kit when he came to work at Lone Harp.

Basil arrived right on time, at the wheel of a Ford Scorpio Estate – I suppose it would be the same one Nick Pearson had seen him in. I peered closely at it, trying to see if it was 'very dark blue', but I couldn't tell under the orange sodium lights. Petesy got in the front beside Basil, while I opened the back door to climb in the back seat, beside the shadowy shape that was already there. The car's interior light came on, showing me who the passenger was – although the first words he spoke would have identified him just as easily.

'. . . 'kin'ell, Kenny, it's good to see there's still a place for us old hands in this modern, high-tech business world.'

Kinnell – big as life and twice as ugly, looking more than ever as if somebody knitted him a long time ago. I managed a grunt; better be nice to him since it looked like we would have to share the back of this car for a while.

Basil drove out to the Alcester road, and turned right, away from Stratford. He started to tell us what was going on:

'You geezers are coming along to learn a bit more about what makes this business tick. We don't just nick stuff on impulse, like a sneak thief; it's all carefully planned. And once we have our supplies, we plan the best way of marketing them. In fact, sometimes it works the other way round – our operations are planned in response to the needs of the market.'

He was interrupted by a loud noise from Kinnell. Something between a snore and a wheeze, if that's possible. Basil stopped talking until it seemed likely that Kinnell wouldn't snore again, then he took up where he had stopped:

'We are now on our way to Redditch, where a number of our people are unloading the contents of a large trailer which came into our possession earlier tonight. It is loaded to the brim with light electrical goods – laptop computers, printers, televisions, VCRs, stereos, CD players, Walkmans, all that kind of high-value stuff. In this kind of situation, it is vital to move like greased lightning to empty the hijacked vehicle – meticulous planning again. Our people will be moving the goods to our own legitimate premises; we don't want to get in their way any more than we can help. We have two jobs to do here on the Wheel's behalf. The first is to check and note the quantity of goods which are being taken into stock – we want to minimise any risk of pilfering by our own people. The second part of our job is to secure samples for marketing purposes. We need one example of each type of article loaded into the boot of this car. That will help our sales and marketing people to feed the goods into the straight economy.'

Petesy was hanging on his every word; giving Basil more attention than I get from him when I'm explaining some of the finer points of stock control. Still, I guess it was pretty much the same thing; either way, he was learning about how business works. I wasn't listening too closely, having plenty of other stuff to think about, as you know. Well, actually I was thinking about Sam Cotteridge, if you must know – and wondering . . . well, never mind what I was thinking.

So there I was, leaning back in the comfortable back seat of the Scorpio, trying to relax, when something heavy landed on my shoulder. It gave me quite a start, which was intensified when I realised that the object on my shoulder was Kinnell's head. The idle sod's fallen asleep, I thought, and shrugged that side, my right shoulder, to shake him off. That just made him slump more heavily against me, so I gave him a solid push, which made him flop the other way.

'Come on, Kinnell,' I said in quite a loud voice, to wake him up. 'We'll be needing you bright-eyed and full of beans in a few minutes.'

No reaction. I began to have a faint suspicion that Kinnell might have been taken ill.

'Stop as soon as you can,' I said. 'I think Kinnell's not feeling too well.' We were barely out of Stratford at this point, so it wouldn't be too far to take him to what was left of the local hospital (just accidents and out-patients now). Basil pulled into the next lay-by, got out, and opened the offside back door to take a look at Kinnell. He loosened Kinnell's tie and collar, and fiddled around for a bit.

'The stupid bugger's gone and died on us – must have had a heart attack or something,' Basil told Petesy and me.

I observed gloomily, 'I suppose now we'll have to take him to a hospital, and report it to the cops and everything.'

'Not on your bleeding life, mate. We've still got a job to do.' Basil was suddenly full of decisive responsibility. 'Here! Help me get this seat belt tight enough to hold him in position.'

'What do you mean, hold him in position?' Petesy protested. 'Couldn't we put him in the boot, or something, out of the way?'

Basil found that an offensive proposal. He was aghast at Petesy for having the effrontery to suggest such a thing.

'Don't talk like a prat. That would be a fucking stupid thing to do. We need the boot free to hold all the samples we have to bring back. Wait a minute ... let's give him a bit of disguise.'

He took a baseball cap out of the glove compartment and jammed it on Kinnell's head, saying:

'There! That'll prevent his face being seen ... looks like he's asleep.'

So that was the end of Kinnell; maybe the Wheel would know what name to have him buried under. We continued our journey to Redditch, with me plastered against the left rear door of the car, to put as much space as possible between me and our friendly local corpse. It was not a long journey, which was just as well, considering the company. There wasn't much conversation. It felt as if we were driving for ever around the network of dual carriageways and roundabouts that seem to be what the new town of Redditch is mostly made of.

At last, we drove into a huge structure ... I suppose it was a shed, really, but it didn't have any actual doors that could close – just a wide gap in the wall in the side away from the road. It did have fairly bright strip lighting, though. The main content of the shed was an extremely large truck – the kind the *Daily Mail* would call a juggernaut – in the livery of a well-known road haulage company, Ted Starboard Ltd.

It looked to me like what is known in the trade as an S and D. That means Stand and Deliver – where a truck driver passes on details of his route and timetable to the villains, who make sure that he gets robbed in exchange for a cut of the proceeds. Later on I found out from Basil that it was far better organised than that. The whole operation was planned well in advance using information out of the haulage firm's computer.

The truck's hydraulic tailgate had been lowered to the concrete floor, loaded with cartons, apparently just the first bite out of the vehicle's enormous cargo. There were three Transit-sized vans waiting near the tailgate, all bearing the words 'Drennan's of Wellesbourne'. A number of men were standing around or sitting on the loading platforms of the vans, some having a smoke, and some just looking as if they were waiting for something to happen.

It seemed that we were what they were waiting for. As soon as the Scorpio stopped, one of the men, who was obviously the boss of this gang, came over to talk to Basil.

'Everything's ready,' he said when Basil slid his window down. 'Is it OK to get started with the loading up now?'

'OK. Just give us a couple of minutes to cast our eyes over each tailgate load as it comes out. We need to make sure we take one of everything.'

It took hours to empty that truck, and Christ knows how many van loads. The whole operation reminded me of an ants' nest – you know, the truck was the queen, and the Transit vans were like the worker ants carrying thousands of eggs away from the queen to nurture and look after them. And all this time, poor old Kinnell went on sitting in the back seat of the Scorpio, taking part in his last crime.

Eventually the truck had given up everything it had to give, all the vans had gone, and no more empty ones were coming in. The three of us, Basil, Petesy, and I, checked over the shed and the inside of the truck to make sure that no signs of our recent activity were left behind. We even had to pick up all the cigarette ends, which Basil put into a plastic bag for later disposal. Then the lights were switched off, and the truck was driven away to be abandoned in some faraway deserted off-road site.

'Isn't that an unnecessary risk? I mean, the cops will be swarming all over the place looking for a hijacked Ted Starboard rig, won't they?'

I felt able to ask Basil the question, since we had become quite matey while working together on checking the truck's cargo.

'Nah! It's not much of a risk,' he replied. 'You see, it wasn't a Ted Starboard truck that we nicked. The livery you see on the truck is fake. It's ours, in fact, and it's just sheets of plastic that we tack on to any vehicle that we hijack. It's all equipped with quick fastening clips, and in any dim light it makes a perfect disguise – and the fake number plates that go with it are duplicates of a number that belongs to a real Ted Starboard rig. Mind you, it does mean that all seven hundred of Ted Starboard's trucks are safe from us. Anyway, when they dump that truck, the van that's following it to bring the driver back will also recover the disguise.' He grinned like somebody who's showing off how dead clever they are, and added, 'Did you think we would be flying the Jolly Roger on it?'

I must admit, I was really impressed. In my experience, the criminal element are usually pretty thick, but this lot were better organised than most commercial firms I've seen.

My problem would be to decide whether I should let Neil know about this ploy. I would have to think about it – this was the kind of information that was useful to keep up my sleeve in case I needed some bargaining chips sometime in the future. Relationships with the police can get very complicated at times.

By the time the truck went away, the Scorpio's boot was crammed full. There was more stuff than I expected, because some of the goods came in, maybe, three different models, and we wanted one of each model.

There was still the journey home to be faced, with me sharing the back seat of the Scorpio with a deceased person. I never liked him much when he was alive; but dead was even worse. Still, at least he wouldn't be picking his nose, or talking to me in that whinging voice of his. I had a half-hearted go at persuading Petesy to swap seats with me, predictably without success.

Anyway, it was a long ordeal, because our first port of call was to a small workshop-type place somewhere in Yardley, on the southern outskirts of Birmingham, where we unloaded the contents of the boot.

It was only then, when we had completed our work for the night, that Basil turned his attention to the problem of our dead companion. Business before pleasure, I suppose.

'Right, lads, what are we going to do about our friend in the back?' he asked. 'Any suggestions?'

'Has he got a wife, or anything?' I glanced at the shapeless lump in the back seat.

'He's been on his own for years,' Basil told us. 'Nobody's going to be in mourning.'

'Couldn't we take him to a hospital now?' Petesy asked.

Basil shook his head.

'No, they would have to inform the police ... and we don't want that kind of attention. Besides, how would we explain being in possession of a corpse that's been dead for ... quite a few hours now?'

I had an idea: 'What about delivering him to the Condiment Brothers? They're equipped to deal with corpses.'

'No way. That's a straight business – and it's got to stay that way. Think again.'

In the end, what we did was, we nicked a car – quite like old times, it was – well, as a specialist in that area of human endeavour, I did the honours. Then I drove it, following the Scorpio to a deserted car-park at a leisure centre somewhere on the south side of Birmingham. Then came the nasty bit. We had to manhandle the stiff –which he really was by this time – out of the back seat of the Scorpio, and into the driving seat of the nicked car. Once he was strapped in, all three of us heaved a sigh of relief.

It would be really interesting to know what the Old Bill would make of a dead body at the wheel of a stolen car at a leisure centre – too early for his morning swim.

Then it was back to Lone Harp Auto in Stratford to let Petesy and me out. And a long night's hard work was over for us.

I was really knackered by the end of that night, and it wasn't all physical exhaustion; there was also the mental stress caused by travelling in such close proximity to a dead person.

On the plus side, it looked as if the Wheel and his gang had accepted me as one of their own, and were opening up their ranks to let me in. On the other hand, they were looking more and more like a tough nut to crack open, given how efficiently and intelligently their operations were run. Their biggest weakness that I could see, was the sheer number of people who had to be involved. No doubt, each person knew the minimum amount necessary to do his job, but still ... for instance, all these van drivers and loaders and Drennan's of Wellesbourne employees must be well aware that they were involved in something extremely shady.

Funny thing, though, I had to admit that I was starting to kind of enjoy my criminal activities, now that I had overcome my initial reluctance. You know, it brought some adventure and excitement into my life.

I admitted as much to my mate Steve the next night, over a couple of pints in the Bell.

Steve and I have been pretty close friends since about the age of seven, but we don't get together so much these days – not since he married that Sheila and saddled himself with a dirty great mortgage. For some reason Sheila thinks I'm a bad influence on Steve, so our long nights at the snooker club and trips to Villa Park to watch the home games are things of the past. Even our get-togethers in the pub have been getting further apart. Another thing is that I don't think Steve likes Aileen very much. He's never actually said so, as such; though he once described her as 'a bit waspish', whatever that means.

My mate Steve has never done anything dodgy in his life; unless you count working in the head office of a big insurance company, where he's steadily moving up the management tree. Still, he's always interested to hear about what I've been getting up to.

It came as no surprise to Steve to hear that I was beginning to get some enjoyment from my renewed life of crime. He just nodded in that way he has, which he thinks makes him look full of wisdom.

'That's you all over, Kenny. I could have told you that something like this would happen – you were bound to be drawn back into a life of crime. You get bored when your life keeps dragging along the same old rut – the kind of routine that most people like.'

'But I like peace and quiet,' I protested. 'I hate hassle, and I can't stand anything that comes along and upsets the smooth running of my life.'

'Yeah, I know,' he said, with maybe a touch of the sarcastic in his tone. 'You're OK like that for a while, and then something throws you an opportunity for change . . . and you grab hold of it with both hands. You can't help it. You can never resist what you called the adventure and excitement. And the danger too – don't forget the danger . . . you're a sucker for that.'

Steve peered into my glass. 'Are you ready for another pint of that processed bat's piss you swill down?' I nodded, and he went up to the bar for my beer and his rum and Coke. While he was there, I considered what he had just said, and had to concede that he had a point, to a certain extent anyway.

It's true enough, I complain when I think everybody is out to get me, but half of that is just me trying to convince myself that

I'm hating every minute of it. Trouble is, I end up not knowing what side I'm on.

Anyway, country cottages can never compete for excitement with all that criminal stuff. I suppose one reason is that I'm quite good at it, and everybody likes to use their skills. The one thing that makes me mad is when somebody gets badly hurt or even killed just because they got in the way of some over-enthusiastic dickhead. And when some innocent person does get hurt, like Del Cotteridge for instance, it does remind me of which side I'm really on. At least nobody had got themselves killed in the current rash of shenanigans ... well so far, only the miserable bastard who gave the orders to have Del beaten up – and I certainly didn't give a shit about him.

When Steve came back with the new round of drinks, the conversation switched to something else, and somehow never got back to my underhand activities.

The next morning, I was late getting to work again; half-past ten by the time I dragged myself to the garage. Well, Senga could run the business perfectly well without me – in fact, I sometimes thought that she preferred it when I was out, for whatever reason. It's true that I would sometimes go out and chat with the mechanics – you know, purely to maintain good staff relations. Senga hates that. She says I'm only giving them an excuse for skiving off their work. But I mean, it's not as if I really want to hear a blow by blow account of the tricky grouting job that Jeff has on his hands as a result of retiling his bathroom.

So I got in about ten thirty, like I said, and was getting back into the groove of planning my used car operation, when I received an unexpected – not to mention unwelcome – visitor.

11

Neil came straight in, as well dressed as ever, and parked his bum on the visitor's chair in my office without so much as a by-your-leave. He started talking right away without even waiting long enough for me to finish the note I was in the middle of. That was a bit bloody rude of him, I thought, at the time.

'Do you know a scummy small-time villain who goes by the name of Nick Pearson?' he asked.

'Yes,' I said.

Just answer the questions; don't volunteer any information. As my Auntie Ursula would have said – a closed mouth gathers no feet.

'When did you last see him?'

I tried to remember. It was when Nick Pearson reported back to me after watching the warehouse at Alcester, and I paid him fifty pounds.

'Er . . . last week sometime. Thursday, I think.'

Neil's brows dropped about an inch and his black eyes were trying to drill a hole right through my head.

'Are you trying to tell me you haven't spoken to Nick Pearson since last Thursday?'

'That's not what I said,' I protested. 'You asked me when was the last time I *saw* him, and that was last week . . . but I've *spoken* to him more recently than that.'

That's a thing about coppers that really gets up my nostrils – they're always trying to make you say things you don't mean, just to confuse you.

'So you admit it?' Neil said.

I tried to put him straight.

'It's not a question of admitting. Nick Pearson called me on Tuesday to tell me he had some information I might be willing to pay him for, and could I meet him. I went, but he never turned up. So I went to his caravan to see if he was there, but he was out. Now what is this all about? Whatever he's done, it's got nothing to do with me.'

'I certainly hope not, Kenny,' he said, all serious. 'Nick Pearson was found in a ditch out the other side of Evesham last night.'

Bloody hell!

'Is he . . .?' I stammered. 'Will he . . . er . . . recover, or . . .'

'Well, whoever it was probably left him for dead, but he got lucky. He's in intensive care. Severe bruising, some internal bleeding, various broken bits . . . but they reckon he'll live to nick another car stereo or two.'

That was really bad news – not the news that Nick Pearson would recover; I mean the fact of him being beaten up. What could I say? I just sat there gaping at Neil, while my brain cells went around asking each other if this meant that I was in any danger. Finally, I managed to speak:

'Who did it? Have you got anybody for it?'

'Not yet,' he said. 'I hope you can account for all your movements over the last few days.'

Oh, yes. Half the villains in the Midlands could have given me an alibi for Wednesday night. We were all out together, robbing a truck. I remembered that Neil hadn't wanted to know about Basil's invitation to Petesy and me. I mentioned it again in the hope that it would take his mind off Nick Pearson – and surprise, surprise – *now* he was interested. So I told him about it, leaving out a few details, like the truck disguise, and the death of Kinnell. The bits he liked best were about Drennan's of Wellesbourne, and the place in Yardley where we dropped off the samples.

'That's quality information, Kenny. Keep hanging in there, and together we'll have them bang to rights sooner or later.'

It was the first time I ever heard anyone actually say 'bang to rights'. I always thought it was one of those phrases that only existed on television. When I got over that, I asked:

'What about these places ... Drennan's ... and the one in Yardley? If you search them, you'll find the stolen stuff.'

Of course, I knew it wasn't that simple, and Neil told me so. But he did admit that it was useful to know, and he would keep an eye on Drennan's. Then he came back round to the subject I was trying to keep away from.

'Nick Pearson's neighbour gave quite a good description of you. Pity she was so vague about the two men who took Pearson away. Any idea who they might be?'

By this time I was wishing that Neil would go away, so I could work out the implications of his news, and then get down to some solid worrying.

'Look for a very dark blue car,' I told him. Then I thought I would wind him up a bit more.

'Why don't you bring in your tame gypsy ... you know, Madame Kazza, or whatever her name is? Sounds like this is right up her street.'

On a normal day, that would have been enough to make Neil suddenly remember an urgent appointment somewhere else, and shove off, leaving some parting insult hanging in the air. But it didn't work this time. Instead, he said:

'Oh, yes, I meant to tell you about that, just in case you could throw some light on it. We got her report . . . you know, from the session we did here – trying to find where that runaway prisoner is hiding out.'

'That's good,' I said, but not sounding as if I meant it. 'What does she say?'

'Well, of course, I think it's a load of crap, as you know. But my bosses insist we have to follow up information from whatever source.'

He was looking kind of embarrassed now, but struggled on manfully.

'She says he is – or at least was at that time – definitely within twenty-five miles of here, in roughly a northerly direction. And then it gets pretty vague. She claims she got a strong impression of tyres.'

'So you think she's telling you to search tyre depots and garages, and any tyre factories you can find as well. There must be thousands within a twenty-five-mile radius. Anyway, she could have picked up the smell of tyres in here.'

'Yes,' he nodded, 'but it wasn't the *smell* of tyres, because she says the odour she was getting at the same time was redolent of decay – these were her very words – redolent of decay. Now the only thing I can think of, that would fit, is a scrap-yard. You know, the kind of place where they break up old cars. What do you think, Kenny?'

I could only agree. 'Well, there would be plenty of decay going on in a breaker's yard . . . and there are always piles of old tyres lying around too.'

But while I said it, my brain cells were busy beating around a completely different bush.

Then I thought, But this psychic business is all a load of garbage, isn't it? Or is it?

'Right!' said Neil. 'There can't be that many breakers' yards to the north of Stratford, and within twenty-five miles. We can bring in the dogs – they'll be easier to work with than Madame . . . er, Heather Thomson.'

93

'Good idea,' I told him, 'a scrap-yard could be quite a good place to hold a prisoner.'

'Oh, there was just one other thing in the report. She said the sound that went along with the tyre impression and the decay smell was like slow classical music. I don't suppose that's very relevant, but it won't do any harm to look for a scrap-yard where the watchman listens to Classic FM.'

I nodded. As you know, I had my own thoughts, which I didn't bother to mention, as such. I was thinking, Tyres – wheels – the Wheel: and decay – death – funeral undertakers. And there *was* the quiet music at Condiment's.

But it really is all a load of rubbish, of course.

When Neil had gone away, I called Petesy in from the store-room, where he was currently under Senga's eagle thumb. I had decided it was time he started giving out with some real information, for a change. Let's not beat up the bush, I thought, and plunged straight in:

'I want to know some more about your uncle and his businesses. When I risk my skin, I like to know that the people I'm working with can be relied on.'

Petesy brought out his captivating grin – the one which I've noticed seems to have an effect on women; even Aileen and Senga, for Christ's sake – but luckily I'm immune.

'Sure thing, Kenny,' he went, brightly. 'What do you want to know?'

'Right, how many businesses has he got, and what are they?'

'Buggered if I know,' he shrugged. 'Anyway, he told me you're not to be told too much, even though he trusts you now. I mean, he works on a need-to-know basis, so even *I* don't know all that much either – not about the businesses. Why don't you ask Basil? He's probably the only person who knows everything.'

'Well, why don't we just see what we can come up with, between the two of us? I'll start us off. There's Drennan's of Wellesbourne ... there's AutoSupCo, the motor trade supplier, and there has to be at least one distributor of electrical goods ...'

'That would be Allison's Appliances. They distribute household stuff too – like cookers, refrigerators, washers, and hoovers. And the Silver Cicada ... don't forget the Silver Cicada and ...'

Petesy stopped. 'Why do you want to know all this stuff?'

I tried to look surprised. 'Why do you think?' I strapped on the voice of sweet reason. 'Look, Petesy, suppose I come across a ... er ... business opportunity – which can happen from time to time. I'll want to have a feel for whether it's within the Wheel's areas of interest. And I'll want to pass the information to where it can be most useful.'

I paused, thinking if he believed that, he would believe in the fingernail fairy. Then I added:

'Besides, I'm risking everything by going in with the Wheel, so I need some assurance, from an intelligent third party, that I'm not going to be ripped off. I owe that much to Aileen. And I need to know I can trust your uncle and his associates.'

Kenny Madigan, you're quite right to be thinking you should go into the used car sales racket.

I seemed still to have Petesy's attention. He was nodding, but beginning to look like he wasn't sure why he was nodding. So I dropped another question on him:

'By the way, do you know anything about the Condiment Brothers firm?'

'Not much,' he told me. 'It must be the most boring of my unc ... er ... the Wheel's enterprises. It's dead straight and legit; but it's a dead end business.'

Petesy looked to see if I had got his little joke. Actually, I hate that kind of obvious humour, but in the circumstances I thought it wouldn't do any harm to encourage him with a forced half-grin.

'Doesn't he ever go there, then?' I asked, dead casually.

'Well, he's got an office there, though he mostly sets up meetings in other places. But I think that's where he keeps his records ... you know ... like paperwork and VAT returns, I suppose.'

He waved his arms vaguely, not knowing too much about business records, adding:

'And of course Basil uses the computer there.'

Bingo!

But I should have got that far on my own, after my brief visit. Anyway, it was nice to have Petesy's confirmation that Condiment's was the Wheel's nerve centre, as such.

'So,' I said, summing up, so to speak, 'this Wheel bloke spends all his time running his own business empire. Right?'

'No, he pretty much leaves them alone to operate under the management that he has put in place, though he uses their facilities whenever they're appropriate to what he needs. He's more interested in what he calls his special jobs, and for these he uses his own private staff – like you and me and Basil and –'

'Just a minute,' I interrupted, 'these special jobs; would they be things like hijacking great big trucks, and moving escaped convicts around the country?'

'That's right,' Petesy said. 'The Wheel calls these kind of things "the core business", and he does all the planning himself – and even takes part, when he thinks a job is really interesting or extra important.'

Wow, what a nest-egg of rattlesnakes I'd got myself into. I changed tack, a bit.

'What about scrap-yards?' I asked. 'You know . . . places where cars are broken up? Does he control any of those?'

He shook his head. 'No . . . not as far as I know – and I suppose I would have come across anything like that during the time I've been working for the Wheel.'

'That's another thing,' I said, 'even *you* call him the Wheel – and you're a member of his family. What's that all about? It doesn't make sense. I mean you could hardly have grown up calling him Uncle Wheel.'

'No, of course not. I called him Uncle Alf.'

'So his name is Alfred, then?'

'No, not Alfred. It's Alphonse . . . and he hates it. Close friends get to call him Alf, and everybody else has to refer to him as the Wheel.'

'OK,' I said, 'now surprise me. Why *the Wheel*, as such?'

Petesy gave me a don't-be-such-a-prat look, and said:

'Because his name's Turner, of course – Alphonse Turner.'

It was late that same afternoon that I got another call from the Wheel. No introduction by Basil, and he didn't identify himself. But then he didn't need to. He had switched his dynamic voice on.

'Kenny? Glad I caught you. Some news for you. We're putting

together a team to carry out the next phase of Project Parcel. I'm holding a kick-off meeting at the Silver Cicada – Monday . . . er . . . two thirty. Bring the lad, Petesy. Oh, and come in through the tailor's shop; I don't like the police to see a lot of daytime comings and goings at the Cicada.'

'All right,' I said, 'we'll be there.'

My brain was in an overloaded state, what with all the information I had had flung at me that day. I needed to talk it all over with Aileen to help me catch sight of the wood through the trees. Not that I was too confused to be scared – well, Nick Pearson had been taken away and severely maimed, hadn't he? And I was the logical next target for whoever had done it, wasn't I? Also, I was not too confused to notice that the Wheel had paused before letting me know the time of the meeting. As if he was running his eye down a whole list of times, and I was just one of the items on that list.

I got out of the garage pretty sharpish that night, only stopping to tell Petesy about our kick-off meeting with the Wheel, and leaving Senga to lock up. When I turned into the street where Aileen and I live, I saw that the kerbside space where I usually park, opposite the maisonettes, was already occupied, so I drove another twenty yards or so, to the next available space. What I didn't notice was that the car occupying my usual space was a big Volvo – a big dark blue Volvo – very dark blue. And there were two people in it.

That was why, when I got out of my car and started walking back along the footpath, there were these two blokes walking towards me with their eyes full of determination. I hesitated, but it was too late. They grabbed me. One held each arm. My brain cells were yelling at me – telling me that this was what happened to Nick Pearson.

The thug on my left said, in a quiet voice:

'Come along with us. We want to have a little chat with you.'

At the same time, I was being propelled towards the Volvo, in spite of ordering my feet to walk in the other direction. Out of all the stuff that was charging through my mind, I jumped on something I read once – that most people, when attacked or mugged, will keep quiet and still, as if they didn't want to kick up a fuss. Which is exactly what the attackers want. So you should kick up as much of a fuss as you can possibly manage.

I sucked in a deep breath and screamed. I lifted my feet off the ground to make myself as heavy as I could. I struggled. I shouted as loud as I could, 'Help, I'm being mugged. Somebody call the police.' And I kept on yelling while the tough guy who was holding my right arm delivered God knows how many punches to my face and body. It slowed them down though; progress towards the Volvo stopped for a bit – until it dawned on my new friends that their best bet would be to pick me up bodily, and carry me to the car. They hoisted me to a horizontal position, still yelling, and one of them even added to the din by shouting at me, 'Shut the fuck up, you chopsy bastard.'

My own yelling was still pretty loud. I suppose it was louder to me than anyone else, but anyway, it prevented me from hearing the new noise for a while. My captors must have heard it, because they froze for a moment. Then it came through to me – the beautiful sound of a police siren. They dropped me, one of them putting a final boot in on my ribs, leapt for their car, and were round the corner before the cops got level with me. The police slowed down to see what condition I was in, and I yelled at them to get after the buggers.

Which they did, after a bit too much hesitation. And they must also have whistled up another cop car by radio, to find out what had happened to me. I was still painfully climbing to my feet when another siren screamed in bearing two nice women coppers, who held me steady while I dragged myself up the stairs to the maisonette. They came in with me, notebooks poised for action, and I gave them the best descriptions I could manage, which weren't great, as you will understand if you have ever been mugged. And no, I didn't get the registration of their car either. The little cute one sighed with irritation, and wondered aloud if Miss Downie would have noted the number.

That was the most surprising thing about the whole episode – that it was Miss Downie, the Neighbourhood Witch, who saved me. As you know, she monitors everything that goes on in the street. Well, she had spotted these two blokes in the car, half an hour earlier, and thought they looked suspicious. Of course, there was no way for her to know that they were lying in wait for me – she thought they were a gang of desperate refuse robbers who were out to hijack her wheelie-bin.

Fortunately, when Miss Downie called the police, she hadn't sounded *too* dippy. So they sent a patrol car round; a half-hour response was pretty good for that lot, I thought. My attackers got clean away, of course. Oh, and Miss Downie had made a note of the Volvo's registration.

12

So that's how it came about that Aileen arrived home from work to find me lying back on the sofa, nursing the sore places where I had been punched and kicked. So I was able to enjoy a bit of extra attention, and didn't even have to help with the washing-up after we finished our lemon chicken with pilau rice.

Unfortunately the evening was spoiled soon afterwards, by the arrival of Neil, with Sally in tow. Neil had heard about my attempted abduction, down at copper headquarters, and he was here flying the flag of sympathetic concern. It was pretty obvious, to me at least, that he only came in the hope of picking up more information. While the two girls went off on an exploratory voyage through Aileen's wardrobe, Neil got down to business.

'The uniforms got descriptions of your attackers from about a dozen witnesses who were drawn to their windows by your yelling,' he said, 'so they're now looking for a couple of tall short men of medium height, whose ages vary from twenty to forty-five, and who are both bald with long hair. The usual reliable witnesses, in fact.'

'That's exactly how *I* remember them,' I said. 'What about the car registration that Miss Downie wrote down?'

Neil did a negative shake of his head.

'That number belongs to a Post Office van in Billericay – so that's no help either. But you must be able to give a better description of these nutters, Kenny. More to the point, you must have some idea of why they liked you enough to want to take you home?'

Put that way, it was a question. In fact, it was the question I'd been asking myself ever since the would-be kidnappers drove off into the sunset. I even thought I knew the answer, but I wasn't ready to confide in Neil yet. However, as it turned out, he wasn't far behind me.

'How about this for a wild guess, Kenny? That escaped convict, Cameron Dalgetty, has two mates who were never collared. As far as we know, they didn't get their share of the robbery proceeds. They are highly pissed off at Dalgetty, and they're desperate to find out where he stashed the loot. So they want to get their hands on the aforementioned Dalgetty, with a view to kicking the shit out of him until he tells them what they want to know. With me so far, are you, Kenny?'

I nodded. I could see where he was heading.

'I can see where you're heading,' I said, 'but how do we know they didn't get the proceeds of the robbery?'

'Oh, come on, Kenny, you're not that thick. Nobody would have gone to such a great deal of bother to spring Dalgetty out of the nick – not unless they knew that he could lead them to the loot. And this pair of ulcers must be anxious to get their mitts on the money they missed out on the last time round.'

He went on:

'Somehow, these blokes have got the idea that you can help them to find Dalgetty. And then there is the question of Nick Pearson . . . I don't know exactly what your recent contact with him was about, though I'm guessing that you sent him on some errand that exposed him to these thugs. But the only place he could lead them was to you. How am I doing?'

I had forgotten how bright Neil was. It should be against the law for the police to recruit graduates like him. So I confirmed his suspicions; what else could I do?

Then I thought of something I could ask him:

'Any progress with your search of breakers' yards?'

'Nothing to report yet. Remember, it was only this morning that you and I discussed Madame Kazza's prognostication.'

Jesus Christ, just this morning. It seemed like ages ago.

There was nothing more I could think of to ask Neil. All I wanted was for him to bugger off out of there and give me some peace and quiet. Trouble is, Neil wasn't finished with me yet. He couldn't resist putting the boot in when I was on my knees.

'The main message I want to leave with you, Kenny, is this:

100

I am not pulling your plonker when I tell you that we've got enough on you to put you out of the game for a few years. And that could easily happen unless you get serious about helping me with my enquiries – and pronto. Keep that in the front of your thoughts, mate.'

No trace of the friendly neighbourhood copper there. Whatever happened to community policing?

When Neil and Sally left, I limped off to bed, feeling about a hundred years old, and guilty about having sent Nick Pearson to what could so easily have become his death. There was very little that could be said in his favour, but he didn't deserve to suffer so much for such a futile cause. Still, I had to admit that I definitely preferred him over Kinnell any day of the week.

Aileen was working the next day, which was Saturday. I woke up feeling completely knackered, and spent the day gently recovering, without trying to think through the mist to the end of any of my personal tunnels.

The day after that, my body – and my mind – felt as if they were getting back to their normal unscrambled states. Aileen and I sat down to our usual Sunday morning breakfast of boiled eggs and toast soldiers. Afterwards, I brought Aileen right up to date with everything – well, almost everything – that had been going on. She went silent for a while, when I told her about Nick Pearson. I could see she was thinking that the same thing could have happened to me if Superwitch Downie had not ridden her broomstick to the rescue.

It was Aileen who pointed out that there were things going on which were not obviously connected to the Wheel's Great Midlands Shit-heap. First, there was the presence of the hard men who tried to abduct me. Aileen took to calling them Hengist and Horsa for some unknown reason. (I mean, I know why she gave them nicknames – it was so that we didn't have to say 'the two blokes who tried to kidnap me', every time we wanted to refer to them. It was her choice of names, Hengist and Horsa, that had me boggling.) She agreed with my opinion that they were probably the ones who kidnapped Nick Pearson – we were both carefully using the word *kidnapped*, though we were really thinking *beat the shit out of and nearly killed*.

And then she went on to analyse it a bit more. She decided there was no chance that Hengist and Horsa could be part of the

Wheel's organisation, so they must either belong to some other gang, or else were working for themselves.

Duh! I could have worked that out all by myself.

But then Aileen's intuition kicked in, and she declared H and H to be definitely the former mates of Grievous Dalgetty, the great escaper. He never grassed on them for their part in the robbery that got him put away, but if he hid the proceeds before being collared, they would be willing to do a lot of nastiness to get to Grievous and make him tell them where to find the money.

So there you go. My Aileen proved she was just as clever as Neil. And she showed she was even cleverer, by going on past the point where he had stopped.

'Right,' she said. 'So there's nothing you can do about Hengist and Horsa. Not directly anyway, because you haven't got a clue where to find them. I mean, the only way to find them would be to set yourself up as bait in some way, so as to attract them. And that would be too dangerous; I wouldn't let you do it. In fact, you've got to be more careful in future, and always check to make sure you're not being followed.'

'Yes,' I nodded, 'and I'll have to watch out at the garage, too. Like never being there alone or being first in, in the morning, or last out at night.'

'Right. So we'll have to tackle it from the other end.'

She was beginning to lose me now.

'What other end, Aileen?'

'Through your Wheel's connections, of course.'

Aileen had taken to referring to the Wheel as 'your Wheel' for some reason. I never mentioned it to her, though I certainly didn't feel as if he was *my* Wheel.

'You think you know where this Cameron Dalgetty is hidden. He's probably still a prisoner, so if you can get him out – help him to escape again – Neil can have him picked up and returned to the real prison, where he belongs. Then there won't be any point in Hengist and Horsa going after you.'

Aileen made it sound easy. As if the Wheel mob would let me walk in and remove one of their most valuable investments; they were obviously after the same stolen money. I wasn't convinced that Grievous would be grateful to get back to a 'real' prison. Also, I could be in danger from him if I got him out – he wouldn't have forgotten who it was that got him soaked in oil and bopped on the head.

'No, Aileen,' I told her. 'There is no way I am going to unleash that Grievous on the world . . . I think I prefer the idea of him being in custody – anywhere. Anyhow, it sounds a bit too dangerous. Still, I quite fancy the idea of having him returned to the real prison.'

I thought about that for a moment.

'How about if I find out where Grievous is, for sure . . . and then tell Neil to raid the place and get him?'

'Hmm.' She considered that, and said, 'Maybe . . . but wouldn't Neil need some evidence to support your claim that Grievous really was where you said?'

'In that case,' I said, 'I'd better get myself a crystal ball – he'll believe his little gypsy assistant, rather than me. That's why he's running about, searching breakers' yards.'

I was quite happy to ignore the fact that I had helped to mislead Neil.

So here I was, girding myself up to spy on the Wheel's activities, now that I was a trusted member of the gang. Well, I suppose that was what I'd been doing all along, but that was just picking up information that happened to blow in my direction. From now on, I would be actively poking my nose into the tiger's dinner.

It's a hell of a life, being a double agent.

Monday arrived, the day when Petesy and I were scheduled to go to the – what did he call it? – the kick-off meeting for the next phase of Project Parcel. I'd had too much to think about over the weekend to devote any brain capacity to the Wheel's kind invitation, as such. Oh, well, not much point in speculating. I would find out soon enough.

Petesy was quite edgy though. I could sense his excitement bubbling along below whatever he was doing or saying. He was psyching himself up, determined to have a great time breaking the law on a large scale. I couldn't help wondering if Petesy had chosen the right profession.

It was then I remembered him telling me that he was on his way to the very top of the organisation. And I suddenly twigged

– he thought he was being groomed as heir to the Wheel's criminal empire. To take over the reins of the underworld in the fullness of time, so to speak. That was definitely a big attraction for him – big enough to make him try to overcome the fact of being shit scared of the job.

Petesy Curtain, the Prince of Wheels.

I couldn't stop thinking about Hengist and Horsa. It was preying on my mind – the thought that somewhere not far away, there were two murderous tearaways looking for a means of spending some quality time with me. Twice, I walked out to the forecourt to look up and down the road to see if there were any suspicious characters in the vicinity. Of course, they couldn't risk being seen in a dark blue Volvo any longer, but it wouldn't take them long to nick another car.

That led me to the thought that there was one thing I could do for my own protection, and to increase my chances of survival. I know I've always said I wanted to have nothing to do with guns, but there aren't usually a pair of murderous geezers trying to make me tell them something I don't know.

I got the Smith and Wesson pistol out of my drawer, unwrapped it, and laid it flat on the desk. It glinted blue under the fluorescent light. I spun it round so that I could read what was stamped on the grip, below the maker's name. Sigma Series, it said. The model number was perfectly legible – SW380 – but somebody had very carefully used a file to remove the serial number.

If you were compelled to carry a handgun, this must be about the easiest one to carry. The barrel was only three inches long, and the whole thing, loaded, weighed no more than a pound – less than half a kilo. As an engineer, of sorts, I couldn't help admiring it as a beautifully designed and well-made machine. I checked that the safety catch was on.

Of course, it was now illegal for anyone in the UK to possess a handgun, now that the government, in its wisdom, has decided that only criminals should have guns.

Seeing as how I would be going to the Wheel's meeting in the big city later in the day, I was not wearing my usual working jeans. However, the pistol, being flat, slid easily into the back pocket of my River Island chinos.

Kendall Madigan, the meanest gun in the Midlands.

* * *

104

Petesy and I both drove our cars to Birmingham, since I pointed out to him that it would hardly be worth his while, dragging all the way back to Stratford for only an hour or so of work. And anyway, I might want to nip over to Evesham afterwards. Going to Evesham had become a sort of code word between Petesy and me, which I used any time I didn't want him along. I mean, we both knew that I wasn't really going to Evesham, at least I thought we both knew it.

Agreeing to meet in a particular city centre car-park, Petesy and I left Lone Harp early enough to make sure we would be in time for the Wheel's meeting, what with him being such a stickler for punctuality. My other reason was that I wanted to hang back a bit behind Petesy to make sure that neither of us was followed by Hengist and Horsa. I was sure that the dreaded duo weren't going to give up just because they failed to reel me in at the first attempt – and they might well go after Petesy next, if they knew that he was in on the action. Anyway, we didn't have a tail this time – probably too soon after their attempt on me.

The result of our early departure was that we shuttled through the tacky menswear store about twenty minutes too early. Basil left us to wait our turn at a table right at the back of the dimly lit main night-club area.

From where we sat, we could see a distant pool of light on the stage. However, it wasn't distant enough to prevent us seeing something of what was going on, although we were unable to hear anything that was being said. The Wheel was on his feet beside an overhead projector, in gleaming white shirt-sleeves and blue tie, doing what he did best, in my experience – talking. His audience, two blokes on chairs facing him, were obviously concentrating hard on the magnified image being thrown on to the screen from the sheet of transparent foil currently laid on the overhead projector that the Wheel was standing beside. He kept tapping the screen with a long pointer. From my distance and angle, I could see that there were lines of print being displayed, but I couldn't make them out.

Eventually, the Wheel took a look at his watch and brought their meeting to a close. As Basil conducted the two blokes out in the direction we came in from, I saw that they were both

Asians. Nice to know the Wheel is an equal opportunity employer, I thought.

Basil came back to conduct Petesy and me down to the stage. As we approached, the Wheel switched foils on the overhead projector so as to display on the screen the words, 'Project Parcel', and below that, 'Phase Three'.

True to his principles, he got straight down to business. Who needs small-talk anyway?

'Right!' he said. 'Project Parcel is not a sudden death job.'

I flinched, not wanting to hear talk of death. The Wheel didn't notice; he just went on ploughing his lonely ditch.

'This is the kind of job where the preparations need to be extremely thorough. And the beauty of it is that we can take as much time as we need, in order to get everything exactly right, at the end of the day. Right?'

It was a theoretical question, so nobody tried to answer it. The Wheel seemed happy enough with that. He was getting into his State-of-the-Union stride.

'Now, I know you must both be desperately keen to know all the details of Project Parcel – Phase Three. Well, you shall, in the fullness of time. However, I insist on running a tight organisation – that means one with no leaks ... and among other implications is the necessity for the implementation of a strict need-to-know policy, in order to promote an optimum level of security awareness. At this moment in time, there is no prima facie requirement for you two to have an overview of Project Parcel in its entirety.'

Christ, he's been on a management course, I thought. He'll be doing risk assessments of truck hijacking jobs next.

Petesy was nodding enthusiastically, as if he understood, but I was still waiting for the Wheel to touch base with some actual information.

'Before assigning your specific task,' he continued, 'I feel it is worth sharing with you the fact that I have had Basil conduct an exhaustive risk assessment exercise to validate the viability of this operation ... not to mention the supplementary quality appraisal that will review the project subjectively in retrospect. I hope this knowledge will assist in sustaining your continued confidence in our enterprise. Any questions so far?'

There was no possible answer to that. Our brain cells were

already paralysed on account of jargon fatigue. We simply shook our heads, which encouraged the Wheel to get on with the next bit. He switched foils again, but kept a blank sheet of paper on top of the new foil on the projector, so that only the heading showed up on the screen. Confusingly, this heading said 'Sellotape'.

Looking every inch a model of managing directorship, the Wheel pointed his pointer straight at Petesy and me and pinned us with his no-nonsense look.

'The people who were being briefed when you arrived are my String team. You two are my Sellotape team, and as such are categorically vital to the successful prosecution of Project Parcel.

'Let me put you fully in the picture. Your assignment is of a reconnaissance nature. You are to accrue data concerning a particular residence, namely – Cressida, 14 Lundy Rise, Solihull.'

The Wheel slid the covering paper down so that the screen showed the first line of the foil on the projector. It said:

'1. Accrue Information re – Cressida, 14 Lundy Rise, Solihull.'

'Memorise this address,' he told us. 'The foils will be destroyed as soon as this briefing is over. What we need to know is the exact layout of that house, so I shall expect you to provide plan diagrams of each floor – as near to scale as you can, please. OK?'

Some actual substance at last. We nodded. Not so much in agreement, as in relief that here, finally, was something we could understand.

'Right!' said the Wheel. 'On we go to the next line item.'

He slid the sheet of paper down to reveal the next line of print on the foil:

'2. Floor Plans of Above Residence Required.'

'As you can see, we have to know the identities of all the residents at this address.'

He turned round to point at the screen, saw that he had cocked it up, and hastily made the necessary adjustment in order to display:

'3. Identities of All Residents at Above Address Required.'

'Finally, I want all the information you can obtain about all of the residents. Their habits, lifestyles, occupations, hobbies, what they have for breakfast – everything that will help us to build up

107

a picture of their lives, so that we can predict their movements and reactions.'

At last, the Wheel was talking as if he really meant what he was saying, without dressing it up in management speak. This must be what it was really all about.

The new line on the screen read:

'4. Comprehensive Details on All Residents at Above Address.'

He looked at his watch, then back at us.

'Use your initiative . . . I don't care how you do it, but the people you will be investigating must not suspect that they are under scrutiny. You have until two weeks from today – but no longer . . . sooner if possible. Generous supplementary bonuses will be paid into your accounts in the usual way, and there will be a further assignment for you when the time comes to wrap up Project Parcel – Phase Four. Good luck.'

The foil was whipped off the overhead projector, and the Wheel dismissed us with a nod of his black curls. As Basil showed us the way to the back door through which we had entered, we saw that there were another couple of blokes waiting for their meeting with the Wheel. I whispered to Petesy, 'Do you think that's his Sealing Wax team?'

I drove slowly south out of Birmingham, not feeling much like going back to work. The recent meeting – briefing, really – with the Wheel was tumbling around in the back of my mind, although I wasn't ready to devote any serious thought to it yet. So I tried to think about something else. Sam sprang to mind. Gradually, two things dawned on me. The first was that I was forgetting to look out for anyone who might be following me. The second was that if I was going back to Stratford, I should have turned off this road some distance back. I seemed to be heading towards Evesham, and the Five Ponds Garage.

I stopped off at a pub I know in Studley to drink a half-pint of lager and have a bit of a think. As you know, I'm not the kind of bloke who makes a pass at every woman who comes along. I'm quite happy with Aileen, and we get on well together, as such. That's why it shook me so much to be knocked sideways by sexy Sam. And there's also the fact that it was a two-way thing; right from the time we first met, Sam seemed to be attracted to me almost as much as I was to her.

I sighed and admitted to myself that Aileen was really the woman for me. Where Sam was concerned, I was thinking with my dick instead of my brain cells. It might be just sex, but as sex goes, it was bloody great.

Anyway, my life was surely complicated enough already. What with Project Parcel getting ready to burst, a pair of no-brain ulcers trying to kidnap me, and Neil expecting me to solve all the crime in the Midlands, woman trouble was the last thing I needed flung into the melting pot.

What I would do was, I would go on to Evesham, seeing as how I seemed to be heading there anyway. I would try to have a word in private with Sam, and I would tell her that I couldn't get into any relationship with her, and it would be better if we just cooled it and didn't allow anything else to happen along these lines. I would tell her about Aileen, and apologise for leading her on – if that's really what I had done.

That would be one of my problems out of the way for good.

I was beginning to feel better already.

13

I parked in the customer parking area at the side of Five Ponds Garage, and was about to get out of the car, when I cleverly worked out that it was probably not a good idea to carry a gun when I go to visit friends. So I took the pistol out of my pocket, and slipped it into the driver's seat. Not under the seat, but actually inside it. See, there's this slit where the upholstery has come partly adrift at a seam, which you can only reach by reclining the seat quite far back; and it was just big enough to let me slip the gun in among the stuffing of the seat.

Sam was in the little reception area when I went into Five Ponds Garage. She lit me up with one of her best smiles.

'Hello, Sam,' I said, and she replied with, 'Hi-ya, Kenny, I was just thinking about you.'

'That's nice,' I said. 'Can we grab a couple of coffees, and go in your office to drink it? I want to talk to you.'

'Well, actually, I've got a better idea,' she said. 'I was just about to go round to the house, so if you come with me, we can have some decent coffee, without being interrupted by customers coming in to demand their car keys.'

Sam hung up her overall and shouted through to Del in the workshop to say she was going. I followed her blue Toyota, while making sure that nobody was following me. We only went a mile or so, before she drove into the drive of a brick-built detached house in a small development of newish houses not far off Cheltenham Road. I followed, and parked alongside her car.

'What do you think?' Sam asked, waving a hand towards the house. 'Nice place for two working girls on their own, isn't it?'

I nodded and followed her into the living-room. I couldn't help thinking that this was exactly the kind of house that Aileen and I should be looking for, instead of some manky cottage . . . if we ever moved out of the maisonette, that is. Standing there, looking round the room, I was so involved in these thoughts, that before I knew what was happening, Sam had undone my belt, unzipped my chinos, and was reaching into my boxer shorts, while nuzzling into my neck with her lips.

My cock leapt to instant attention, being apparently more ready for this development than my thinking facilities – but who needs a brain at a time like this? Sam's T-shirt came off very quickly, and her jeans slid easily to the floor, once the tight part was clear of her hips. She slid my chinos and boxers right down my legs, and shoved me backwards on to an armchair in order to pull them completely off. Then she removed my shoes and socks, while telling me:

'A man who is naked except for his socks is the biggest turn-off in the world.'

Very philosophical, that.

By this time, my hormones were thinking that there had been quite enough delay, but the dog was not allowed to get chasing the rabbit just yet. Sam kissed me briefly, and then, taking hold of my dick, she led me by it, up the stairs to her bedroom. She had me completely naked, while she was still wearing a flimsy white bra, and little white lacy pants. I thought this was a bit unfair, so, on the way upstairs, as she was slightly ahead of me, I placed my left hand high up between her legs, and did some gentle stroking of the smooth skin at the top of her thighs. We both seemed to enjoy that.

Sam was still firmly in charge of the situation. She got me flat on my back on the bed without letting go. I wondered if I would ever get my cock back – and didn't really care whether I did or not. Next thing I knew, she leaned over and kissed me passionately, our tongues playing hide and seek with each other. At the same time, she must have been using her free hand to peel her panties off, because they were stunningly absent when she got on to the bed, and knelt, straddling me, with a knee on each side of my chest.

Of course, my tool was now free, which I thought was a mixed blessing. Sam leaned forward so that we could kiss again, and so that I could reach around her to undo the catch on her bra. Then I was able to view those beautiful breasts again – to caress them – to kiss them, and run my tongue around the hard nipples . . . at that point, Sam began to lower herself on to my penis – and we were both in heaven at last.

Well, I certainly was, and from the moans and other noises Sam was making, I worked out that she was also having a great time.

Afterwards, we lay there feeling contented for quite a long time. I was on my back, with my left arm round Sam, who was lying on her side with her head resting on my shoulder and her left leg across my thighs.

A long time later, I felt Sam's lips moving across my chest, and then there was a gentle tugging of teeth on my left nipple. Not surprisingly, this had the effect of reviving my interest. I reached my right hand over and used both arms to give her a tight hug. To my surprise, she winced, and her whole body tensed up.

'What's wrong?' I asked. 'Did I hurt you?'

'A bit,' she said, 'I still hurt a bit where my ribs were cracked by those nutters who broke into the garage.'

My brain cells were suddenly in free fall, on account of having just tripped over something they didn't understand.

'But . . .' I must have spluttered a bit, 'but . . . that was Del. You told me it was Del who was in hospital . . . that time we made love in your office . . . Remember?'

111

The thunder struck me all at once. 'Oh, Christ . . .'

I couldn't get any more words out.

Sam or Del giggled.

'I'm so sorry, Kenny. We didn't mean to . . . the first one of us that you met was the one called Sam, and we both quite fancied you, so we agreed that whenever one of us met you, she would be Sam. Kind of a competition . . . you know . . . to be the first to get into your underwear.'

I was about ready to apply for admission to a home for the bewildered.

'So, you must be Del, then, because of the cracked ribs . . . you were definitely the one who got beaten up, because you were in hospital at the time we did it in the office . . . Right?'

'Well . . . that depends on whether the one you . . . er . . . fucked in the office was Sam or Del. That was cheating, 'cos I was in hospital at the time.'

I gave up. All I could be sure of, was that I had now definitely shagged both of them. And she had now started kissing her way down my stomach – and down – and down – until her talented lips and tongue reached the place where I keep my brains.

Eventually, we did have a coffee; fully dressed, and back downstairs on the living-room sofa. While I was there, Del . . . well, the other one – the one I had to call Del – she came home from the garage, threw us a knowing look, and went off upstairs to change. Sam (perhaps) leaned over to whisper in my ear:

'Maybe we should arrange a threesome sometime . . . that way, we would be absolutely certain we've both screwed you on the same day. We would probably have to carry you out to your car afterwards.'

We both laughed. If you'd asked me a month ago how I would enjoy being used as a sex object by two gorgeous women, I would have said it would be great beyond my wildest dreams. But now I wasn't so sure.

Shortly after that I made my excuses, and left, promising to be in touch.

Aileen had held off preparing our dinner, having realised that I might be late getting back from the Wheel's meeting, so we did manage to eat together. Over our chilli con carne, I told her about the briefing, and we discussed how Petesy and I should go about the tasks that the Wheel had handed out.

Aileen was strongly in favour of taking it gradually; she thought we should spend quite a lot of time just watching the house. That way, she said, we would get to know, at least by sight, all the people who lived there, and their habits – the times they went out and came back and so on. And then, if we needed to break in, so as to get the layout and more information, we would be able to do it at a time when everybody was out. I couldn't disagree with any of her arguments, but neither could I help thinking it was never going to be that simple.

'Wait a minute,' I protested, 'it must be a lot harder than *that* to get into the house. I mean, there must be something pretty valuable in there, for the Wheel to be interested. So if it was possible to break in just to get the layout and such, it surely wouldn't be necessary to find out all that information, and . . .'

'No, I don't think that's it.' Aileen shook her head, sending her fair hair swishing around her head. She liked showing off what she called her golden tresses. 'Your Wheel seems to be just as interested in the people as in the house . . . maybe he wants to kidnap somebody who lives there.'

I gave that some serious consideration before replying.

'I don't think so. He could have a person kidnapped when they were somewhere else . . . you know, where they would be more vulnerable than in their own home.'

We both went quiet for a while, thinking. I was thinking how terrible it would be if Aileen suggested an early night, after my exertions in Evesham. She was still thinking about Project Parcel, as she proved five minutes later.

'It's just like usually. We need to think about it from the other end. I mean, it must be connected with something else your Wheel is involved in, mustn't it? And it's obvious when you think about it.'

She was beginning to sound quite excited, as if she had cracked it. I waited, knowing it would be worth waiting for. I'm dead proud of Aileen's brain. She stacked our empty plates, and carried them into the little kitchenette, before coming back to the table to explain to me what it was that was obvious.

'Look, Kenny, your Wheel has told you himself. He still calls it Project Parcel, so it must be something to do with that escaped

113

convict, Dalgetty. See, getting him out of jail must have been Phase One; passing him up the country like a parcel was Phase Two; and now you're involved in Phase Three.'

I was well impressed. The bits had been there all along – I just hadn't fitted them together, as such. Keep going, girl, I thought, and asked, 'So, what does that tell us?'

'Right!' she said, to give herself more time to think. 'Remember what we said last night . . . about everybody being after the robbery money that Dalgetty has hidden somewhere.'

Aileen held her hands out, palms up in a now-all-is-revealed gesture.

'Well then!'

She sat up straight, flushed with victory, which made me feel as thick as pig shit.

'Well, then . . . what, love?' I said, frowning.

'Well, then . . . your Wheel must have persuaded Dalgetty to tell him where the money is hidden – and it could be somewhere in that house in Solihull.'

It sounded good, but I was firmly on the doubtful side. Too neat maybe. But worth giving a bit of thought to. Surely, if the Wheel knew, or even suspected, that the money was in that house, he would be inside like a dog on fire, regardless of who was there. Anyway, I found it hard to believe that people could live in a house for any length of time and not find any stash of loot that might be sharing the premises with them.

Aileen's bringing up of Grievous again made me think of something else.

'Oh yes,' I said, 'that reminds me. I'll have to postpone my research on the place where I think they're keeping Grievous Dalgetty. I'll be too busy doing my survey of that house.'

'Surely you won't need to bother. Your Wheel would let Dalgetty go free once he told him where the money was hidden . . . oh, of course . . . he'll have to keep him until the money is found in case he wasn't telling the truth.'

I was smiling. 'Yes, even big nasty villains sometimes tell fibs.'

Another thing came into my mind – and no, it's not what you're thinking; the randy twins couldn't have been further from my thoughts.

'By the way, love,' I said, 'I may crash out at Petesy's flat the odd night while we're doing our surveillance act in Solihull. We might have to be at it very late some nights.'

'OK,' she said. 'In that case, we'd better have an early night tonight. Just in case we don't get the chance for a while.'

Petesy was all excited about our mission. It seems he actually went to Solihull the previous evening, to see what our target looked like – the house, that is. He swore blind that he only drove past slowly, without stopping.

'And I was dead lucky, Kenny,' he told me. 'As I was passing the entrance, I looked in, and there was this chick getting out of a car in the driveway. I only got a quick glance at her, but she looked like a real babe. It gave me an idea.'

I had to laugh. 'Yeah, I know what kind of an idea that would give you, but your sex life will have to take a back seat for a while. We haven't got time to waste.'

'No, no,' he said, 'that's not what I meant. Well, it is, in a way, I suppose . . . See, if I was to pull that chick, she might invite me back to the house, and I could get all the information we need.'

I thought about it. Not a bad idea.

'That's not a bad idea,' I said, 'but what makes you think she'll be interested in you? Anyway, she might be married, or have a bloke in her life already – or . . . how's this? . . . she might puke out of control at the sight of a smarmy git with his hair slicked back.'

Petesy didn't laugh. In fact he looked a bit put out, so I made him feel better by agreeing it could be worth a try. At least we would find out if he was telling the truth about his great chick-pulling abilities.

We agreed that the sooner we got started on our voyage of discovery, the better. So we decided to take a preliminary look at the place that evening, and then the next day we would start into some serious lurking.

Lundy Rise was a quiet leafy road inhabited by the well-heeled. Not that many of the well-heeled were on display to the casual eye. Their occasional comings and goings took place mostly inside cars, which they got in and out of behind thick hedges or garage doors.

Petesy's BMW 320i was in its native habitat, so it merged right into the background. We sat in it, watching number 14, or Cressida, as it was probably better known to its inhabitants. This was exactly the kind of place where people feel the need to give their house a title – even though it already has a perfectly good number.

The street was not very well lit by imitation Victorian lamp standards which splashed widely separated puddles of yellow-ish light on to the grassy verges at the edges of the road. The dark inter-puddle space where we parked, half on and half off the verge, gave us a good view into Cressida's driveway, which was on the outside of a bend.

There was something white on the ground just inside the entrance. It could be a McDonald's burger container that had blown in. I hoped it was bio-degrading. Beyond that, we could actually see part of a lit downstairs window, and even occasional movement behind it. Nothing that meant anything, though.

At 10.25 p.m. (I made Petesy write it down in the notebook we brought along to use as an event log), a pair of headlights swept past us and turned in at the target house. It was a Toyota Carina, no more than two years old, and it parked alongside a little Vauxhall Corsa which was already there. The front of the house was now flooded with light from one of those doodahs that switches on when it detects movement. A woman got out of the Toyota, and locked it, before using a different member of the same bunch of keys to open the front door of the house. She was a stylishly dressed middle-aged woman; about forty-five as far as I could tell at that distance. I got the impression that she was probably quite well preserved, though.

We heard the door close behind her, and the whole street was plunged back into stillness and silence. After another couple of minutes the automatic light went out – and the night's excite-ment was over.

I wondered how many cars were in the double garage. Lots of people, I've noticed, keep their garage full of useless junk, and leave their cars lying around outside. Hard to understand, that, except for company cars, of course – nobody cares about looking after company cars carefully. Anyway, I decided there must be at least one car in this garage, because the two cars parked outside were placed so as to leave the garage door clear for any vehicle that might want to get in or out.

We stayed another hour, watching various downstairs and upstairs lights winking on and off. Finally, when there were no lights left, Petesy was all in favour of boldly going closer.

'I bet we can find a way round the side of the house to scout out the back. I read somewhere that you can find out almost everything about people by analysing their garbage. Do you think they'll have a wheelie-bin?'

I shuddered a bit at that, as my brain conjured up a mental image of Miss Downie's wheelie-bin. I contented myself with pointing out to Petesy that we still didn't even know if there was a dog. And there could easily be another automatic light at the back. We gave up for the night. Petesy took me back to where my car was parked, and I drove back home to Stratford.

14

Next morning I walked to the garage, where I gathered together a few bits and pieces, and shoved them in a supermarket plastic bag. About ten o'clock, I got Senga on her own, when she was having her tea break.

'Can I borrow your car for an hour or two, please, Senga? Aileen's got mine today, and I've just remembered I have to go and see one of our suppliers in Coventry.'

'Aye,' she said. 'No problem. Just make sure ye bring it back before five thirty. I never feel up tae walking home after a hard day here . . .'

Then she gave me a vicious look and added:

'. . . and don't you insult me with stories aboot suppliers in Coventry, Kenny Madigan. Ah don't want tae know where ye're going. Ah'm just warning ye that if I find out you've been two-timing my friend Aileen, ye'll get yer heid in yer hands to play with.'

As if I would.

About an hour later, I threw my Tesco bag into Senga's little white Ford Fiesta, and drove to the pay-and-display car-park in Solihull where I had arranged to meet Petesy. On the way there, I made one stop – in a quiet lay-by, where I removed the number plates from Senga's car, replacing them with the ones from the plastic bag. Probably an unnecessary precaution, but you never know when a number will stick in somebody's mind, and be remembered days or even weeks later, when the coppers come round asking questions.

I knew a bloke who was fingered because some housewife could place his car near the scene of a crime. The reason she remembered his registration was that the number consisted of her birth date and month, followed by the initials of her three kids. It just goes to show you can't be too careful.

In the car-park, Petesy helped me put the finishing touches to the Fiesta, and off we went towards Lundy Rise, with him driving. We had given ourselves a licence to drive slowly around the residential area for hours on end. If we stopped and stayed inside the car for five or ten minutes, no one would be bothered. We could even reverse in and out of people's driveways if we felt like it. That's the beauty of a car with L-plates front and back, and a big sticker that says 'Driver Under Instruction'.

We lurked around there for several hours, from midday till about half-past three. We got to know the surrounding area very well, considering the number of times we crawled in and out of all the little cul-de-sacs, and along all the crescents and such.

During our tour of the neighbourhood, we discovered how to get access to the rear of the house called Cressida. It turned out that the garden backed on to a rugby field, with only a six-foot wire mesh fence between. The only other thing we found out was that the house was almost certainly unoccupied in the daytime – at no time did we see any comings and goings.

Petesy was quite disappointed that we had added very little to our stock of information. Of course, I tried to explain that we had really discovered quite a lot. See, it's dead important in this kind of business to know the whole vicinity like the back of your hand. I told him about a bloke I used to know, who nicked a car from a posh area like this, and ended up doing three-point turns in four different cul-de-sacs before he finally found the way out to the main road.

I got Petesy to draw a rough plan of the area in our notebook.

He also recorded the stuff about access to the back garden, and – probably most important – the fact that the place was likely to be empty in the daytime. We knew of two members of the household; the middle-aged woman, and the chick that Petesy fancied.

As I said, by about half-past three, I was satisfied that there wasn't much chance of finding out any more useful information. So we went back to the car-park where we restored Senga's Fiesta to its normal state. Then I headed south to Stratford, leaving Petesy with instructions to take his BMW back to Lundy Rise by five o'clock in order to watch out for the natives coming home from work. I would join him later.

In fact it was later than I intended when I joined Petesy. This was because it's harder to tell if you're being tailed in the dark. On the way to Solihull, I became suspicious of what seemed to be a persistent pair of headlights behind me. I did a few turns down side streets and thought I must have shaken them off, but when I went back to the main road, it looked like the same lights behind me again. I was probably just being paranoid, but took evasive action which involved a network of country lanes with sharp bends and unexpected junctions. When I finally arrived at Solihull, I was dead sure there was nobody following me.

I left my car a few streets away from Lundy Rise, and walked to where the BMW was parked with Petesy inside. It was well dark by then, being nearly seven thirty. Petesy had clocked – and noted – the times of three people arriving home to Cressida. The first was the middle-aged woman in her Toyota. Soon after her came the young woman driving the Corsa. They both parked in front of the house where we spotted them the previous night. The third arrival was a middle-aged man (Petesy was almost sure) in a Saab, which drove into the garage. The automatic garage door had closed behind the Saab, so the driver must have entered the house either through the back door, or directly from the garage.

'Well done,' I told Petesy, and we settled down – heads low, so as not to be visible to the casual observer – to the boring routine of watching the movements of shadows on the other side of the downstairs windows. The McDonald's wrapper didn't seem to have bio-degraded much since the previous night, and we just kept on waiting. Waiting ... for the unlikely event that would answer all our questions.

At eight fifteen, it happened. A small Honda swished past us from behind, and stopped across the entrance to Cressida. The driver got out, revealing herself to be a female in a short skirt, who went towards the front door. We couldn't hear the ring of a doorbell, but there must have been one, because the door was opened to admit the new arrival.

Ten minutes later, the door opened again. Two silhouettes came out and turned into two young women when the automatic light came on. They both got into the Honda. One of them was the recent arrival, and the other – the young woman from the house.

'Follow them,' I whispered to Petesy. Christ knows why I was whispering, but he started up the BMW without saying anything. We drifted along some distance behind the Honda through several corners and roundabouts. We had only gone a couple of miles, when the girls' car turned into the car-park of a pub. The big gilt lettering across the upper storey said this place was called the Royal Oak. It was a big 1930s boozer, set back from the road, with most of the parking space at the front. I got Petesy to stop at the kerb, short of the pub. From that position, we were able to watch our quarries as they entered the Royal Oak.

'Do you think you could pick up that girl?' I asked Petesy.

'No problem,' he said, 'I told you – I never miss. Here's what we do; we buy them a few drinks ... get chatting, you know, be really friendly and nice to them ... and I'll pull the one we want to know about. Oh! ...'

He looked at me doubtfully.

'You might find yourself left with the other one, Kenny. How will that go down with Aileen? Still, it's all in the line of duty –'

I interrupted. 'Aileen doesn't have to know, as such. All right? Anyway, if I do find I've got to take on this other chick so as to give you a clear field ... well, I'll make some excuse and get away from her as soon as I decently can.'

Petesy put the car into gear, and we moved ahead into the car-park of the Royal Oak – babe-hunters swinging into action.

120

Leaning against the bar while the barmaid poured our pints of lager, we took a scope around the premises. Nicely modernised place; no plastic pretend beams or fake horse brasses, thank God. The main bar was in a big room with lots of tables, a wide area for people to mill around in; food was being served in a dining area through an archway. A fruit machine stood over against the back wall. A light sprinkling of customers were making a faint background buzz of conversation. Very civilised.

All that, we took in with a single glance before homing in on the real target. We copped our first clear look at the two girls we had been following. They were quite a bit younger than me. Twenty – maybe twenty-one.

The one we wanted to know more about was pale, with light-coloured short hair. Her friend had longer, black hair. They both sported black skirts which stopped well short of their knees. Not that they were showing any worthwhile leg, as such, since they were encased in those horrible legging things – one plum-coloured, and the other olive green. Both girls were above average in the looks department, in their own ways, although not raving beauties.

'What do you think of the boobs on that blonde bit?' Petesy said, under his breath. 'I'm really going to enjoy this job . . . and to think I'm getting paid for it.'

I looked. Yes, I could see what he meant. They weren't enormous, as tits go, but what you might call very prominent, very nicely shaped, and very much at home inside the burgundy sweater. Personally, I preferred the dark-haired girl. I guess I'm just not so much of a tit man as Petesy.

Our survey was interrupted by a cough from the barmaid, who was waiting to be paid. As she took Petesy's money, she winked at him and said:

'If you don't get anywhere with that pair you've been eyeing up, I could take you to a nice little club when I finish here . . . eleven thirty. Right?'

Christ, I couldn't help wondering what the hell women see in him. Still, it made me begin to feel optimistic about our mission for tonight. Petesy was as stylish as usual, while I was wearing my expensive Austin Reed jacket over my best dark blue silk shirt. We took our drinks to an empty table adjacent to the one occupied by the two girls.

Don't ask me how he did it, but within about ten minutes Petesy was exchanging banter with the young ladies, and even I was throwing in the odd comment. I've always been absolute crap in the chatting-up department. When I was younger, I used to envy the blokes who had that kind of easy magic. Usually, by the time I thought up the right thing to say, the lucky girl had already left, hand in hand with one or other of my mates.

It wasn't too long before I found myself up at the bar ordering two glasses of dry white wine for our new friends. That provided a suitable excuse for Petesy and me to join them at their table, where our presence seemed to be quite welcome.

The dark-haired chick who had been driving the Honda was called Sophie; her friend from Lundy Rise was Emma. First names only, at this stage. We chatted about this and that. You know, what sort of music we liked – that kind of thing. The girls had been best friends since they were at school together, at which time they were rampant Take That fans. But of course they were now much too grown up for boy bands, so they had moved on to various bands that I had never heard of. Well, not quite; I had heard of Verve – or is it The Verve?

Petesy surprised me by having better taste than I would have expected – Van Morrison, Crowded House, et cetera. I decided to keep quiet about my taste in music – they were all too young even to have heard of the heavy metal bands I liked in my teens, and they would just sneer at my current liking for The Beautiful South and The Lighthouse Family. So, what with one thing and another, I was fairly quiet, compared to the rest of the party.

Sophie had a job at the airport – Birmingham airport, that is – as what she called a ground steward. She lived in a flat that she shared with two other girls, not far away, in Acock's Green. Emma was learning her way around the ropes as a trainee or apprentice or whatever, in a stockbroker's office. She was slightly shame-faced to admit that she still lived in her parents' house, because of it being so much cheaper and easier.

Petesy and I poured out the story we had agreed in the car. We were sales representatives, working for a company that distributed automotive parts and supplies – not too distant from the truth, and something we knew enough about to keep up the pretence. We got away with being vague about where we lived.

122

It ended up being quite a pleasant evening, really. Sophie and Petesy were being careful about their drinking, as they were both driving. I was being just as careful, on account of I would be driving home to Stratford later on, although just then I was a bit hazy about how I would be reunited with my car. The only person drinking wholeheartedly was Emma. Not that she was falling-down drunk, or anywhere near it. Just pleasantly tipsy, and probably a bit more chatty than I think she normally would be.

With 11 p.m. edging in our direction, our new friends were starting to look at their watches and make remarks about having to get up for work in the morning. That was the signal for them to make the ritual women's trip to the loo, presumably to discuss strategy, as well as carrying out unnecessary repairs to their make-up.

As soon as the door of the ladies' room swung closed behind the girls, Petesy and I took the opportunity to visit the men's room. Back at the table, we had plenty of time to review our own progress, or at least Petesy's, since he was the one in the spotlight with a mission to close in on Emma.

'I think I'm well in there,' he said. 'I want to avoid taking her back to my place, because it's her house I'm interested in, so I'll take her home now. It's not very likely that she'll invite me in, because of her parents being there. But I'll make a date for tomorrow or the day after, and somehow or other I'll find a way to get into the house. I hate sex in the car anyway.'

I nodded in agreement. We were working in an area where Petesy was the acknowledged expert, so it was up to him to set up the ground rules. He went on:

'I can't see how you're going to get out of this, Kenny. Maybe you can get Sophie to drop you at your car. You'll think of some plausible explanation for it being where it is . . .'

He grinned. '. . . and you can tell her you've got a head-ache.'

'Don't worry about me,' I told him, 'you just get on with the job in hand, and . . .' I broke off as Sophie and Emma came back to the table.

'Well!' Petesy grinned round the three of us. 'Time to hit the road, eh?'

Nobody argued. We trooped out to the well-lit car-park, and

what a coincidence – the girls' car turned out to be parked right next to ours. That was when it all started to go wrong. Out in the fresh air, Emma seemed a little more tipsy than she had inside. Still far from drunken, though. She came right up, and leaned against me and murmured:

'Kenny's my strong silent man. I want Kenny to take me home.'

'I haven't got my car here,' I said, but put an arm round Emma just in case she would stagger, or lose her balance, or something. The four of us stood silent for a moment or two, then Sophie claimed Petesy with a hand on his arm.

It was Petesy, the man in charge, who did the decisive thing to pull our burnt chestnuts out of the frying-pan.

'Here you go, Kenny,' he said, and tossed his car keys to me. I caught on, and threw him *my* keys.

'You know where my car is, Petesy. Catch up with you tomorrow.'

Emma directed me to Lundy Rise in Petesy's BMW. All the way there, I was wondering how I should handle the situation. I reckoned the best outcome, from my point of view, was to put up with a bit of kiss and cuddle in the car, and I would have to make a date for a couple of days ahead to try and get more information about her house and family.

When we got to Emma's house, she told me to park outside the hedge that marked the boundary between the front garden and the road.

'Come on in and have a coffee, Kenny . . . meet my parents.'

It was like being invited into the Holy Grail. How could I refuse, especially as there would be no danger of getting involved in any sex, what with her parents being on the scene.

As we approached the front door, the automatic security light came on.

'That's my car, there. Isn't it cute?' Emma said, indicating the Corsa in the drive. I didn't bother looking, because I had seen it before, as you know – and more importantly, because I was taking advantage of the light to read the tiny nameplate beside the door. 'Prof. R. Ormiston', it said.

I was ushered along a deeply carpeted hall and into the living-room, which was a lightly furnished place with a nice peaceful atmosphere. The walls were white, the floor was polished wood, and the lighting was supplied by various wall and table lamps. In the fireplace, there was the flicker of one of those gas fires that shoots out real flames. I couldn't see a television, but there could have been one in an expensive-looking cabinet that stood closed in a corner. All nicely modern and comfortable.

The middle-aged woman from the Toyota was on a black leather sofa, holding an open book, and the man of the house sat about fifteen feet away from her, on a matching armchair, reading a very large newspaper. Very cosy.

Emma introduced them as Carole and Reg, adding that these were her parents. I thought they seemed like nice enough people.

'Come and sit here, Kenny.' That was Carole – Mrs Ormiston, I supposed – inviting me to share her sofa. She went on, 'You can talk to me while Emma brews up some coffee in the kitchen.' To Emma, she said, 'Coffee for Reg and me too, dear, if you don't mind.' Reg went back behind his newspaper, after aiming a polite nod and a welcoming smile in my direction. I could now see that he was reading the *Guardian*.

So there I was, with Carole on the sofa, exchanging pleasantries about the weather, and what a nice pub the Royal Oak is, how good the food is there – I must try it sometime – and how busy the roads are getting, and she put her hand on my knee. I stiffened – no, not that, I mean my muscles tensed up, but I decided she was just being friendly. Perhaps there was a son, now left home, whom she used to pat affectionately; and she was missing him, and patting my knee out of habit.

Yeah, perhaps.

When Emma came back into the room, carrying a tray of coffee mugs, Carole gave my thigh a final squeeze before letting go. I was sure Emma had clocked her mother's grip on my leg. I hoped they were not the kind of family who share everything.

The coffee mugs were handed out, Reg put his paper down, and the four of us had a pleasant chat. I said all the right things, like what a lovely house you have, which pleased Carole no end, and she told me I would be welcome there any time, and what an improvement I was over most of the young men Emma brings home.

My coffee mug was down to the dregs, and I sneaked a look at my watch, thinking it must be about time I hit the road out of there. Carole must have noticed this, because she did a little yawn and said:

'Oh, well, it's been a long day. I'm feeling quite sleepy now.' She turned to Emma and me and added:

'And I expect you two young people will be anxious to get up to bed. I can remember what it was like when *I* was young and free. Off you go, upstairs.'

Bloody hell! There was no escape. Emma jumped to her feet and took me by the hand. We exchanged pleasant goodnights and left the room.

On the way upstairs, Emma whispered:

'Don't be put off by Carole. She always turns a bit competitive any time I bring a boyfriend home. She doesn't mean it, really.'

Emma's bedroom was really nice – a bit girly, of course, but what else would you expect? It was huge, compared to any bedroom I've ever had, and it had its own bathroom as well. I looked around it while Emma was in the bathroom.

When she came back into the bedroom, Emma was wearing a flimsy night-dress thing which was very nearly transparent, and showed what a really great figure she had.

'Wow, you look terrific,' I said. She did, too – even though I would rather have been somewhere else. With Aileen, definitely. With Sam, even – or did I mean Del? So it was no hardship to put my arms round Emma, and give her a hug, before excusing myself to visit the bathroom.

I used the loo, washed, and put some of Emma's toothpaste on my finger, with which I then rubbed my teeth. Ready for the fray, I stepped back into the bedroom to find that the light had been turned off. Not that that was much of a handicap, as there was enough light to be getting on with, spilling through the open bathroom door. Certainly enough for me to see the bed with an Emma-shaped bulge under the duvet, and her night-dress draped over the bedside chair.

I undressed, and slipped into bed. Leaning over the pale face on the pillow, I kissed Emma on the cheek – and was answered by a gentle snore.

I suppose I was quite relieved, really. I considered getting dressed, slipping out of the house, and making a getaway in Petesy's BMW. On the other hand, here I was, in a position to find out everything the Wheel could ever want to know about this house and its inhabitants. There might even be a clue as to why the Wheel needed to know all about some nice middle-class people in a nice middle-class house.

15

Something fairly pleasant is going on. I just lie back and let it happen. After a while, a dim ray of curiosity breaks through, and makes me open one eye. The room is steeped in daylight. There is no duvet on the bed I am lying on. A pair of hands is taking liberties with a part of me that enjoys a bit of liberty – under the right circumstances, that is. It responds by increasing like the National Debt. The hands decide there is no more scope for growth in the economy, and the one that is gently squeezing my balls – that one, leaves its task for a moment. When it returns, it is holding something. The two hands now co-operate in rolling something all the way down – a condom. I open the other eye, and turn my head so that my lips can nuzzle an adjacent breast. Emma goes down on to her back, pulls at me so that I roll over to end up between her open legs. Now I come fully awake, and grab her with both hands.

'How do you like my tits?' Emma asked, when we got our breath back.

'Beautiful,' I told her – truthfully, as it happens.

'Good', she said. 'They're my best features; everyone says so. Now I've really got to rush. What with one thing and another, I forgot to switch on the alarm last night . . . so I'm disastrously late for work. Carole and Reg have both left long ago.'

Emma was now charging around the bedroom, opening and closing drawers in a frenzy and making her breasts jiggle around in an interesting, though slightly alarming, way. I asked:

'What do your . . . er . . . Carole and Reg do for a living? Isn't he a professor or something?'

'Yeah, that's right,' she said absently, concentrating more on the tights she was trying to straighten out, 'he's a professor in Warwick University. Dead boring.'

'And Carole?' I pressed on. 'Does she work at the university too?'

'What? No . . . Carole works for the Leek and Chester . . . you know . . . the building society. She's branch manager in the main Coventry branch.'

Bingo! One of them had to be involved with money.

Already, Emma was looking highly presentable in a crisp white blouse and pinstripe skirt. I watched as she put on her shoes and took the matching pinstripe jacket out of the wardrobe. Very fetching – but I think I preferred her jiggling phase.

'Are you in too big a hurry even to brush your teeth?' I asked, rather cheekily, I thought.

She grinned at me.

'I did all that, *and* showered, *and* blow-dried my hair, before I . . . woke you up to fulfil your destiny as a man.'

She came over to where I was still flaked out on the bed, and planted a kiss on my cheek.

'Now, I've absolutely got to get off to work, Kenny. Pull the front door firmly shut when you leave. Oh, and help yourself to coffee if you want some – you'll find the kitchen downstairs . . . there'll be hot water on the Aga. Thanks for everything. Call me – I've jotted down my number for you on the pad on the bedside table.'

And she was gone.

What a wonderful girl, I thought. She's only gone and left me alone in the house I'm supposed to investigate in depth for some scam being planned by the top criminal brain in the Midlands.

Being late in for work at the Lone Harp Auto garage was getting to be a habit with me. Of course, going home to change into my working clothes made me even later. Lucky I was the boss – a fact that I would remind Senga of, if she followed up her disapproving looks with any verbal criticism.

Petesy knocked and came into my office as soon as I got there.

'What happened?' he asked anxiously, putting my car keys down on the desk, and picking up his own. 'I thought I was on a sure thing with that Emma. She must have been really pissed to the eyeballs, to come on to you like that.'

'You bloody cheeky sod,' I said, quite miffed. 'I think she was just showing what good taste she has. She's a very nice girl, you know.'

I brought out the sheets torn from Emma's A4 lined pad, on which I had drawn my rough diagram of the house in Lundy Rise. Well, the diagram was on one sheet, while I had noted the dimensions of all the rooms on another. A third sheet listed everything I knew about the Ormiston family – all three of them.

'Job well done,' I said. 'I should get a bonus for gallantry in the teeth of the enemy. How did you get on with Sophie?'

Petesy was already poring over the information I had slapped on to the desk. I don't know why, but I got the idea that he was trying to be evasive when he said:

'Oh . . . it was like throwing a sausage up the High Street. No thrill at all.'

He turned to see me looking at him – and his face went bright red. I kept on looking at him – and finally, he admitted it:

'All right, so I didn't get anywhere with Sophie. She dropped me off at your car. I never even got my hand on a tit. I must be losing my touch.'

Somehow, I knew that he was still holding something back. There must be something he didn't want to tell me. I let it go for the moment.

'Never mind, Petesy. Why don't you take all this stuff . . . draw a scale plan of the house and its grounds, and make a neat list of all the information. You know . . . a businesslike report for the Wheel. I shouldn't have to do *all* the work by myself . . . it's time you contributed something to this operation.'

'No problem, Kenny,' he said, sounding relieved, as if he was pleased to be off the hook. 'Can I use one of the computers in the back office? The Wheel would be really impressed with a well-formatted printed report.'

'Fine, if you can get one of these damn things to work, go ahead,' I said.

I hadn't realised that Petesy was computer literate. The two computers in the back office had been used by the crooked previous owner of the garage, mainly for criminal purposes which had nothing to do with Lone Harp. I had vaguely thought of trying to sell them and the printer, but had never got round to it.

Another thought came into my head.

'We must have a talk sometime, about the used car business I'm going to start. If you can drive a computer, maybe these machines could be useful in helping us to run it. You could be a real asset there.'

Jesus Christ. Here I was, treating this bloke like the long-lost son I never had. He looked back at me with his head slanted to one side.

'Well. I can help you get it started ... I mean, with the computers and all. Of course, if I didn't already have a great career in front of me, I might be interested in this kind of business. As it is, I'll be out of here as soon as the Wheel sets me up in a more permanent position.'

While Petesy was working his magic on the computer, I started to get on with planning the start-up of Madigan Motors. It was hard to concentrate, though, because I couldn't stop trying to work out what Petesy was trying keep from me. Surely there was more than just embarrassment at Sophie blowing him out. Wait a minute – she dropped him at my car, which he must have driven home to his flat, and then to Stratford in the morning.

My car!

I went out to look at it. Bog-standard transport – my three-year-old grey Ford Mondeo. I don't like to be conspicuous. It looked just like always. Well, of course it did. If Petesy had got it bashed up, he wouldn't be evasive about it. We're in the motor trade, after all.

I opened the driver-side door, and pulled up the lever that allows the seat to recline. I reached in, feeling for the bulk of the hidden pistol. Yes, it *was* still there. I walked back into the garage scratching my head.

What I should have done then was, I should have shaken Petesy within an inch of his life till he told me what it was all about. That way I might well have saved myself some grief and distress later on. Of course, I did nothing.

Back inside, I made sure that Petesy was fully occupied in the inner office. Then I shut both doors of my office and called Neil. I told him about the Wheel's interest in a certain house in Solihull, and its inhabitants. He seemed intrigued, but when I suggested he might want to investigate, or put a surveillance on the house, he gave an incredulous snort.

'Look, Kenny, I can't go chasing your rainbows. Find out what the scam is, get me some solid evidence, and then maybe I can do something about it. Meanwhile I've got my work cut out, trying to track down the escaped convict that you let slip through your hands.'

Suddenly, it was all down to me. Typical.

'You bloody useless bastard,' I said, 'you hustled me into this situation, and now you won't lift a sodding finger to support me in doing your dirty work. Well, sod you.'

'Sorry, mate ... it's a hard life,' Neil told me.

'Listen carefully,' I said. 'Foxtrot-Uniform-Charlie-Kilo ... Yankee-Oscar-Uniform.'

'Calm down, Kenny,' he said. 'If you want to do something useful, why don't you go and visit your friend Nick Pearson in Warwick Hospital? He's out of intensive care now ... maybe he'll tell you something he wouldn't tell us.'

'He's no fucking friend of mine ...' I started to protest, but gave up when I realised I was talking to empty space. Anyway, I knew perfectly well that Nick Pearson had nothing to tell me.

It was nice to have a quiet evening at home with Aileen, for a change. Over our microwaved chicken Kievs, she asked me how the surveillance of the Solihull house had gone. That got my brain cells running around in circles asking each other how much I should tell her – I hadn't given a thought to what Aileen should be allowed to know.

To give myself time to think, I filled her in with a full description of our house-watching activities right up to the point where we followed the two girls to the pub. After that, I had to get a bit cunning. I said that we had talked to the girls in the pub, and that Petesy made a date with the Emma one, for the following night. ('So right now he'll be getting ready to go and meet her.') Oh, and we stayed the night at Petesy's flat, where we went in

131

a taxi, on account of having had quite a few drinks and a cab to Stratford would have cost a fortune. Tomorrow, I could tell Aileen that Petesy had penetrated the objective and come up with the goods.

I had just got to the end of my story, when the doorbell rang. Aileen went to answer it, and ushered our visitor into the living-room.

Petesy.

Who seemed to think I should be pleased to see him.

'I thought you would want to see this right away, Kenny. I kept on working till I finished the report for the Wheel. See . . . accurate floor plans of the house and everything to scale, from your measurements . . . all neatly printed out.'

He had done a really great job, as far as I could tell. But I wasn't actually much interested in looking at it, at that particular moment. My brain cells were running around looking for the lifeboats. Aileen smiled sweetly at Petesy, and asked him:

'Shouldn't you be at home getting ready for your hot date, Petesy?'

'What hot date?' he asked. He looked blankly from Aileen to me, and back again. His forehead wrinkled with the mental effort going on behind it, but all he could come up with was:

'Oh . . . sorry. Am I interrupting something?'

'Nothing worth a kick in the pants,' Aileen said. 'Just Kenny and me – our relationship, or whatever it used to be.'

Petesy suddenly decided to leave. He muttered something about having to get on home, and found his own way out. I risked a look at Aileen's face, and wished I hadn't.

'I can explain, love,' I lied.

Ignoring is not a strong enough word for what she did to me. It was more that she made me feel as if I didn't even exist – had never existed. Then she had the door open and was shouting to our departing visitor:

'Wait for me, Petesy. I need you to buy me a lot of drinks.'

Bloody women.

Aileen came home late, reeking of that sweet brandy stuff she sometimes drinks, ignored me, and went to bed. In less than a minute, she was snoring steadily. That was how I knew it was safe for me to crawl under the duvet, being careful not to get too close in case I would wake her.

In the morning, she was up long before me, bustling around the bedroom, getting ready for work. I knew she wouldn't be feeling the effects of the previous night's brandy – Aileen has never had a hangover in her life. Sickening, isn't it? Anyway, I tried to set up some peace talks.

'Aileen, I just want to say –'

She cut me off, which was perhaps just as well, since I had no idea what I just wanted to say.

'I have no desire to hear another farrago of your lies, Kendall Madigan. I am fed up with being played fast and loose with . . . and I am not going to put up with it any longer. I shall let you know when I have given full consideration to my position and decided on my next move.'

The maisonette was beginning to feel colder – and I was feeling well gutted. I mean, Aileen and I have had our differences in the past, complete with tiffs, and shouting, and foot-stamping and tantrums, while I always try to stay cool. But this time it was different – she was the one staying cool, and that was something for me to worry about.

And what the fucking hell is a farrago?

I tried a different tack:

'I hope Petesy took good care of you when you were out drinking last night.'

'Oh, yes,' she said. 'Petesy took *very* good care of me all right. There we were, going at it for hours, shagging like bunny rabbits in the back of that posh car of his.'

I didn't believe a word of it, of course.

Nothing else was said until Aileen was about to leave for work. With the door open, she turned round and said:

'By the way, there was one thing you were right about . . . your Wheel *is* keeping the escaped convict, Dalgetty, at that mortician's place in Shirley.'

Typical of Aileen to jerk me into a different dimension. I struggled to catch up.

'How on earth did you find out about that?'

'I asked Petesy. What else? It seemed to me there was a good chance that he would know, what with his family background and all. Why don't you try using your brain for a change, instead of your dick?'

I couldn't help wondering what else Petesy might have told

133

her. If Aileen had used even half of her grilling capability on him, there was no doubt that he would have told her all about Emma.

Petesy was straight into my office as soon as I got there, wanting to know how Aileen was feeling this morning. 'Fine,' I said, in a tone of voice that made it clear I was not interested in plucking any more feathers off that owl. Then I remembered what Aileen had told me about Grievous, our favourite escaped convict. I said:

'You never told me about the Wheel keeping Grievous stashed away at the Condiments' place.'

'You never asked,' he said. 'How was I supposed to know you were interested?'

I didn't even think about trying to answer that question. I was finding it hard to keep track of the different spins I had put on the different amounts of information I had handed out to Petesy, Neil, Aileen, and everybody else I had recently been involved with. I said:

'You didn't hesitate to let Aileen know. I hope you haven't been going around telling the whole world about Grievous.'

'Of course not.' Petesy was trying to sound indignant, but there was the unmistakable clink of guilt in the background of his voice. I had to chase that one. I proceeded to grill him, Aileen style, until he admitted:

'Well, all right, I might have mentioned it to somebody, but only once.'

He tried to avoid my eyes, but I didn't let him off the peg. I just kept on staring at him without blinking, to show that I was waiting to hear the details. Eventually, Petesy took a deep breath, and dropped the bone:

'It was these two guys ... the other night ... when that girl Sophie dropped me off ... I got into your car, and they grabbed me from behind ... they were waiting for you ... hunched down in the back seat.'

'Hengist and Horsa,' I exclaimed. 'The bastards who beat me up. Why didn't they beat the shit out of *you* then?' At that moment, I was wishing they had.

'They recognised me. When they realised it wasn't you, one of them shone a flashlight in my face. They've done the odd casual muscle job for the Wheel, and they know of my connection. It would have been suicide for them to cause harm to me – and they knew it.'

'So you're fireproof, Jack,' I said. 'How come you had to tell them where Grievous is?'

He shrugged. 'They asked me,' he said, simply.

Suddenly, the whole world seemed to twist around, and left me reeling, as if I had stumbled on to an alien planet without noticing. Too many things were happening today that didn't make sense – and I had no control over any of them. What with Aileen behaving like a pregnant nun, and now Petesy. I mean, he may be a bit green round the horns, but he's definitely not thick.

'Let me get this straight,' I said, as if I was a TV-show private eye repeating the clues in order to let the more backward members of the audience catch up. 'You freely handed out information that could cause a load of problems for the Wheel – your own uncle – and maybe even get somebody killed?'

While these words were coming out of my mouth, the sun was coming up in my brain. I realised that I was the backward member of the audience, who hadn't understood what was going on.

I asked him straight out:

'What makes you so anxious to puncture the Wheel's operation?'

16

One thing I had to do, was get that report to the Wheel. You know, the one with the details of the Solihull house and its owners. Normally, my first impulse would have been to send Petesy to deliver it, but considering how unstable he was becoming, I decided that might not be such a good idea.

So what I did was, I picked up the phone on my desk, and called Basil to ask for an address where I could mail my report to the Wheel. He gave me one – a box number in Birmingham, it was. I photocopied the report, before putting it in an envelope and sending Peasel to the post office to put a second-class stamp on it. There was still plenty of time before the Wheel's deadline, and I had reasons of my own for not wanting him to get his hands on the report *too* soon. But at least I had now discharged my current responsibilities to the Wheel.

My next move was going to be a dead clever one. I would do nothing at all. Let the bastards get on with their slimy manoeuvrings, while I watched from the sidelines or preferably didn't watch at all. I'd had enough. My priority was to placate Aileen, and prove to her that I had done nothing wrong. Why should I take all these risks and ruin my digestion, not to mention my relationship, when it would suit me so much better to drop back into my comfortable life where the only threat was having to look at the occasional crummy cottage in the country?

Yes, why *should* I et cetera? I kept asking myself the same question right through the day – until late afternoon, when my favourite copper turned up to give me the answer. Neil breezed into my office and parked himself on the visitor's chair.

'It's finger out time, Kenny,' he said, without so much as a good afternoon or how are you. 'I need results, and I need them yesterday . . . and you're just pissing about, enjoying yourself in a game of cops and villains. Well, you just keep reminding yourself that I can have you put away for a long time if I choose – and that option looks more and more attractive every day that you spend pratting around. All I get is a load of nonsense about some bleeding house in Solihull, for Christ's sake.'

I couldn't help thinking Neil sounded as if he had been taking nagging lessons from Aileen. I said:

'What about your happy medium, Madame Kazza . . . surely you haven't given up on her?'

He gave me a shrivelling look.

'Come on! You know, and I know, that's a load of crap. We're trying to let all that unfortunate fortune-telling business slip quietly down the back of the sofa. There are two things you are going to do for me. First, find out through your bent contacts where that bastard Dalgetty is hiding. Second, get me evidence that can put a stop to the plague of stolen goods that the whole Midlands is awash with.'

I sighed and said, 'OK, OK, you've got me by the balls. I think I might have a lead on where your runaway is.'

It occurred to me then that it would suit me fine if the cops picked up Hengist and Horsa for the damage done to Nick Pearson. It would suit the cops themselves too, on account of they would be cutting out someone who was after the same parcel as they were. But *they* didn't know that, and I don't really like the police to have information they don't actually need. I asked Neil:

'How about if I were to point you at the thugs who beat up Nick Pearson?'

Neil was less enthusiastic than I had hoped for.

'Well, I suppose it's always a good idea to put villains behind bars whenever you can, but it's not as important – well, not to me, anyway . . . I mean, catching a pair of low-grade tearaways won't get me transferred to where the big-time action is. You don't get to the top in the job when you're stuck in a backwater like Stratford.'

I found that last bit a damn sight more persuasive than all Neil's threats. I would fight my way to the front of the queue for anything that might get Neil transferred out of my life. Now both the carrot and the stick were pointing straight at me.

However, I still didn't feel like rushing headlong into telling Neil everything I knew, or thought I knew. I would have to think about how to go about it, how much information he could be trusted with, and how to get hold of some actual evidence.

Then there was the problem of Petesy. I supposed he was kind of a friend now – so I would have to try to protect him, even though he didn't deserve it. If only he could abstain from doing bloody foolish things, like telling Hengist and Horsa where they could catch up with Grievous. At least it didn't seem that his reasons were malicious – well, not towards me.

I could hardly bring myself to believe his so-called 'frank admission' – it was just too far-fetched after all the macho stuff he had previously been handing me about his criminal ambitions. Anyway, this is what he told me:

'See, if I'm honest with myself, I've got to admit that what I really want is to get my arse out of this crime stuff,' he said. 'I'm just not cut out for it – working for the Wheel and all.'

Petesy sighed, trying to make himself sound tragic.

'The trouble is that I know too much about all his bent operations, so I'm gonna be in dead trouble if I try to just walk away from it. I saw what happened to the last bloke who tried to run out on the Wheel.'

I thought Petesy might have a point there. I didn't ask exactly what had happened to that bloke – I didn't want to know. He shrugged, and went on:

'So there's no alternative. I'll just have to do anything I can to make the Wheel's whole empire fail and fall apart. Then I'll be able to get on with the next bit of my life in safety.'

It didn't seem to occur to him that he might pull it down on top of himself – or on top of me, for that matter. Christ knows what his next move would be – or how dangerous. Talk about loose cannons!

At that point I still wasn't too worried about Aileen. I knew from past experience that it was mainly a matter of time before she got back to normal. I sometimes think she drums up the occasional tantrum as a matter of policy, just to keep me on the straight arrow.

It was becoming more and more obvious that the whole world and everyone in it were united in a conspiracy which could only result in one thing. Me having to do something about the Condiment Brothers' place in Shirley. Not only was it Grievous Dalgetty's current address, I had become pretty certain that it was also the nerve centre of the Wheel's entire organisation, as such. There was no doubt that the files and records in that office could put a lot of people away for a long time.

And it would have to be done at the first possible opportunity – that very night in fact; before Hengist and Horsa had time to act on the information that Petesy had presented them with.

But first there was Aileen. If I hadn't had so many other things on my mind, I would have been getting very worried about the danger of losing her. And I would really hate that to happen.

When I arrived home at the maisonette, she was seated at the dining-table, busily writing on a sheet of paper in red ball-point. I gave her the benefit of the doubt and greeted her as if nothing had happened. But no – she shrank away from my attempted peck on the cheek and blasted me with her strongest don't-you-dare-touch-me-you-heartless-swine glare.

'Don't you dare touch me, Kendall Madigan,' she said. 'If I

had a car of my own, I would be staying with my dad now. He's got plenty of room in his bungalow . . . it's just too inconvenient for getting to work. So this is a . . . a relationship of convenience until I decide what to do about the next part of my life as a one-person family.'

That shook me. Aileen had never gone this far before. She took her attention away from me, and back to the sheet of paper she was writing on.

'Look, love,' I said, 'whatever I've done, I'm sorry. There's no need for any of this . . . I can explain –'

'Don't bother.' She cut me off without even looking up. 'I don't want to know what you've done, or who you've done it with, and I especially don't want to hear any more of your lies.'

She brandished two sheets of paper; the ones she had been writing on.

'These are our rotas,' she said. 'I'll stick this one on the bathroom door, so we know what times each of us can occupy the bathroom. The other one is for the cooking and washing-up facilities. Oh, and I've put the spare duvet out on the sofa, so you should be quite comfortable . . . unless, of course, you'll be going elsewhere to sleep with one of your floozies.'

Floozies, for Christ's sake. Where does she dig up these words?

I was starting to wonder how I would get through an evening of sharing the house in a state of daggers, when Aileen solved the problem for me, by going out. She didn't say where she was off to – or anything else for that matter – but I assumed she was on her way to dramatise every detail of my suspected wayward behaviour so that Sally could join her in condemning me. Anyway, it made it easier for me to get ready for my night's work at the Condiments'.

My preparations didn't take long. The shower cubicle in the maisonette has a light-fitting set flush into the ceiling, and if you give it a quarter turn, the whole unit comes loose and dangles by its wires. This leaves a seven-inch hole through which I can reach into the recess above the ceiling. The space is about six inches high and stretches off in all directions. This is where I keep various things that a completely law-abiding citizen would be unlikely to have in their possession. I took a chair into the bathroom to stand on, and got my burgling equipment out of its hiding place. I also changed into more appropriate clothes.

I dug Aileen's little camera out of her knicker drawer, where she keeps it. It was one of those small automatic jobs that does everything for you; it has automatic focusing and film winding, and decides for itself whether a flash is needed.

Then there was this little black leather bag which I keep for occasions when I need to carry a number of smallish items that would clutter up my pockets. Aileen's camera went in there along with her spare spool of film. The other things I put in the bag were my burgling tools, a small flashlight, a couple of screwdrivers, and a pair of black gloves made of some thin material.

When my preparations were complete, it was still too early, so I tried to relax in front of the television until it was time to leave, but found I couldn't concentrate.

When I finally went out, I did so silently, on my black sneakers to match the black jeans and sweatshirt. I could have been a crack SAS man.

Nothing moved in Tagley Road. The Condiment Brothers building was the only place that showed any sign of life; and that was only because the lights of the reception area had been left on to spill a yellowish glow out through the plate glass door.

On my one previous visit, I hadn't really taken in the details of the premises from the outside. I studied it now, from my car, parked on the other side of the street and maybe thirty yards along. It was a three-storey building with the top-floor windows jutting out from the roof – dormer windows, I think they're called.

The main reception entrance was not a suitable way in for me, it being so well lit. I had thought there would be a vehicle entrance of some kind so that the hearses could get in. Now it was obvious there was no such thing – not at the front anyway – so there must be a way in for vehicles at the back, from the next street, or an alley. I should probably find it and try there.

On the other hand, there was a second person-sized door at the front. It was discreetly recessed a couple of feet back into the building, and was positioned at the extreme left of the

Condiments' premises, only inches from the adjoining building. It looked good to me. While I worked on it, I would be hidden by the door being in deep shadow.

Decision made, I drove off and parked a couple of streets away. As my Auntie Ursula would have said, there's no need to let the cat out from under the blanket.

Before locking my car, I picked the pistol out of its nest in the driving seat, and slipped it into my little black burgling bag. As you know, I really hate guns, but this had the potential to become a very sticky situation, seeing as how I was walking right into the spider's den. Fully equipped, I walked back to Tagley Road, keeping in the shadows as much as possible.

It was reassuring to find that some of my old skills still lurked not far below the surface. It was a pretty good lock, though, and was taking longer than I hoped, so I was soon sweating with impatience. That's why I was scared shitless to hear a police siren coming fast. Not far behind the sound was a flashing blue light. I had sudden thoughts about alarms that ring in the nearest cop shop, and cowered further into the shadows with my heart thumping ten to the dozen – just about the most useless tactical manoeuvre known to man or beast.

It turned out to be a jam sandwich – a red and white traffic cop car – and it shot past to turn into Stratford Road with howling brakes. Common sense leaked gradually back in as my brain cells pointed out to each other that underworld gang bosses tend not to have their offices equipped with police alarms. I calmed down and finished opening the door.

The beam of my little flashlight showed that I was in a long passage which looked like it went straight through to the back of the building. I moved along it, carefully leaving the door not quite shut behind me. A few yards in, I found a door on the right.

If there was a manual of breaking and entering, one of the main rules it would specify for burglars would be: *Always thoroughly explore the space you are in before moving on*. So I made a mental note and carried on down the corridor. The next thing I found was a staircase going up at right angles. Then another door. Nothing after that until I came up against the end of the passage, featuring another external-style door which must lead to whatever was behind the building. My flashlight revealed a Yale-type lock – relatively simple compared to the lock on the front door. Trust me to do it the hard way.

I turned my light off, opened this back door with the handle provided, and stepped gingerly out into the night. There was enough light to tell me I was in a large yard bounded on the left and the back by a brick wall, about ten feet high. The stretch of wall at the back was interrupted by a pair of wooden gates, now closed, but which are presumably left open during the day, to let vehicles in from the street on the other side. Over on the right was a single-storey open-fronted garage – really just a shed, wide enough to shelter maybe six cars or vans. Dimly gleaming chrome bits indicated four vehicles crouching in the deeper shadows inside.

I stepped back into the passage, leaving the door open. Then I noticed a hook attached to the wall, and dropped it into the matching metal loop fixed to the door. I supposed it was left like this during opening hours, so that employees could get in and out easily. Another rule of burgling: *Always leave an easy exit.* Maybe I should write that manual. As I turned to go back along the passage, my flashlight snagged on something on the other wall, just inside the back door. A board, with a row of hooks; and on the hooks – bunches of keys. I grabbed the biggest bunch, in the hope that they might save me some lock picking later on. Then I headed back down the passage and closed the front door.

OK! I could pause to draw breath, now that I was safely inside and unlikely to be disturbed. It was a fair-sized building, but I knew roughly where my destination was – or my first destination, at least. It was the Wheel's office upstairs, behind a door falsely marked 'Embalming'. I was actually quite pleased not to have to search the downstairs rooms; you never know what unspeakables you might find in a funeral parlour. I guessed it was unlikely that bodies and coffins and such would be taken upstairs, for weight and handling reasons, so the ground floor would have all the undertakers' work rooms, as well as the public areas.

Then there was the matter of Grievous Dalgetty, the dreaded escapee. I reckoned it was a safe bet he would be held on the top floor, two storeys up from the ground. That was simple common sense, since he would need to be well tucked away from the prying eyes of the mortician's staff. I wasn't quite sure how I would go about the task of checking for his presence. I mean, this bloke was dangerous, so I was not much in favour of breaking into the penthouse suite to shine my flashlight on the (presumably) sleeping robber. Well, I left my brain cells to chew on that one. The office came first.

So, it was up the stairs for me, where I found the Wheel's room quite easily, in spite of coming at it from the opposite direction, and in the dark. The office was locked up, of course, but it had another Yale-type lock. I checked out the bunch of keys I had picked up downstairs – and cursed when I realised they were all car, or at least vehicle, keys. I flung the useless things into my bag.

Never mind, a few minutes of fiddling with my trusty lock-picking tools, with the little flashlight held in my teeth – and I was inside the Wheel's office.

I bee-lined straight for the filing cabinet, which took no more than five seconds to unlock. It was crammed full of files, all neatly labelled and arranged in alphabetic order. I grabbed the one marked 'Madigan-K', and stuffed it into my bag. After a moment's hesitation, I also took the 'Curtain-P' file.

Then I went to work with the camera. Conditions were not good for reading through wads of paper, so I took pictures more or less at random, with four sheets of A4 in each picture. I went first for files with names I recognised, like 'AutoSupCo', 'Drennan's of Wellesbourne', 'Cicada-Silver', and so on. After these I just guessed.

There was no file for Project Parcel – must be in use, I thought. By the time my film, about one and a half spools, was all used up, I had pictures of more than a hundred pieces of paper. Surely that would be enough evidence to put the Wheel away for ever. Or at least enough to persuade the cops that it was worth getting a warrant to come in and seize the rest of the files.

Of course, that took a lot of flashes, and I ended up with my eyes so dazzled that I could hardly see to lock up the filing cabinet. Now I was sure I had something valuable, I put the two exposed spools away in the pocket of my jeans. It was conceivable I could be parted from my black bag, but not from my jeans – well, not unless Sam or Del were lurking somewhere in the building.

Back in the corridor, I looked around for the stairs to the next floor. It took me a couple of minutes and quick looks into several rooms, before I realised that they must be behind the only other door that was locked. A sign said 'Private – no admittance'. Another Yale; I was getting plenty of chances to practise my lock-picking skills. Sure enough, it opened towards me to reveal the stairway, narrower than the one going up from the ground floor, but neatly carpeted – more like stairs in a house.

I decided to go up these new stairs just to have a look around – there must still be at least one more lock between Grievous and me. That was when the sky started to fall down the grid. I had done everything in almost total silence since I entered the building. Not that I thought there was anybody around to hear – just good burgling practice. So when the sound came, it pummelled my eardrums like an avalanche.

17

Actually, it's a fairly muffled cracking, or splintering noise. At first I wonder if it could be Grievous moving around upstairs. But this noise is coming from below. I freeze. I switch off my light. The noise comes again. Somebody is breaking in. Somebody who doesn't care about covering his tracks – or maybe lacks my level of craftsmanship. Anyway, it sounds like a crude jemmy operation.

Footsteps move along the passage downstairs. I suspect there is more than one set of feet. Doors are opened – and closed. A voice says:

'Grab one of these chairs and use it to prop the door shut . . . so's it looks from outside as if it ain't been busted.'

Scraping and bumping sounds. Feet pass the foot of the staircase. More door activity. When the feet reach the end of the passage, a voice says:

'Hey, would ya look at that . . . the careless buggers have only gone and left the back door wide open. If we'd a' come in that side, we wouldn't a' had to smash the bugger down.'

Christ, I think, they don't come much thicker than Hengist and

Horsa. It's amazing they've stayed out of jail long enough to find Grievous. But no time for philosophy – the footsteps are starting up the stairs and light is dancing on the wall at the bend in the staircase. I'm still at the foot of the carpeted stairs to the top floor, with an urgent need to avoid becoming visible to the snooping eyes which are walking up the stairs towards me. I pull the door closed behind me with the handle turned so that there will be no sound of a lock springing shut. I slowly release the handle and tiptoe in the pitch dark, up to the top floor.

Some discreet use of my flashlight shows me a carpeted passage. The doors I see at first have a flimsy look. They can be ignored. The last one on the left looks more fertile, because of being substantial and also because of the two large bolts which are preventing it being opened from the other side.

I'm reaching a hand out towards one of these bolts, when I get distracted by a commotion from downstairs. Voices are raised in what sounds like anger. I move back to the top of the staircase I have just come up, and hear more shouting. I should have known that the Wheel wouldn't leave his headquarters unattended, especially while it was harbouring a prisoner. See how right I am to be dead silent? If Hengist and Horsa hadn't turned up, I would have been in and out without disturbing the nightwatchman.

Now there is lots of grunting, stumbling feet, and other sounds of struggling bodies. This goes on for maybe a minute before there is a multiple thud – like a limp body collapsing to the floor. Then it all goes quiet again. I'm pretty certain it *is* a limp body making its way to the floor.

But whose limp body?

However, there's no time to worry about other people. The seriousness of my own predicament is just starting to filter through my brain cells. There is only one way out of the top floor of this building; and that involves getting past a pair of murderous nutters (the struggling sounds stopped when *one* limp body dropped to the floor, so H and H must have claimed the victory – logic, see). And it won't be long before they get round to exploring in my direction. I make the discovery that I'm sweating though it isn't a hot night, and I wouldn't be surprised if they can hear my heart thumping. The only point in my favour is that they don't know I'm here.

I go back to the door with the bolts, and slide them back –
carefully, for the sake of silence. I use the handle to ease the door
open, and slip through, closing it behind me. No time for creep-
ing around in the dark. I grope for a switch. The place floods
with light.

It's quite a big room, comfortably furnished, and equipped
with television, stereo, cooking facilities, a dining area, and a bed
in the farthest corner. An open door leads to a bathroom. I am in
a well-appointed bedsitter like many you would find in a big
city.

Except for the steel bars across the window.

The bed is occupied by a long thin figure which is in the act
of waking up, on account of the sudden bright light. I shake him
to speed up the process. Drowsily, he asks:

'What the fu . . . wha' are you doin' here?'

'Get dressed quick,' I tell him, 'I'm getting you out of here. I'll
explain while you get dressed. Just do it as fast as you can.'

Credit where it's due; Grievous doesn't waste any time. And
as I get the situation across to him, it becomes obvious that he
has no great wish to be reunited with his former accomplices. We
barely have time for some makeshift preparations before the
invaders arrive muttering outside the door. They could just turn
the door handle and come in, though I am hoping they will
fiddle with the bolts in the dim light of their torches, thinking the
door needs to be unbolted.

However, it turns out that I've drastically over-estimated their
intelligence, because what they do is, they solve the problem
with the jemmy – and they don't stop until they've converted the
door jamb to matchwood splinters. I would laugh if I wasn't so
shit-scared. Eventually, the door swings slowly open, and the
nutter with the light shines it round as much of the dark room
as he can from outside. Of course, this doesn't allow him any
sight of Grievous and me huddled behind the door, but the beam
settles on the bed, where it reveals a lumpy shape under the
covers.

Instead of coming straight in, the stupid sods stop to hold a
conference. I hear one say:

'I'll go in and wake him up. You go to the foot of the stairs and
keep watch. There might be another guard wondering why his
mate hasn't come back.'

146

It sounds to me like somebody is intent on double-crossing his partner, by getting him out of the way while he tries to make a deal with Grievous. Anyway, Horsa (or Hengist) just grunts and moves away down the passage. The other one comes into the room and tiptoes towards the bed. That's our moment to nip round the door, pull it shut behind us, and slide the bolts home.

About this time, it is becoming obvious to me that my cunning plan has sprung two leaks. The first is that only one of these blokes was caught in the trap; and the other is that the door jamb has probably been damaged too much to hold the bolts for long. Still, we have improved the odds, at least for the moment.

I'm in front, as we charge down the narrow stairs, in the hope of an element of surprise. The geezer on guard there hears us coming. He shines his flashlight our way. At the same moment, my light sparks highlights off the jemmy that he's swinging at my head. The chaos intensifies as the nutter in the room upstairs throws in some confused shouting for his mate to stop arsing about and let him out.

I twist aside as much as I can in the confined space. The jemmy misses my head. It thumps into my right shoulder. Grievous is a couple of steps higher. He lashes out with a foot. It's either well aimed or lucky. It knocks the jemmy out of the bloke's hand. My forward impetus brings me into forcible contact with this guy, and we bundle each other through the broken door at the foot of the narrow stairs – into the first-floor corridor.

We fall to the floor, fighting like starving weasels, though I am at a definite disadvantage on account of my right arm is too numb to be much use. My memory of that fight is a bit hazy, though I know it hurt more afterwards than it does at the time. Anyway, it is brought to an end by Grievous, who has picked up my flashlight so he can see well enough to deliver a shower of kicks on any bits of my opponent that can be reached. This has the desirable effect of making him back off to seek safety further down the corridor.

I take a deep breath and get to my feet, almost tripping over something bulky.

'Shine that light over here,' I tell Grievous. 'There's something on the floor.' And then I wish I hadn't bothered. It's the man I saw in the reception area on my first visit to the Wheel; the black beetle – maybe a Condiment Brother? Whoever he is, I can tell that any future involvement he might have with a coffin will have to be from the inside. His skull is seriously caved in, and sticky-looking stuff is oozing out. Somebody has crushed this black beetle.

The villain trapped upstairs is still yelling to be let out.

My look at the body only takes about five seconds, but that is enough. I forget how much I'm hurting.

'Let's get the fuck out of here,' I say, postponing for later the urge to throw up. I grope around for my black bag which I have dropped in the confusion, and lead the way downstairs to the ground floor and straight out the open back door to safety.

What safety?

There we were, in the back-yard. Even in the half-illumination that was leaking over the back wall from a street light, it didn't take us long to realise that there was no clear exit. Of course, I could have had the vehicle gate open in a few minutes, but we didn't have a few minutes, what with two enraged ruffians regrouping to come after us.

I grabbed Grievous by the sleeve, and told him, 'Front door.' We wheeled round and went back in the way we had just come out. Too late. Feet were thundering down the stairs. Two voices were asking each other which way we went. Even blokes as hard-of-thinking as these ones couldn't have thought we had gone out the front, so they would be on to us in a flash.

So we ended up back out in the yard, crouching in the shadows, while the villains were shining their torches around in search of us. They were not in so much of a rush now, because they knew they had got us bottled up.

We were in the vehicle shed, huddled against a car in the deepest shadows, watching the flashlight beams draw nearer, when I got the idea of hiding *inside* the car. Well, it wasn't locked, so we crawled in, Grievous first. He slid across to the driver seat to leave room for me. It was a big car, so we weren't cramped. I just lay curled up on the seat with the smell of leather in my nostrils, clutching my shoulder, while the hairs on the back of my neck tried to crawl away to a safer place. It felt like ages, but couldn't have been more than half a minute, before I got another idea. I rummaged around in my bag for that useless bunch of keys. I whispered:

'See if one of these fits the ignition.'

There was quite a long pause while Grievous tried several of the keys. Then, 'Bingo!' he said. 'Fasten your seat belt.'

The noise of the starter motor changed the world. The engine caught on the second attempt. We were sitting up now; no point in hiding any more. Grievous slipped the automatic gear lever into drive – and a whole bundle of things happened, all too fast for any thinking to take place; and in a much shorter time than it takes to tell.

We started moving forward. Grievous found the headlight switch. Either Hengist or Horsa jumped into our path. His mate stayed off to one side. Grievous started to accelerate. The bloke in the headlights didn't move. I got worried that we were going to hit him. I stuck my head out of the open window and yelled for him to get out of the way. He didn't. With my left hand, I whipped the pistol out of my black bag, which was already open because of the keys. I leaned out of the window and fired it at the ground in front of him. He went down, clutching his leg, and rolled out of the way.

I was pleased. I didn't want him to get run over. I hadn't shot *at* him, as such, but the bullet must have ricocheted off the ground, and hit him in the leg.

The front of our car crashed the wooden doors at about thirty miles an hour. For a dreadful moment I thought we were going to bounce back, but the gates rended apart with a shriek of complaint, to deposit us slewed sideways on to the street outside. Grievous kept his foot on the accelerator, causing us to travel down the street with a piece of gate clattering along behind.

I looked round. The car we had hijacked was a hearse – a Rolls-Royce, in fact. With the weight that thing packed, you could barge your way out of Fort Knox.

A couple of corners later, I decided we had gone far enough, and told Grievous to stop. We got out, and I led the way through the back streets, to my car. I told him to get into the driving seat, on account of my right arm was still in no condition to be used for anything. The good news was that I was pretty sure no bones were broken.

'Just drive,' I said. 'I'll tell you where to go.'

In fact, I hadn't a clue where to go; I just wanted to lay down some distance between us and the mayhem we were leaving behind. Grievous just did what I said, without opening his mouth. In fact, this bloke had not uttered a word since I woke him. I had no idea whether he even wanted to be rescued from the clutches of the Wheel. The only thing I knew for sure was that he was quite anxious to avoid a reunion with his old mates from his robbery days.

He never even said a word when I shot at that bloke to save his life. All this silence was continuing beyond the call of duty. I suppose he must have been thinking things through.

Still waters run deep, I thought. My Auntie Ursula would have sniffed at that, and pointed out that still waters don't run at all – that's what makes them still.

Anyway, I wasn't in the mood for idle chatter myself, because I now had the problem of what to do about my new companion. As you know, I had never intended to let him out of his penthouse pad; it was only the intervention of Hengist and Horsa that caused that cock-up.

When we had put several miles between ourselves and the Condiment Brothers' premises, Grievous pulled in and stopped the car in a shallow parking bay across the front of a row of shops.

'Right,' he said, 'thanks for gettin' me oot of that fucking place. It wis worse than the Scrubs.'

I tried to look modest in the dark, and was about to say something to indicate that I was graciously pleased to accept his gratitude, when he added:

'But yer bloody interference has left me wi' a quandary. Ye see, I just wanted tae do my time. I would have been oot and free in another nine months, wi' maximum good behaviour. And I had plans. Then you and yon soddin' Wheel have to go and stick a spoke up my plans. So what does he want now – your bastard-ing boss? Is he no satisfied wi' the information I gave him?'

'How the hell should I know?' I said. 'I wasn't working on his behalf when I broke into the mortician's. More kind of . . . you know . . . private enterprise. As far as I'm concerned you can go any place you bleeding want. You're free.'

'Huh!' he snorted. 'It's no' that fucking easy. That becomes obvious when ye examine my range of options. I can turn myself in, and do a longer stretch wi' nothing to look forward to when

I get oot. I can keep on the run wi' no visible means of support. My only chance is gone; yon Wheel said he wis goin' tae cut me in on the loot if I told him where to find it. In the end there was nothing else to be done ... I caved in and told him what he wanted to know. He said he was making arrangements.'

'Well, I happen to know that he *is* making arrangements,' I said, at the same time thinking that the chances of Grievous ever getting anything out of it were pretty remote, if I knew anything about the Wheel.

'Aye, maybe so, and maybe no',' Grievous said, 'but I canny go back tae the undertaker's. It'll be swarming wi' the filth, now that it's the scene of a murder.

'Not to mention a shooting,' he added. Getting at me now.

My brain cells had been beavering away all by themselves, during that conversation, and they chose this moment to come up with a suggestion. I put it to Grievous – very carefully, because this was a bloke who was not averse to performing violence on people. On the other hand, I knew from recent experience that he was capable of keeping his head straight in a crisis, and that he would support a mate as long as he thought it was in his best interests. We examined my proposition from every angle we could think of. He turned out to be quite bright, and finally agreed.

Before we did anything else, I had a priority task of my own. Following my directions, Grievous took us to where the road crosses a river, and I threw the trusty Smith and Wesson pistol off the bridge, into the dark waters below. Now there could be no danger of me ever using it again.

Then, while Grievous got on with the driving, I turned my thoughts towards the planning of the daring operation ahead of us.

Kenny Madigan, the big-time criminal brain.

18

The bungalow was in darkness. I knocked on the front door.
Nothing.

I got Grievous to hammer on it with both fists. After a couple of minutes, a light came on inside, and we heard movement behind the door. It opened.

'Hello, Kenny. Great to see you. Don't tell me Aileen's kicked you out of the nest, yuk, yuk.'

Peter didn't seem the least bit surprised to find me outside his front door at three o'clock in the morning. He was wearing a white bathrobe with blue piping, and what looked like a regimental badge on the breast pocket.

'Come on in and have a drink. And your friend.'

'Oh, yes,' I said. 'Meet Grie ... er ... Cameron. Actually, Cameron needs a bed for the night, or what's left of it. Could you do us a great favour?'

I turned to Grievous.

'This is Peter, my ... a good friend.'

'No problem, dear boy,' Peter said. 'Always glad to help strays, you know. Dogs, cats, hamsters, whatever ... Yuk, y ...'

Peter broke off in mid-sentence as the light came on. While he was talking, we had been moving in through the porch and hallway which were only lit indirectly by the light in Peter's bedroom further back. Now we were in the living-room, where Peter switched on the light.

'My God, Kenny. You look as if you've been in the wars. These bruises must hurt like hell. Come on, let's get you cleaned up.'

I didn't understand what he was talking about until I took a look at myself in the mirror above the mantelpiece. I hardly recognised my face. It was covered with bruises and scratches, and was stained with dried blood that had run down it from a glistening cut above my eye. I touched the other eye – the one that had all the colours around it – and winced with pain.

'Bloody hell,' I said. 'But I think my shoulder is the worst. It still hurts to use my arm, so I don't think I can drive yet. The way I feel now, I just want to get home and crawl into bed – and Aileen will be worried. Any chance of a lift?'

Peter was one of those rare people who will do anything for anybody, any time, with never a complaint, and no questions asked. I felt guilty about taking such outrageous advantage of his good nature, but I had the clever idea that Aileen might be reassured by the fact that I was delivered home by her dad – and sufficiently worried by my injuries to forget about her grievances.

Peter got Grievous installed in a spare bedroom. Then he dressed himself in a well-pressed pair of flannels and immaculate blazer over a clean white shirt and silk tie – ideal kit for a run to Stratford in the middle of the night.

It worked for me. Aileen came out of the bedroom looking sleepy – attracted by the sound of her dad's voice, which is seldom used quietly. She gasped at the sight of my face, and went into her mother hen act. Once Peter left, which he did almost immediately, I was tenderly sponged, band-aided, had my shoulder massaged, and put to bed. I lay there feeling pleased at having started my comeback into Aileen's good books. Still, I knew very well that there was still a long way to go before I redeemed myself enough to break free from the dark looks and pointed remarks. Maybe I could suggest going to look at cottages in the country.

That last idea sent me off into a well-deserved sleep.

The next day being Saturday, I didn't have to try to go to work. I woke up about 11 a.m., feeling refreshed and starving. I got up, threw some breakfast together, and decided to take it easy for the rest of the day, to let my aches settle into the background. Aileen had gone to work, of course, so I had the maisonette to myself.

An examination of my face showed me that it didn't look all that bad with the dried blood washed off. The bruises would soon fade, and my right hand and arm were back in working order, though the shoulder still hurt like hell.

Once breakfast was over, my brain slipped back into gear, and suggested switching the radio on, to find out whether any of my recent activities had caused waves in the news. I was in time to catch the midday bulletin from BRMB in Birmingham.

There were a few interesting scraps: a humorous item about a hearse being stolen by joy-riders from a mortician's yard in Shirley; in another part of the city, a man had been brought into a hospital Accident and Emergency department to have a bullet extracted from his leg. The gunshot injury was said to be 'not life-threatening, and in fact, quite superficial'. Both the wounded man and his companion were helping the police with their enquiries, but were not themselves under suspicion for any crime.

I suppose I *should* have been pleased to hear it was superficial.

Not a word on the radio about a vicious murder – or even a break-in at that mortician's premises in Shirley. The Wheel's people must have done a terrific cover-up job, considering how little time they had to do it in.

I wondered how the Wheel would react to the loss of his precious human package. Would he cancel Project Parcel now? Somehow, I didn't think so. Then I remembered something that had slipped my mind in all the excitement. It was, in a way, the most important outcome of my trip to Condiment's – the camera spools that contained the power to end the Wheel's reign of terror. So with a bit of luck, the police could close down his operation almost immediately, and it wouldn't really matter whether the Wheel cancelled the operation or not.

I knew from Grievous (I supposed I should call him Cameron, now that we were in some kind of partnership – but I still thought of him as Grievous) that he had told the Wheel the truth about where the hidden proceeds of his robbery were to be found. Of course, he had only done so in desperation, and with the promise of being cut in for a share.

The main thing I didn't understand was what problems the Wheel could be having in his attempts to get his hands on the loot. I mean, it must be a hell of a set of circumstances that involves a whole family who live in a particular house in Solihull. As my Auntie Ursula would have said: it's a flat fish that seeks the shallow water.

And I now knew straight out of the horse's mouth that the money was not stashed away anywhere in Solihull. Unfortunately, I didn't know where the money actually *was* hidden. Grievous hadn't yet let *me* in on the big secret – there's a limit to trust among villains – but *he* didn't see how there could be any great problem about getting hold of the money. He was as puzzled as me, when I told him about the Wheel's elaborate preparations.

Well, we would discuss it the next day, Sunday, and make detailed plans to return the loot to its wrongful owner.

I was beginning to enjoy my day of relaxation, when there was a knock at the door. Petesy was there, being lectured by Miss Downie on the evils of alcopops. I gave the old baggage a cheery wave, and rescued the lad, by letting him in.

'I had to come and see you, Kenny,' he began anxiously, as he stepped through the door.

'Yeah, yeah,' I said. 'Save it while I make some coffee. Just go in there and sit down quietly for a minute.' I indicated the living-room.

When I handed Petesy his mug of coffee, he gave me a funny look and said, 'Have you been in a fight, or something? You've got –'

I cut him off right there.

'Don't ask,' I said. He looked a bit doubtful, but closed his mouth.

'So what's so important that it brings you all the way here on a Saturday afternoon?'

I was actually wondering if he'd got wind of some of last night's events and the Wheel's resulting problems. But no – he went on:

'Did you mean that? What you said the other day . . . the day I did that report for the Wheel? Oh, by the way, I gave him his copy last night . . . he was very impressed, and he told me the reason for wanting all that stuff about Emma's parents and the house they live in.'

Bloody hell! Isn't initiative a terrible thing? If I'd known Petesy was going to deliver a personal copy to the Wheel, I wouldn't have needed to go to all that trouble getting it posted. But then I remembered why I sent it through the post, and pointed out:

'Wait a minute, you're the one who wanted to bring the Wheel's empire crashing around his head, and now here you are propping it up again. Have you mucked about with the data on his copy of the report, by any chance?'

'No, of course not . . . but that's kind of what I've come to see you about . . . in a way. You see, I've been thinking about all that stuff, and I've decided that the Wheel will probably let me off the hook if I want out. I'll stay until Project Parcel is finished, so as not to let him down, and then I'll tell him. You see, I've realised that he'll have enough dirt on me, to guarantee my silence.'

I nodded. 'Well done, Petesy. That's about the most sensible thing I've ever heard you say.'

Kenny Madigan, the well-known pompous git.

What I was actually thinking was that it no longer mattered what the Wheel did or didn't do. As soon as my spools of exposed film were safely passed on to the police, the Wheel would be finished for good. And I would be in touch with Neil just as soon as I felt up to it – hopefully that very evening.

'So tell me,' I said, 'why did we have to spy on the Ormiston family?'

'Oh, yes . . . that. It's because one of them has the keys and knows the security codes to get us into the place where uh . . . Grievous hid the loot from his robbery.'

I had vaguely thought of something along these lines, so I nodded wisely:

'So he'll be wanting us to break in and hold a knife at the throats of the rest of the family, to encourage . . . Carole, or Reg, to co-operate in getting him into wherever . . . Wait a minute. How would Grievous be able to hide the money in a place that's got that kind of security?'

Petesy shrugged. 'How the hell should I know?'

I quickly changed the subject.

'But what's all this about something I'm supposed to have said the other day?'

'Right,' he said. 'It was when you said you were thinking of starting a second-hand car business. You dropped a hint . . . you said something about . . . putting me in charge of that part of the business. Did you mean that?'

'Sure, why not!' I told him. 'We'll give it a whirl and see how you get on. I'll need to give you a bit of training, but after maybe six months you should be able to handle it mostly on your own. We can have a serious talk about it at work next week. OK?'

Soon after that, Petesy left, looking pleased with himself, and I turned my attention back to the spools of film. They would still be in the left front pocket of my black jeans.

My black jeans had disappeared. I finally tracked them down – spin-dry damp in the washing machine. All the pockets were empty. Great! Aileen was always dead careful about checking pockets before she washed things. I decided she must have put them somewhere safe, but Aileen's idea of a safe place can be a bit unpredictable at times.

I looked in all the likely places before starting on the unlikely places. Eventually, I got round to my clean sock drawer. There, at last, were my burgling tools, my little flashlight, the camera – with no film inside – and the 'Madigan-K' and 'Curtain-P' files I took from the Wheel's office. Aileen had taken her tidiness to new heights, and cleared out my black bag.

But no sign of any camera films. Aileen must have thought the spools deserved an even better hiding place. I had to know; I called her at work, even though it was Saturday and the Jonathan Phillips shoe store would be up to its ears in customers. I nibbled my nails for several minutes before she came to the phone.

'What spools?' she said, sounding puzzled for a moment. Then she caught up with me.

'Oh, you mean those camera films? Don't worry about them. I took them in to the chemist's at lunchtime . . . to be developed.'

'Aileen, you're wonderful,' I said, hoping there was nothing too obviously criminal in those snaps. I had been going to let the cops have them developed. I asked:

'So you'll be collecting the developed photos later this afternoon, then? It's a two-hour service, isn't it?'

'Don't be silly, Kenny,' she said. 'The fast service is ruinously expensive. The three-day service costs less than half as much. I'll pick them up on Wednesday.'

I groaned down the phone. Aileen is at her most dangerous when she's trying to be helpful. But I still love her in spite of it.

'Anyway,' she continued, 'I can't stay here chatting all day. I've got three customers limping around the shop on one shoe. I'm sorry to hear you sounding so much better . . . you deserved to suffer a bit longer. See you tonight.'

Bloody hell, she wasn't letting me off the peg yet. The only good thing is that Aileen didn't find out about my adventures with Sam (and Del). I really did feel guilty about straying in that direction, because I gave into temptation on account of getting over-excited by an attractive woman (or maybe I mean women). The case of Emma Ormiston was completely different – that wasn't my fault at all, as you know. I was just a leaf blowing in the tide.

I certainly wouldn't be going back to Five Ponds again, if I could help it. It wasn't the prospect of going to bed with a pair of gorgeous twins that scared me off; it was the feeling of being treated as nothing more than a sex object.

As long as my brain cells were giving me a hard time, and making me feel guilty, there was one other thing I ought to feel guilty about. Peter didn't deserve to have a desperate and violent criminal dumped on him. Not that I thought that he would be in any danger, as such.

I remembered that I had no transport, having left my car at Peter's bungalow. So I called his number, hoping to arrange for either him or Grievous to pick me up sometime on Sunday, and take me over there to get on with some detailed planning. Then I could drive my car home. I tried several times, and let the phone ring and ring, but there was no reply – which got me worried. I mean, all the coppers in England were quite anxious to meet Grievous, so it wouldn't be a good idea for him to be gallivanting around the countryside.

At a loose end, I went back to my clean sock drawer to look at the Wheel's file on me. It was really just a single sheet of paper with printing on it, though you can get an awful lot of printing on a single sheet of A4. What was more surprising was the photograph that was attached by a paper clip. It showed Aileen and me together – just our heads.

We spent a quiet evening in front of the television. Aileen was still treating me like a smelly dog, so I crawled away to bed early in order to be sure of meeting the day bushy-eyed and full of beans on Sunday morning.

Peter answered his phone in the morning, and agreed to come over to collect me. Aileen insisted on coming along, though I tried to discourage her, but you know what she's like when she gets the bit between her legs; and I could hardly prevent her going to visit her own dad.

On the way, I asked Peter why there had been nobody answering his phone the previous day. He said:

'Work, old chap, work. Some of us have to get things done, you know ... yuk, yuk.'

'Ah,' I said, 'so you told Gr ... Cameron not to answer the phone while he was alone in the house.'

'Not at all,' he said. 'The both of us were down the field all afternoon, mucking out the chickens and the geese. So we had to recover in the evening by getting round to the Seven Stars, the Butcher's Arms, and the Tuppeny Bucket. Good bloke, that mate of yours ... hard worker, as well.'

Grievous was there when we arrived. It was the first time I had ever got a proper look at him in daylight. When I introduced him to Aileen (as Cameron Dalgetty, of course), I had to admit that he didn't look quite so sinister now. Especially as he was decked out in a pair of fawn cavalry twill trousers and a light blue button-down shirt, courtesy of Peter. It was just about the most effective disguise possible; the chances of anyone recognising him in a pub were pretty minimal.

'Aye, Ah know,' he said when he saw my eyebrows going up, 'but Ah drew the line when Pete wanted me tae wear the regimental tie.'

'Were you still in your prison clothes when you got here?'

That was Aileen jumping in with both hands, as usual. She has this knack of homing in on a person's most sensitive areas, and coming straight out with the most tactless questions. The amazing thing is that she gets away with it; they usually just tell her anything she asks. Anyway, this time I changed the subject.

19

'Right,' Grievous said, 'I suppose I should start by tellin' ye how this whole mess came aboot.'

He had supplied us with mugs of coffee from Peter's kitchen, and the three of us – Grievous, Aileen, and me – were seated round the dining-table. Peter had tactfully removed himself by going down the field to collect duck eggs. When I asked Aileen if she wouldn't like to go and give her dad a helping hand, she refused, and said:

'No way! I'm staying here to make sure you're not planning to hijack any more floozies ... and besides, I might be able to prevent you doing something even more stupid than usual.'

I apologised to Grievous, but he seemed quite taken with Aileen, and didn't seem to mind. At least it showed that he still had good taste, even after being in prison.

He told us about the robbery that got him put away. His biggest mistake lay in his choice of accomplices. Apparently, he was not the one who clubbed the driver of the security van, it was one of the others (but he *would* say that, wouldn't he).

'It was when we were doin' our getaway act, that it all went doon the plughole. I was driving the car, the canvas bag full of money was on the passenger seat beside me, and these two bastards were in the back. It was only about a mile to the Range Rover we had pinched and left parked in a quiet street, for us to transfer into. We got there all right, and I stopped behind it. Thae two scunners jumped out and ran to the Range Rover. I was still reaching over to get the money, when a polis car appeared round a corner a few hundred yards behind us, and switched its siren on.'

Grievous was enjoying telling the story. He took a sip of coffee, put the mug down, and held out his hands, palms up, in a theatrical gesture of helplessness.

'What could I do?'

He was building up the suspense now, knowing he had our full attention. I nodded to encourage him.

'Well, I gets off the mark right away ... I pull out and shoot past the Range Rover, and it starts up behind me. So here we are ... in a car chase. Me in front in the getaway BMW, then these two plukes in the Range Rover, followed by the howling cop car. Now, the reason we choose a four-wheel drive vehicle for transferring to, and also why we leave it in that particular spot, is to give ourselves a better chance of getting away, in case the police are catching up with us. Ye see, there's a golf course just up the road. Well, of course, the blokes in the Range Rover put my contingency plan into operation ... drive straight across the golf course, where the coppers can't follow. So naturally, they keep on chasing *me*.'

'But you must have got away – for a while, at least,' I said. 'You managed to hide the robbery money, didn't you?'

'Aye, right enough. Here's what happens. I can see I'm never

160

going to get clean away in the car. Even if I outrun them, they must already have called for reinforcements to head me off, so I gets a bit ahead, and try to go where they would never expect . . . and I end up driving into a car-park – a multi-storey. I leave the car on the ground floor, blocking both entry and exit, and me and the bag of money have it away on foot down the rows of cars.'

Grievous paused and grinned at us.

'It doesnae sound the most sensible thing to do, in retrospect, like . . . but it's hard to chase somebody through a maze of cars, especially when it's starting to get dark, and the lights haven't come on yet. I get out through one of the pedestrian exits at the back of the building, and look round for somewhere to go. It's not like any kind of place I recognise . . . separate buildings, all different styles and sizes, with grass and wide spaces between, and roads and pathways connecting them. Not a lot of people about, either. Then I see something familiar – a construction site, down to my left, just past the last building on the road I'm standing on.

'That's where I head for. See, I'm right at home in a building site, 'cos I've always been in that line of work – served my apprenticeship as a bricklayer in Glasgow, in fact. And it's a good bet that nobody's going to climb all over a load of scaffolding in the dark, on the off-chance of finding me. So I gets inside the building that's under construction, and settle doon to get my breath back . . . and do a bit of thinking, by the way. That's when it occurs tae me to hide the dosh. Well, I know the rozzers will be covering all the ways out of the area, and then in the morning when it gets light, they'll comb the place till they find me. I don't believe I've much chance of getting out free.'

Grievous stopped for breath and a gulp of coffee. Aileen, who had been listening enthralled, said:

'So the money from the robbery is hidden in that building? But why has nobody found it?'

'I was coming to that,' he said. 'Ye see, one of the rooms on the ground floor of that building is fourteen inches shorter than it was intended to be. I found a run of about six feet of internal dividing wall, and built a duplicate wall aboot a foot away from it . . . it was just breeze-block, and all the materials were lying around, and there was enough light coming in from the road. So that's where the loot is – in the cavity between the two bits of wall.

'Later on that night, I tried to get away on foot, but there were too many open spaces to cross, and they nabbed me before I'd gone more than a mile.'

'Wow,' I said, 'that's a great hiding place. But it could be tricky to recover the money.'

'Right!' Aileen said. 'Why don't we go and take a look at this place? Maybe we'll be able to see why your Wheel thinks it's so hard to get into.'

Both Grievous and I stared at her in surprise. She stared back defiantly.

'Well, why not? It can't be terribly far from here.' She turned to Grievous and demanded, 'Can it?'

Warwick University is not actually in Warwick. In fact, it's in a suburb of Coventry. We drove into what I suppose would be called the campus, and Grievous pointed out which road I should take, and there was the multi-storey car-park. We passed it slowly, and he said:

'Here we are, right enough. It's the last building down that way.'

We followed his pointing finger, and stopped opposite the last building. A sign above its entrance identified it as the Gerald Fritwell Memorial Laboratory. Grievous said:

'There's something wrong here. That's no' the right place.'

After a look round, he found the right building; it was now the second last one on the road. Both buildings were of a similar size and configuration – it hadn't occurred to Grievous that the university might have added on a new last building while he was in prison. A broad grin appeared on his face.

'Here's the good news. I've given yon Wheel a bum steer. He'll be lookin' in this laboratory building.'

My brain cells were trying to work out what this meant to me, when Aileen surprised us all by slipping out of the car. We watched her as she crossed the street and spoke to a passing group of students. When she got back in the car, she said:

'Right! They told me this is a lab that does medical research, and guess who its director is – only Professor Ormiston.'

I had been looking it over, and could spot the tell-tale signs of high security.

'Medical research ... that's it. There must be loads of drugs and expensive equipment in there,' I said. 'That would explain the high-tech locks and alarm systems.'

Grievous turned to Aileen: 'What aboot the building next door ... the one we're really interested in? Did you find out anything about that one?'

'Oh, they said it's nothing special – mostly lecture rooms and rooms used for tutorials and such.'

I was beginning to realise that the Wheel's elaborate and expensive Project Parcel had hit the fan, although he was still not aware of it – and if he ever found out that I was responsible, I wouldn't have the life expectancy of a bat in hell. I mean, if I hadn't inadvertently taken his prize captive away from his clutches, he would presumably be taking Grievous along when going to pick up the hidden money, and the mistake would get corrected. As it was, the Wheel would need a stroke of genius to get back on track. He would probably just believe that he had somehow been double-crossed, when he failed to find the money in the place Grievous pointed him at; and the loss of his prisoner would support that belief.

Aileen and I picked up a couple of takeaway pizzas on our way home, having turned down the chance of exploring several pubs in the company of Peter and Grievous. It was getting dark by the time we got back to our maisonette, to find Petesy sitting outside in his car, waiting for us – well, waiting for me, really. He was as jumpy as a bag of frogs.

'Where the bloody hell have you been?' he demanded.

I ignored the question. The only reasonable answer would have been, 'None of your fucking business' – and the look I gave him carried the same sentiments.

He tried again:

'The Wheel has been trying to get in touch with you all day. I've never seen him in such a state ... something has happened ... I don't know what, exactly.'

I could have told Petesy what, exactly, had happened. But, of course I didn't, on account of I wasn't supposed to know about the events at the mortician's. In any case, I was too busy wondering who was on the other end of the icy hand which had just grabbed a hold of my testicles. For some reason, my voice came out higher than I intended:

'So what does he want with me then? What does he think I can do?'

'It's all to do with his precious Project Parcel . . . he's brought forward the next phase of it . . . that would be Phase Four, I suppose. Anyhow, he wants his Sellotape team – that's you and me, remember – to meet him at eleven thirty tonight, ready to swing into action. There isn't time for a proper briefing, so he'll tell us all about it when we meet. I'll drive us there, if you like.'

Petesy came inside with us, and copped a share of our pizzas. Well, actually, I was lucky, because it turned out that Petesy had the same taste in pizzas as Aileen, so he had more of hers than mine. I've never been able to understand how somebody who is perfectly normal in most ways, can enjoy eating something as cheesy as a pizza, with lumps of hot pineapple on top. Still, everyone's got to run on their own legs, as my Auntie Ursula used to say.

The meeting place was a pub car-park up towards Knowle. It was a good place to leave Petesy's car, as anyone spotting it would assume that its owner had drunk too much to drive, and taken a taxi home – a common event, these days.

Basil was driving the Scorpio (a different Scorpio this time), with the Wheel in the back. Petesy got in the front with Basil, while I was invited into the back seat beside the boss. I was pleased it was night-time, on account of there wasn't enough light for the Wheel to make out my bruises and start asking questions.

Once we got on to a road where there was some street light leaking in, I could see that Basil was dressed in black jeans and sweatshirt, just like Petesy and me. The Wheel was also all in black, but his trousers had razor creases, his pullover was probably cashmere, and his dark curls were tucked into a black beret. I guessed it just wasn't dressing-down day for management in this man's organisation.

The Wheel, who was just tucking his mobile phone away, was in no mood to waste time. As soon as Basil got us on the move, he shifted his mouth into gear.

'Right! We're into Project Parcel – Phase Four, in a somewhat premature operation. At the end of the day, I've had to bring it forward for . . . uh . . . compelling technical reasons, which I need not trouble you with. Suffice to say that, so far, everything is going according to plan. My String and Wrapper teams have successfully penetrated the house at Lundy Rise, Solihull – thank you for your excellent report, by the way. Wrapper team remain in possession of the Solihull house, where they are responsible for the security of Professor Reginald Ormiston's wife and daughter. String have taken custody of the Professor, who will perform a certain service for us, in return for the safety of his family. We shall rendezvous with them in due course.'

Meanwhile, the silent Basil obviously knew where he was going, as he threaded the car through the roads and junctions which would eventually bring us to Warwick University. Petesy was the only person present who was unaware of our destination, and of course I wasn't *supposed* to know it.

'Where are we heading for?' I asked, now that the Wheel had stopped talking. But he hadn't finished – it was just a breath break.

'All in good time, Kenny . . . all in good time. As my most reliable team, you two shall join Basil and myself in performing the most crucial role in Project Parcel. We shall enter the target premises, and bring the whole thing to a successful conclusion.'

Petesy put his foot right into the next gap in the Wheel's briefing.

'Why are we doing it in such a rush? Last time . . . at the Silver Cicada . . . you said we could take plenty of time to plan Phase Four, and make sure we got everything right.'

Luckily, we were on an unlit stretch of road at the time, so the Wheel's expression wasn't visible. There was a longer pause before he answered.

'Yes . . . well, there's no point in delaying once all the necessary elements are in place . . . and, as I said before, there is also a technical reason which there is no need for you to be aware of at this moment in time.'

For the first time ever, I thought I could detect flecks of doubt in the Wheel's voice. But he immediately changed back into a more confident gear.

'This is the most complex operation I have ever planned, and I am determined to pursue it to a triumphant conclusion.'

Ha – pride as well as greed, I thought, and decided that the next hour or so was going to be very interesting. Probably not too comfortable – but definitely interesting.

20

Basil stopped the car about a half-mile short of the university campus. We waited with the lights off, Petesy and I wondering what we were waiting for. After about five minutes of dark silence, we found out. The Wheel's phone rang. He answered it with a grunt.

Faint squawks.

'You're sure everything is switched off and de-activated?'

Faint squawks.

'And the cameras?'

Faint squawks.

'The Professor – he's OK and still co-operating?'

Faint squawks.

'Right! Take him back to the car now. Let him call his wife. That'll keep them sweet . . . and it'll let Wrapper team know that the operation is going according to plan.'

Faint squawks.

'No. You take him to the car. Tell Sorab to wait inside the main door till we arrive.'

The Wheel switched off, and said, 'Right! Let's hand out the equipment and get on with it.'

As Basil got out and went round behind the car, the Wheel explained to Petesy and me:

'I am now in a position to divulge to you the information that we have come here to retrieve a large amount of money which Cameron Dalgetty, our parcel, hid inside a wall during the construction of our target building.'

The equipment was packed in a large suitcase that Basil

166

brought out of the boot. We each got a pair of black rubber gloves and a light attached to a headband so as to leave both hands free. There were two walkie-talkie sets, one of which Basil tucked away in a shirt pocket under his sweatshirt. He handed the other one to Petesy, to whom the Wheel explained:

'Basil is our look-out . . . he stays near the entrance. You pass on any messages between him and me.'

Basil never said a word. Funny thing about Basil; he was a nice friendly bloke any time the Wheel wasn't around. But I never heard him utter a single word in the Wheel's presence.

The rest of the equipment consisted of two of Black and Decker's most expensive cordless hand tools with a variety of interchangeable sharp ends, all in their own special loops and holsters around a leather belt. Petesy and I were put in charge of the Black and Deckers and I got to buckle the belt around my waist. The Wheel took responsibility for two lightweight nylon bags, which were currently folded up very small.

When he was satisfied that we were fully equipped, the Wheel said: 'OK! Take us closer, Basil. Just don't park right outside.'

The Wheel's man emerged from the shadows as we merged into them. Then he was outside and we were inside with the door closed, but of course, not locked.

'Keep your lights off while we're still near the door . . . it's got a lot of glass panels.'

The Wheel was casting around on the right of what must have been an entrance hall. Finally he must have found what he was looking for, and led us into a passageway that looked as if it ran to the end of the building. All our lights were switched on now, and we went all the way down to find the last door on the left; then back to the second-last door, through which the Wheel ushered us.

It was a large room, with mysterious instruments and equipment on various tables and benches. There were some set-ups which glowed with a bluish light, while others made an occasional gurgling sound. The windows in here were covered by dark curtains, presumably to prevent anyone outside from viewing the experiments – so we could be more free with our forehead lights.

As you and I would have expected, the Wheel was interested in the wall between this place and the last room on the right off the same corridor. He seemed a little taken aback to find that this piece of wall went all the way across the end of the room in an unbroken run – about twenty feet, I suppose. Still, he acted as decisive as ever when he indicated a section that didn't have cupboards standing against it, and told Petesy and me to get to work. We were to strip off the plaster, preparatory to removing a breeze-block. That would allow us to locate whatever might be in the wall cavity, and then we could cut the wall at the right place.

It was pretty easy really. The Black and Deckers worked fine, and were quieter than I had expected. We were soon lifting a block out of the wall, to place it on the floor. The Wheel shoved his head into the gap, and swore in disgust and surprise, when his light showed the next room. He found it so hard to believe, that he went into the other room, via the corridor – just to make sure that there was a hole in the other side of the wall.

Knowing what I knew, I could sense the Wheel's confidence dropping off him in great lumps. Petesy and I watched him open out a folded piece of paper that he took from his pocket. As far as I could tell, it looked like a rough sketch of a floor plan. He shook his head over it.

The Wheel was still trying to salvage something. He had me drill through the matching wall between the last two rooms off the other side of the corridor, while he watched on the other side until the drill broke through. Then the same thing at both sides of the other end of the building. All the 'just-in-case' things that anybody would try in desperation.

Then we were out of there, with the Wheel keeping very quiet, though I had the impression that if there had been enough light we could have seen steam rising from him. In the car, Petesy foolishly suggested:

'You'll just have to go back and make Dalgetty tell you the truth. If we had brought him along, he would have had to own up to the lie before we did all that work. Wouldn't he?'

There was what I can only describe as a ferocious growl from the Wheel. He busied himself on the phone for a while – ordering the String and Wrapper teams to return Professor Ormiston to the bosom of his family and pull out of the Solihull house. Then he got back to answering Petesy's question.

'That technical reason I mentioned . . . for bringing the operation forward. It was because that devious bastard Dalgetty has got away from me, and I wanted to get to where he said the money was, before he did. As of this moment in time, I haven't a clue where to look for him. He must have known he was going to get out of there; and that was why he lied about where the money was hidden. Fucking ungrateful sod – after me getting him released from prison and everything.'

'Oh,' said Petesy, 'so that's it all over, then. Project Parcel is a bummer, and you'll just have to write it off. Can't win them all, and all that.'

The lad was just trying to help him get over it, I suppose. But the Wheel wasn't ready to give up yet.

'Don't you fucking believe it. I'm not finished with that fucking Scotch git yet. I'll find him . . . and when I do, he'll wish he had never been born.'

I thought it was interesting how our boss had suddenly dumped all his management techniques, just when he got into trouble and presumably had most need of them. Maybe they didn't have much to tell him about how to handle an enterprise which has gone belly-up.

The Wheel went on:

'We're now going to do something I should have done sometime in the last two days. I was too busy getting this operation under way, to do any more than grab the cassettes for safe keeping. Basil – take us to my office at Condiment Brothers . . . we're going to watch the tapes from the closed circuit television cameras. With a bit of luck, we'll get a clear look at the bastards who broke in and ki . . . er . . . took Dalgetty out. This is where our foresight pays off . . . now I'm glad we went to so much trouble and expense to make sure these cameras were well concealed.'

That came as a hell of a shock to me, as you can imagine. Bloody hell, I thought, there goes the rest of my life if I don't get the hell out of here before the cows come home to roost. Aloud, I said:

'OK, then, if you could just drop me at a convenient phone box, I'll call for a cab to take me back to Stratford. I've had a long hard day, and –'

The Wheel broke into my desperate babbling:

'No fucking chance, mate. I need all the brains we have at our disposal. We're all going to watch these tapes together. The more of us who watch them, the better chance there is that one of us will recognise the intruders.'

We sat in gloomy silence for a while. I was having my own private panic all alone inside my head. Meanwhile, the Wheel must have been getting his brain back into gear, while he cooled down and eased back into his management role. So he was back in his icy cool mode when he finally broke the silence to tell Basil:

'OK, maybe Kenny's right. Better drop him back in Stratford ... we'll all benefit from getting some of our night's sleep. There's nothing to be gained by rushing at the problem without having some kind of a plan. We'll look at the tapes tomorrow when we've all calmed down a bit.'

The next morning was Monday, as I'm sure you know. It was Aileen's day off, so she was still sleeping peacefully when I left for work. I walked up to the garage, so as to leave the car for Aileen, who needed it to do what she called a whopping shopping at the Safeway supermarket.

It was a fairly quiet day at Lone Harp, so I had plenty of time to worry, and watch for Petesy's arrival. I was hoping he would be able to tell me more about the Wheel's plans to watch the tapes from the CCTV system at Condiment's, and whether I would be invited to join the party – an invitation I would have to refuse.

There was no immediate need for me launch myself into any serious panic just yet. Probably. These automatic video cameras are pretty unreliable – and even if they were working continuously, and even if there was no dust on the lens to blur the picture ...

Anyway, it was dark all the time I was in there, so there must be a good chance that my face was never lit up while I was facing a camera. Besides, Hengist and Horsa were there too, making bigger waves than I did.

Of course, if that closed circuit TV system happened to feature an infra-red capability for seeing in the dark ...

Nah! The Wheel wouldn't go to all that trouble. Would he? But anyhow, I should be pretty safe because I've got incriminating

(I hope) pictures which I can hold over his head. Only I haven't actually got them, as such – not until Wednesday.

Of course, Petesy would have to choose today to be late.

The morning dragged on past the eleven o'clock-ish cluster of tea and coffee breaks. Still no Petesy. Eventually, at ten to twelve, the phone rang on my desk, and there he was, apologising for not being at work.

'It was the Wheel's fault,' said Petesy, 'he wanted to see me at ten o'clock this morning . . . and he said not to tell anybody.'

'That's OK, mate,' I said, trying to sound casual. 'Will you be coming in this afternoon?'

'No, I'm afraid not. The Wheel wants me to go somewhere with him and Basil. Actually, it's in Evesham, so if I drive my own car there, maybe I'll still have time to come over to Stratford afterwards.'

Christ in a bucket! What the bloody hell could the king of the underworld be after in Evesham?

I asked Petesy:

'Didn't the Wheel mention anything about me going along? I'm supposed to be his representative in this area, after all.'

'Well, no . . . not exactly,' he said. 'But it's got something to do with you, somehow. I don't know.'

I didn't shout at him, though I would have been completely justified. Instead, I sucked in a deep breath and said in a very gentle voice:

'Petesy, why don't you just tell me about your whole conversation with the Wheel . . . as it happened?'

'Right,' he said. 'It was mainly about where that Dalgetty bloke – you know, the one we called Grievous – where he could be hiding out. Well, the Wheel called his police contact on the phone, in case the cops had caught up with him. The chief inspector told the Wheel that Dalgetty still hadn't been picked up. He said the police have a reliable lead, and they're checking all the junk yards . . . you know . . . car breakers, in the Midlands.'

Good old Heather Kazzandra! The cops must be really desperate, if the fortune-teller's information was still the best they could do.

'How do you know all this?' I asked Petesy. 'Did the Wheel tell you in so many words?'

'No,' he replied, 'I was there in the Wheel's office. I heard his end of the call . . . and it was after he hung up that he started asking me about you.'

Here it comes, I thought, and kept my mouth shut. He was about to tell me anyway. He did.

'He wanted to know if you had been going off anywhere with any regularity recently. Like – any place where you never let me go along, or which you acted secretively about . . . so I had to tell him.'

He had me there.

'Tell him what, for Christ's sake?' I yelled down the phone.

Petesy injected a note of it's-so-bloody-obvious-you-pillock into his voice:

'Well, about you sneaking off to Evesham, and being evasive about it, of course. Did you think I never noticed, Kenny? Not that it was any of my business.'

'All right, then – so what? Why would the Wheel give a shit about me going to Evesham?' It seemed like a reasonable question.

He couldn't know anything about my visits to the Five Ponds Garage to see Sam – or Del. And what has that to do with the price of bananas anyway?

'How should I know?' he said. 'All I can tell you is that he asked Basil to suss out the locations of scrap-yards in the Evesham area. Bas came back five minutes later and said there is only one worth considering. It's called Sprott's Spares.'

I knew the place. It has been there as long as I can remember. Not that I went there often – only if I needed a part for something like a 1978 Austin Allegro that had miraculously held on to its rolling death-trap status down through all the rusty years. It isn't fair to charge a customer the full price of a brand new part, when even an oil filter is worth more than the car. Anyway, old Sprott had hung on to his precious scrap-yard, in spite of several charges of allowing noxious substances to leak into the river.

I remembered a funny thing, though, Sprott always had classical music playing on the radio he kept in the dilapidated shed that was the nerve centre of his junk-yard business.

'By the way, Petesy,' I asked, 'do you know if the Wheel still wants us all to look at those tapes from his hidden cameras?'

'Oh, no,' he said, 'the Wheel stayed up the rest of the night, going through them himself, so we're off that hook.'

From where I was sitting, it looked like I was now firmly *on* the hook.

'OK,' I said. 'Have a nice time in Evesham. I'll see you when I see you.'

Much as I was getting to like Petesy, I was forced to the conclusion that he was more dangerous than piranhas in your beer. Talk about lack of discretion. I mean, any information he might have, seemed to be anybody's for the asking. It was certainly no asset for someone serving an apprenticeship for a career in crime. Or second-hand car sales, for that matter – an enterprise that requires pretty much the same standard of ethics.

There must be something I could do to improve the odds against me emerging unscathed out of this complicated farrago (I looked it up) of treachery. I got my brain cells on to the job, but the best they could do was to suggest inviting the cops to swing into action in their usual impersonation of a well-oiled brick.

I had been hoping to put police involvement off until Wednesday, when I would have the photographs which could drop the Wheel into the shit, where he deserved to stay for ever. However, needs must when the cat has died. I sighed and reached for the phone.

21

Neil was at his desk, jumping on me right away with questions about some mysterious break-in at Warwick University, where much mess was made but nothing stolen; and how I must know something about it because of the link with the people in that house in Solihull that I had told him about – and blah, blah, blah ... I switched my ears off until he paused.

Then I knocked the bee off his bonnet by using the words 'car breaker's yard' and 'Dalgetty'. He immediately dragged his feet back to the ground and wanted to hear more details.

'It's in Evesham,' I said. 'It goes under the name of Sprott's Spares.'

Not an easy name to say in a hurry, I discovered. I could almost hear Neil frowning at the other end of the line.

'Evesham? That's not north of here . . . she said it was north. It's further south, if anything. That gypsy moron definitely said north.'

'True,' I admitted, 'but it *is* within twenty-five miles . . . besides, he could easily have been moved.'

'All right,' he said, trying to sound as if he didn't really care, 'tell me more . . . Why should I bother to do anything?'

So I told him:

'OK, Neil, brush me off if you like, but you'll regret it. We both know that Cameron Dalgetty, the great escapee, is rightly your prisoner. But even as we speak, somebody else is heading for Evesham with the intention of getting possession of him.'

'Who?' Neil was starting to sound anxious, in spite of himself.

'Only the Wheel . . . the man responsible for most of the crime that goes on in the Midlands,' I told him. 'If you hurry, you could still get there first.'

'Right!' he said decisively, in a voice that suggested he was about to spring into action. 'I'll meet you there in . . . thirty minutes. OK?'

I protested, 'No, you don't need me –'

But he wasn't having any of that.

'Get to the scrap-yard. That's not an option, Kenny . . . if you want to stay out of prison. I may need you to help identify the villains. And don't start thinking you're off the hook over the Solihull kidnapping . . . we'll get back to that when I have time. Meanwhile, I need to know where you are. Be there.'

The line went dead to prevent any more argument.

Neil had left me with some good stuff, and some bad stuff.

The good stuff was that I had actually got him to do something; and it sounded like he was flinging himself into doing it without putting too much of a burden on his logical abilities. I didn't need him to start wondering about the surrounding bits of the jigsaw puzzle – or asking me questions I knew too many answers for.

Then there was the bad stuff. What possible *real* reason could

Neil have for wanting my presence at what might well become the scene of a crime? Anyway, it looked as if I had no way out of having to make a personal appearance at Sprott's, which might well damage my health, considering who else was going to be there.

Be that as it might, I had to find a way of getting myself to Sprott's scrap-yard in Evesham. As you know, Aileen had my car; and after the last time I used her car, Senga said never again, because she thought something underhand was going on. So I got Brian Miller to give me a lift home, in the hope that Aileen would have finished the shopping and her need for transport.

Luckily, when I got out of Brian's Escort, Aileen was in the process of locking up my car, having already taken the provisions into the maisonette. At first, she was indignant about me wanting my car back – she wanted to go to the health food store for her weekly supplies, as soon as she had tidied away all the groceries. Of course, all that changed as soon as she understood the urgency of my mission. The trouble was that she decided she should go along with me to Evesham.

'For goodness sake, Aileen, it could be dangerous. I'm not having you taking risks like that,' I told her firmly.

Before I knew what was happening, we were in the car, and Aileen was driving us out towards the Evesham road, with me still protesting.

'Shut up, Kenny,' she said.

I shut up. After all, there was plenty for me to think about.

On the road from Stratford to Evesham, not far past Bidford, you come to one of those huge roundabouts that British road planners can't resist sticking in whenever they become afraid they might have provided more than a mile or so of unimpeded roadway. Aileen stopped the car there to give priority to the traffic flowing out of the dual carriageway on our right, past the road we wanted to emerge from, and into the dual carriageway on our left.

If you were driving from Birmingham to Evesham, you would be very likely to do what that traffic was doing – something that was proved by the sight of Petesy's BMW doing it in front of us. He didn't notice us, but his presence made me look out for the Wheel and Basil. They weren't there, of course. Not in that knot of traffic, anyway. But I did see something else of interest. About three cars behind Petesy, and presumably tailing him, were the ugly mugs of Hengist and Horsa in a grey Rover. So they still weren't giving up. It looked as if these bastards would go through anything to get their hands on Grievous and his money.

I pointed them out to Aileen, remarking:

'They needn't have gone to the bother of following Petesy. If they had just asked, he would have given them everybody's address and phone number, and everything else anybody has ever told him.'

Half-way between there and Evesham, a big black Scorpio rocketed past us. It contained the Wheel and Basil. Even if they had been keeping their eyes open, they would only have seen a lone woman driving a nondescript Ford Mondeo. I had the presence of mind to slide right down into the passenger footwell when I detected the distant presence of a Scorpio in the door mirror. Just in case it was them.

It was beginning to look like we were invited to a party – or at least a get-together with all the interested parties. What with the Wheel, Basil, Petesy, Hengist and Horsa, Neil and potentially all the Midlands police forces all converging on Sprott's Spares, why couldn't they do without Aileen and me?

The only person who wasn't going to be there was the one they were all hoping to find – Grievous Cameron Dalgetty.

I told Aileen to coast slowly down the road leading to the scrapyard, and give me a running commentary on what she could see. I was keeping my head well down, so as to be invisible from outside the car. My intention was that we should park in the street where we could watch Sprott's entrance.

'I think that's the gate ahead,' Aileen was saying. 'There's a big wooden door, and it's propped open. I can see the ... oh rats!'

She broke off with a gasp, and said:

'I have to keep going. Your Wheel's car is parked just here ... and they're both sitting in it ... checking out the lie of the land, I suppose.'

I tried to remember the exact layout of the scrap-yard.

'OK, Aileen, drive in, slowly. Tell me what you see.'

'Right!' she said. 'Turning in now ... that big door has seen better days . . . it's in a bad state . . . the road goes straight ahead, full of pot-holes . . . there's a – like a Portakabin on the left . . . some kind of office. A few – four cars parked untidily in the clear area next to the office . . . living cars, that is . . . not like the dead cars which are piled up all over the place. Oh, and there's Petesy's BMW. It's one of the parked cars. He's not in the car; perhaps he's gone into the office. On the other side, there's like a crane thing, and machinery and all that kind of stuff.'

'All right, just keep going, past the office,' I told her. Her words reminded me that the old rotting car skeletons were piled up two or three high around here, more or less ready to be picked up by the crane attached to the nearby crusher, a fearsome device for reducing stripped-down vehicles to half-metre cubes of saleable scrap metal.

But the yard covered quite an extensive area, and I remembered that further on were to be found the more recent additions to stock, in the shape of crashed write-offs, and superannuated geriatrics. They were kept on the ground with fairly easy access.

These last were the ones that provided Sprott's actual Spares. First, Sprott's fat son, Trevor, would reclaim the tyres, wheels, batteries, radios, and any other easily saleable bits. After that, anyone was allowed in to do their own dismantling of the parts they needed. That way, Sprott got paid for doing nothing, except writing out an invoice and receipt. In practice, most of his spares customers were in the garage trade, although there was nothing to prevent members of the public coming along to find a replacement for a broken headlamp or a bent bumper.

Word gets around fast in the garage trade, so nobody in or around the office would think it strange for a car to drive right in; they would assume someone was heading for a particular model of car that they had heard was in a particular position.

'There's a chain-link fence ahead,' Aileen said.

I told her to turn right, and go along the rutted perimeter road, then park near the river bank. I was sure that would put us out of sight of the office. When she told me we couldn't be seen, I came up for air, and we got out to see what was going on, if anything. There was no *visible* sign of life, but the hairs on the back of my neck kept telling me that eyes were watching us from most of the thousands of hiding places all around.

I took Aileen by the hand and we started to thread our way through the dumped cars, on a route parallel to the main drag. I was aiming to put us in a position level with the office, but screened by wrecks. After only a few yards, we came upon an ancient blue Triumph Acclaim with its bonnet up, and a denim-clad bottom sticking out of the engine compartment. As Aileen and I edged our way round this museum piece, the bottom reared up, and its owner turned towards us, holding aloft a handful of large mole wrench.

'Hi-ya, Kenny,' she said, treating us both to a happy smile that made my heart jump with some really mixed feelings. 'Looks like we all have trouble getting our hands on all the parts we want, doesn't it?'

I stammered out an introduction. 'Sam . . . runs the Five Ponds Garage here in Evesham . . . Aileen Morrison . . .'

Not that I was a hundred per cent sure it was Sam, and not Del.

Whoever it was, she used her dirty hands as an excuse for not shaking hands with Aileen. I could see the laughter in her gorgeous brown eyes, when she said:

'Isn't this a great guy. You've no idea how much he helped us out over some crooked parts, a while back.'

I jumped in. I had to say something to keep the conversation moving in a safe direction.

'Look, that's what we've come here about. Remember I told you how I'm helping the police to catch up with these villains? Well, with a bit of luck, they'll be picked up here today.'

Sam laughed. 'Not old Sprott, for heaven's sake? He's a miserable old git, right enough, but –'

'No, of course not old Sprott,' I said, 'but maybe you should get out while you can . . . it could be dangerous.'

'Don't worry about me,' she said, 'I'll just quietly get on with dismantling this steering box, thanks very much.'

Maybe it *was* Del. Who could tell?

She turned back to the Triumph. Aileen and I moved on.

'You must tell me all about her later,' Aileen said.

When we were among the last of the unpiled cars, I pulled open a door of a blue Cavalier that looked as if it had come off worst in a front-end argument with a combine harvester.

I bundled Aileen into the back seat before she knew what was happening.

'Stay here, and keep your head down and you'll be safe,' I told her. 'Hengist and Horsa must be around here someplace, though Christ knows where, exactly.'

And Detective Inspector Neil Cornfoot, for that matter, I added under my breath.

Without giving Aileen time to protest, I shut the door on her as quietly as I could, and picked my way to a position where I could peer through a gap in the piled cars, to get a decent view of the door to the office.

Sprott himself was standing outside. Imagine a really ugly midget, under five foot tall, looking like the top half of Arnold Schwarzenegger in a cloth cap. This vision of loveliness was currently pointing towards the back of the yard for the benefit of Petesy, who was standing beside him. I assumed that Petesy had dredged up enough wit to go into the office and ask where he could find a particular model of wreckage.

Petesy walked off in the direction indicated. Not very convincing, I thought, as he didn't seem to be carrying any tools or getting any out of his car. But nobody got time to notice, because Neil chose that moment to arrive in his inspectorly Vauxhall Omega and a cloud of dust, to claim Sprott's attention. They disappeared into the office.

For the next five minutes or so, Sprott's scrap-yard was like a ghost town – or at least like a ghost scrap-yard. No sound; no movement – the calm before the deluge. I watched and waited.

Neil broke the spell by coming out of the office. He looked around, as if he was making a rough estimate of the number of potential hiding places. Thousands, he must have decided. He took his phone out of his pocket, and used it. I thought he was probably calling for hordes of policemen to come and help him search for Grievous.

As Neil was tucking his phone away, some movement, or something, must have caught his eye, because he started running towards the piled-up hulks a little farther down the yard.

'Stop,' he shouts. 'Police,' he shouts.

Then he gets it together, and shouts, 'Stop, police.'

I move around a pile of cars to keep him in view, while still staying out of sight. So I am watching Neil when it comes – a shattering explosion that echoes round the whole place for several seconds. He goes down without a word, or any other sound for that matter.

Neil remains face down on the weed-riddled tarmac, not moving, but now moaning quietly. A small puddle of blood oozes from somewhere. After a few moments, two figures appear out of the jumble and edge carefully round the stricken copper, before breaking into a trot towards the gate. One of them is limping and has a gun still in his hand.

Hengist and Horsa, of course. They must have felt a need for armament after their escapade at Condiment's.

There is no chance of them having it away through the gate. See, the sound of a gunshot tends to attract moths out of the woodwork. In this case, the moths consist of Basil and the Wheel, who come quite carefully through the gateway from the street outside. Their arrival causes the gun-toting thugs to cancel their flight, and skid to a halt. The limping one fires a shot, which thuds into the timber of the gate. It doesn't sound quite as loud as the first shot.

Basil and the Wheel scatter – if it's possible for two people to scatter. Hengist and Horsa keep close together as if joined at the hip. I suppose they don't need to scatter, them being the ones with the gun.

The one thing all four of them do is, they all take cover among the crippled cars. I retreat a bit deeper into the jungle of jumble, hoping that none of these people know anything about my presence. But I still try to find a hidey-hole which can give me a view of any action that might take place.

I can't make my way back towards Aileen yet, but I know she has enough sense to keep her head down. Anyway, nobody is likely to hurt her.

A tense lull drags on for something between thirty seconds, and for ever. Then I catch a brief glimpse of movement, and shift my eyes left about a foot to get a better view.

Basil. He is stalking something. Presumably Hengist and Horsa. His attention is focused on a particular three-car vertical pile-up. He creeps closer. He must think they are cowering behind this rusty heap. Reaching it, he stretches his huge bulk upwards to clutch at the middle car of the three-hulk sandwich. Pushing it. Trying to tip the unstable pile over on top of the gunmen.

It seems to be working. The middle and top car bodies are creaking, sliding, and starting to topple. As they do so, two shots ring out.

Now it's all in slow motion, but nothing can stop it. The cars seem to take ages to crash to the ground on the side away from me. Basil crashes slowly to the ground on this side. He has been shot at close range, through the glassless windows of the bottom car.

After a decent interval containing nothing but silence, I risk a careful approach. I reckon that Basil has fiddled his last income tax return – two bullets, probably through the heart. He makes an imposing corpse.

Round the other side of the collapsed pile-up, there isn't much room to move. Not that I am eager to get much closer. None of the various body parts that protrude from the wreckage look as if they belong to either of the two human beings who are crushed underneath it. No chance of either one of them coming out alive.

Oh well, no tears for that pair.

Back at Basil's side of the wreckage, I stick my head in the window of what used to be the bottom car – and I get lucky. When Hengist (or Horsa) was firing, he was reaching his gun hand as far as he could into the car, to get a point-blank shot at Basil, whose body had been pressed right up against the opposite window. I reach in and pick up the gun – a revolver, I notice.

Now at least I can defend myself against the Wheel, if it comes to that. I'm thinking it might be a good idea to collect Aileen, and get the hell out of there before the police arrive, when I hear the surging hum of machinery lurching into life.

Electrically operated machinery – and now the hum is intensified and joined by some mechanical clanking. It's the car-crushing machinery, which has a crane attached so that the operator can pick up cars with the electromagnet, and drop them into the hopper on top of the crusher.

The first part of that sequence seems to be happening now, as a car rises out of the jumble, and begins its leisurely swing over the crusher.

A blue Cavalier with the front bashed in.

Aileen!

Her pale face is looking helpless from a window of the Cavalier. I rush out to the open area in front of Sprott's office, where I can look up at the operator's cabin of the crane. The Wheel is firmly in the driving position, looking out of place in his immaculate business kit, and concentrating on lowering the car towards the crusher. With only a couple of feet to go, he stops its descent, and turns to talk down to me.

'Madigan – I was hoping that would flush you out of hiding. You have double-crossed me for the last time.'

He doesn't need to shout very loud, since we must be only about twelve feet apart. He goes on:

'Let me touch base with you; put you fully in the picture. Here is the scenario; as of this point in time, your impending death is assured. Got that? I cannot permit your continued existence. OK?'

He paused to wave a hand towards the dangling, Aileen-containing Cavalier.

'You can, however, purchase the survival of your girlfriend . . . Eileen . . . isn't it? You, Madigan, are going to tell me exactly where to find that other lying, double-crossing, ungrateful . . . Dalgetty. When you do so, I shall lower this car safely to the ground. As insurance, I will keep your girlfriend by my side until I know that you have told me the truth about Dalgetty's whereabout.'

I raise my hand, so that the Wheel can see I am holding a gun. He shows off his teeth in a grim smile.

'You can't scare me off with that, Madigan. I know you're not stupid enough to shoot me. The instant you do, my hand will release this lever, the blue car will drop into the crusher and trip the sensors. That will cause these powerful hydraulic arms to start the process of reducing it to a block of scrap metal . . . only it will probably look as if the original car was red. You will not be able to get her out in time.'

He's put my Aileen in such terrible danger – and he looks so fucking smug about it. And I realise that I can't face the future without Aileen. I love her too much.

I raise the gun. I line up the sights on that infuriating smile.
I squeeze the trigger.
Twice.

22

The dangling car made the two-foot drop. At the instant it thumped on to the crusher, everything stopped. Silence. No sound of machinery. No humming of electric motors. It was as if all power to the crusher and crane combination had been cut off at the split second of the first shot.

Actually, the power *had* been cut off. Out of the corner of my eye, I had registered the appearance of a figure at the side of the crushing machinery.

Out of the Wheel's line of sight, but right beside the big red emergency power off push-button, in fact.

That was when I knew – I knew that there was nothing the Wheel could do to me – and there was nothing I wanted more than to end his reign of terror. Besides, it was my own life I was saving, as well as Aileen's.

Kenny Madigan, deadly hit man for the good guys.

I turned towards the person who had given me the chance to grab revenge by the balls.

'Thank you, Sam. Can you help me get her down?'

The three of us – Petesy was suddenly in our midst, now that the danger was over – got Aileen out of the Cavalier and back to the ground.

Well, to be honest, it was really the other two who climbed up the crusher – I was in no condition to do anything. My knees didn't want to hold me up, and the visible world was spinning around me; or maybe my head was revolving. When Aileen came down, I put my arms around her and let her hold me up for a while.

I needed to stay there for ever, clinging to Aileen, but she had other ideas. In fact, now that she was back on the ground, she seemed to be the only person around who wasn't paralysed, or wounded, or dead.

So it was Aileen who took charge.

Five minutes later, the whole place was saturated with police.

The media made a ten-course banquet of it, of course. Aileen and I held hands on the sofa while we watched the television news reporters wallowing in the biggest crime story the Midlands has seen for many years.

No less than four dead bodies, and a police detective inspector recovering from his wounds in hospital.

Nobody could explain why Sprott's car scrap-yard became the venue for a gangland feud, but various crime 'experts' were wheeled in front of the cameras to talk a load of crap about a power struggle between rival criminal organisations having come to a head. For the most part, they were making it up.

However, one point everyone agreed on was that it was lucky that several innocent members of the public – ordinary motor trade customers of Sprott's Spares – had had enough sense to remain hidden among the scrap cars. Sprott had locked himself in the toilet when he heard the first shot, and his two sons were out collecting a crashed car. So, unfortunately, there were no actual eyewitnesses to any of the killings. The police were trying to piece the story together from evidence found at the site, and were sure that the copper hero, Detective Inspector Cornfoot, would be able to help when he was well enough to talk.

After the news, all the channels had cookery or gardening programmes, so we switched off the television. I asked Aileen about something which had been puzzling me.

'Why didn't you get out of that car before it got too far off the ground?'

'I tried to . . . but I couldn't get the door open . . . the handles didn't work – both sides.'

I smacked my forehead with the palm of my hand.

'Bloody childproof locks,' I said. 'But you could have wound down the window to reach the outside handle, couldn't you?'

Aileen shook her head. 'Electric windows . . . no power.'

I was stunned, as such.

'Oh, Aileen, I'm so sorry. I got you into something . . . and you

184

couldn't get out . . . and you were in danger. I let you down, love.'

For some reason, there were tears in her eyes when she said:

'That's the story of my life, Kenny . . . or at least our life together. I don't know why I still love you.'

I hugged her as hard as I could. Obviously, the tears were a delayed reaction to the ordeal she had been through. Aileen is quite a sensitive soul, at heart.

The next morning, I was back at the helm of Lone Harp Auto Repair, feeling as if a tremendous weight had been removed from my shoulders. Then Petesy turned up. I had been kind of hoping he might have the grace to just fade into the horizon and never be seen again – well, not by me. But here he was, slipping into my office as if he thought he was still employed at Lone Harp Auto Repair.

'Good morning, Kenny,' he said, eager as ever. 'Can I have a word?'

I nodded at the visitor's chair, and he sat down.

'How is Aileen?' he asked. 'Has she recovered from . . . er . . . yesterday? Tell her to double her intake of ginkgo biloba tablets for the next week or so. That should help her to get over the shock, and . . .'

I held my hand up, palm outwards, to put a spoke in his words.

'Don't you worry your pretty little head about Aileen,' I said. 'She'll be fine. Now, why don't you just get on with whatever you came here to tell me?'

'All right,' he said. 'When can we get started on setting up our second-hand car business . . . you know, Madigan Motors?'

Christ, here was I looking forward to relaxing back into my normal easy-going lifestyle, having just managed to paddle my canoe out of Shit Creek by the skin of my teeth, and I was getting demands already. I looked at Petesy's big brown spaniel eyes. Aw, what the hell.

'OK,' I sighed. 'Give me a couple of hours to catch up with what's been happening on Senga's side of the business, then we'll start planning. Meanwhile you can get on with setting up the computer to get ready for it, or whatever you need to do.'

It was more than two weeks later before I saw Neil. By that time, the police had suspended the operations of a number of Midlands companies, as a result of having gone through the files at Condiment's. Luckily, it turned out that they never needed the photographs I took there. Aileen and I happily destroyed them.

It was Neil's suggestion that the two of us should get together in the Lamplighter. He was pale and not completely recovered yet. I got the drinks in – real ale for Neil, and run of the mill rubbish for me – and carried the two pint mugs to a far corner table.

'Here's to the hero of the gunfight at Sprott's Corral,' I said, clinking beer mugs with Neil. He grinned in quite a friendly way that I wasn't used to.

'Thanks, Kenny. I wanted to have a talk with you – all unofficial and off the record, of course. And I didn't want Sally or Aileen around, either . . . which is why I suggested meeting you here.'

'Fine,' I said. 'No problem. What is it about, as such?'

'Well, I thought there might be a chance that you could fill in some of the blanks for me . . . about our little adventure in the scrap-yard.'

'Christ, Neil, I've already told the police everything I know. You must have read my statement. I kept out of sight of these thugs . . . I mean, I had Aileen to take care of. I heard six shots – end of story.'

Neil didn't seem convinced. He said:

'Well, for a start, your statement makes no mention of the fact that it was me who asked you to go to Sprott's. I'm actually quite grateful for that omission, by the way. And then there's the incredible coincidence that everybody who was looking for Dalgetty, the great escapee, turned up there at the same time. Everybody except Dalgetty himself, that is. It looks to me as if someone engineered the whole thing.'

I shrugged. 'Can't help you there, I'm afraid – unless it was your crystal-gazing gypsy trying to justify her predictions.'

Neil took a swig of Old Peculiar and tried again:

'The coppers in charge of the case are really puzzled about certain aspects of the affair. For instance, there's the revolver. It's been established that all the shots were fired from the same gun, which had only one set of fingerprints on it – they were the prints of the corpse whose hand the gun was found in.'

'Well then,' I said, 'there's the proof that he was the one who fired all the shots.'

He gave me a funny, calculating kind of look and shook his head.

'But Kenny, I got a good look at the geezer who shot me – and it was the other one, not him. No . . . if I didn't know better, I might think that someone wiped the revolver clean, and then put it into the only hand that was sticking out from under those fallen cars. By the way, it was in the bloke's left hand . . . and he was known to be right-handed.'

In the end, we had to agree that some things are destined to remain mysteries, and hell, what's the point in worrying about it when a certain rough kind of justice seems to have taken place.

Neil must also have been interested in hearing my views on Grievous. He approached the subject sideways, as if he hoped I would accidentally come out with something he didn't know.

'I don't think we'll be using that clairvoyant woman again, that Madame Kazzandra,' he said, 'after her failure to help us discover that Dalgetty was locked up in that mortician's place all the time.'

'Yeah,' I said, 'and she might have had the decency to give you the gypsy's warning about getting shot.'

I wasn't volunteering to talk about Grievous. Neil would have to get more specific. He tried again.

'Dalgetty will be out in a year, I suppose. The fact that he was sprung out of prison against his will . . . and has now turned himself in – all that will weigh in his favour.'

'Yeah, I suppose it will,' I said.

Neil persisted:

'He still says he doesn't know where the money is . . . from his original robbery. But everything points to the likelihood that he was the only one who *did* know. Oh, by the way . . .'

Neil turned to face me, and raised his eyebrows as if he had just remembered. 'I checked up on where Dalgetty was picked up after the robbery, and do you know what?'

I went along with his sense of drama.

'No – what?'

'It was at the university . . . not too far from the scene of that stupid break-in by your criminal mates, Kenny. Do you think they got the money? If they did, they must have hidden it again; we've never had sniff of it.'

'How should I know?' I said. 'Maybe you should get Madame Kazza in to help you look for it.'

As I said, Neil had this crazy idea that I knew more than I was telling. He seemed to think there was some way he could get more information out of me, about the events that swirled around Grievous during his holiday from prison.

No chance. Especially not about what happened shortly before Grievous walked into the police station in Shirley.

When I stopped shaking after the carnage at Sprott's – two days later, it must have been – I drove over to Peter's bungalow to have a talk with Grievous Dalgetty. I gave him a suitably edited version of the story. Then I suggested that there would never be a better time to put our plan into action.

So, that night, Grievous and I went and got the money out of its wall in the university building next to the one that was so badly vandalised by the late Wheel's mob. It would have been pretty stupid to leave it there, because somebody might just start thinking a bit too logically one of these days.

It was as easy as I've just made it sound. We more or less walked straight in, with the help of my lock-picking equipment. True, there were a couple of heavy filing cabinets against the wall we needed to get at, but it didn't take too long to move them out. Then we hammered and chiselled (with a padded hammer for the sake of quietness) a couple of breeze-blocks out of the wall – and pulled out a plum in the shape of a bulky black canvas bag.

Grievous was all for us getting the hell out of there at that point but I suggested it would be worth taking a few minutes to hide the evidence. So we scooped up as much of the broken plaster and mortar as we could manage with just our rubber-gloved hands, and dumped it through the hole in the wall. Grievous then roughly wedged the two breeze-blocks back into their previous positions, and we covered up all the damage with the filing cabinets, making sure to leave a couple of ten-pound notes behind them. Probably it would be months before some-body discovered anything was amiss – and it would be assumed that the break-in happened on the same night as in the laborat-ory next door. Thus the Wheel would collect the blame, and with any luck, the cops would decide that he got the money out before his unfortunate demise.

Then it was back to Peter's place to drop off Grievous and the loot. We would leave the rest for the following day.

'Right, that's the lot,' Grievous said.

Peter looked up and said:

'Where do I have to apply for a bank card that lets me get this much out of a hole in the wall, yuk, yuk?'

It was the next day. There were the four of us, Grievous, Peter, Aileen, and me, seated around Peter's kitchen table, gazing in wonder at the bundles of banknotes piled all over the table. Well, three of us were – Aileen was too busy adding up the columns of figures she had been writing down as the rest of us compiled the bundles and put a rubber band round each one. We were quite happy just to gaze at it, while waiting to hear the grand total.

'Right,' said Aileen. 'I make it two hundred and eighty-seven thousand, six hundred and twenty pounds.'

'I thought it was supposed to be four hundred thousand,' Grievous said. 'Not that I'm complaining, ye understand. But that's the figure that was quoted in the news, and flung aboot during the trial.'

'Well,' I pointed out, 'everybody piles on a bit extra when they put in their insurance claim. And yes, I know it's dishonest, but it's what they do.'

'Oh well, then, they must be quite pleased it was never recov-ered, yuk, yuk, yuk,' Peter observed.

Cameron Dalgetty picked up a couple of the ten-thousand-pound bundles of money from the table. He flipped one of them across to Peter.

'Here, Pete, this is for taking me in when Ah needed a place to stay – an' for takin' me as ye found me.'

The other bundle came in my direction, with the words:

'An' here's what you an' I agreed ... fair payment for getting me oot of the clutches of that Wheel maniac, and helping to recover the money.'

Cameron stood up and said:

'Now, here's something I've agreed with Peter. The three of ye are goin' down tae the Seven Stars for an hour or so, to enjoy a celebration drink. Pete is willing for me to use his car while ye're away ... and when ye get back, the money will have gone back into hiding. It's not that I don't trust you; I just don't want you to have the burden of knowing, ye understand.'

We all nodded as if we believed that last sentence. Grievous went on:

'Aye, and when you get back, by the way, you can give me a lift ... drop me off in Shirley near the police station. You'll hear in the news that I've given mysel' up.'

Late that night – in fact, it was when Aileen and I were lying side by side in bed, her head on my left shoulder. We were both wide awake and sharing the feeling that we had just emerged from a long and very dark tunnel, into the sunshine. Aileen was going over various points about Grievous and the Wheel and Hengist and Horsa and the money and Condiment's. She likes to know that all the ends are properly tied up, whereas I'm not always desperately keen for her to have them all tied up.

'Where do you think Cameron could have hidden the money this time?' she asked.

'How should I know?' I said, and added, 'But I put my hand on the bonnet of your dad's car after we got back from the pub ... and you know what? It was cold ... he hadn't gone any-where. So I reckon somewhere under the chicken shed would be a good bet.'

'Well, even if you could find it ... don't you dare touch it, Kendall Madigan. It's not yours.'

'Of course not,' I said. 'What do you think I am?'

Aileen was also wondering what would happen to the Wheel's industrial empire, now that he was gone.

'Will Petesy get involved in running any of the businesses, do you think?'

'Christ, I hope not,' I said, 'he's too green-horned. Petesy will be better off absorbing a bit of experience here, in our second-hand car enterprise. No, I think what's left of the Wheel's business after the Fraud Squad are through with it will just limp along like a fish without a rudder.'

'Hmm,' she said, dreamily, and changed the subject. 'That woman who runs the garage in Evesham ... she seems like a nice person. What's her name – Sam, isn't that short for Samantha?'

'Maybe,' I said, 'either that or Delilah.'

I was suddenly overcome with tenderness for Aileen. I gave her a hug, and said:

'Tell you what, love. Let's get serious about looking for that cottage in the country. We'll both picket all the estate agents until they find one you really like. How about it?'

Kenny Madigan, the reconstructed man.